SHOWDOWN

When Roselyn reached the Council Chamber, the reception desk in the anteroom was empty. *What am I supposed to do? Wait? Knock? This is ridiculous.* She pulled the door open and strode in.

All eyes turned towards her.

She let the silence stretch, then gave a polite smile. "I gather you have something important to discuss with me."

Head Councillor Isaac gave a serious nod. "We do."

"Important enough to pull me away from my teaching in the middle of the day?"

"You were the subject of some heated discussion, and I thought it best to have you present."

"I thank you for that, sir." She scanned the faces. *So, I do have some support. That's nice to hear.* "What is the problem that upsets everyone so much?"

Isaac shifted in his seat. "Well, it has to do with your fitness for your duties."

She choked down a reaction. "Fitness for my duties, you say." She held the Head Councillor's gaze, but made a gesture towards the Pastor. "I've been expecting this. Let him have his say."

Isaac sat straighter. "Who?"

She shook her head. "Pastor Josia, of course. You all know about his vendetta against me since I refused to marry him." She faced her opponent squarely. "What have you dreamed up this time?"

The man rose, his face reddening. "If you insist." He took a pose and looked down at her. "Roselyn Jacobsdotter, you are not fulfilling your duties as a teacher in a proper and equitable way. Your classroom is rife with favouritism. You waste your valuable time on those who neither deserve nor can benefit from your teaching."

She regarded him coldly while she settled her wits and stilled the fright that choked her throat. "Miriam. You have finally stooped to attacking me through the weakest child on the ship."

"You spend too much time with that girl. Some people are suggesting it's unhealthy."

"Unhealthy! She's a little girl with no parents and a socially debilitating handicap. You're right. I don't have time to give her the attention she needs. That no one else on this vessel will give her."

He drew himself up. "And that is where you step outside your area of responsibility and training."

"What?"

"Her deformity is a religious matter. If you read your scriptures, the tribulations that come from the womb are holdovers from an earlier life. You are not supposed to be making it easy for her. Her punishment is for the good of her soul."

"Are you saying that Miriam's deformity was created to make her atone for sins committed in another life? Nothing, for example, to do with the fact that her mother and father are too closely related, and the geneticists' desire to create the perfect mind overwhelmed their humanity?"

"Oh, and now you're an expert in that field, too."

She sighed. "Of course I'm not. And neither are you. And you've taken a very twisted view of the Scriptures to get that interpretation." She held up a hand. "No, don't lecture me now. Save it for Sabbath where I'm sure we'll hear a lengthy sermon on the subject."

His face beet-red, the veins on his neck pulsating, the enraged man turned to the Head Councillor. "You see? She wants to run everything. She wants to be in control of the children and this council, and now she's telling me what to say in my sermons. This girl is not fit to hold any position in this society, especially such a sacred one as the teaching of our children!"

CENTAURI TRIANGLE

Gordon A. Long

Delta, B. C.

2021

Centauri Triangle

Gordon A. Long

Published by

Airborn Press

4958 10A Ave, Delta, B. C.

V4M 1X8

Canada

ISBN: 978-1-988898-32-2

Printed by Amazon

Cover Design by Gordon A. Long

CONTENTS

PROLOGUE: THE BEAST ATTACKS

INTERSTELLAR EMIGRANT TRANSPORT *JERUSALEM'S HOPE*

Roselyn Jacobsdotter jerked upright out of a sound sleep, alarms ringing in her head. Her glance skipped around her tiny cabin, but she could see no danger, hear nothing amiss. As her wits settled, she found the source of her anxiety. A small figure in a nightdress hesitated in the doorway, radiating fear and uncertainty.

"Miriam! You scared the life out of me. What's wrong?"

The little girl took this as permission to enter and dove onto the bunk, burrowing under the blanket and squirming as close as she could. Her whole body was cold, and she was shivering. Her powerful little mind radiated a scene, over and over again.

Image: A nondescript spaceship, very similar to the one in which they travelled, attacked by a huge, ravening beast, its back and shoulders covered with armour plating. Its mouth gaped with rows and rows of triangular teeth. Hard hooves pawed at the Ark of the Covenant, denting its hull and sending it flipping away across the stars. The Beast jumped high and came down on the vessel from above...

...and then the scene shut off. Completely, like switching a light. The terror abated, and the ship, miraculously unhurt, sailed on through space.

Roselyn stroked the girl's soft hair. "There you are. It was only a dream, and it ended when you woke up. It's all over. Our sistership is safe in Barnard System, at the Planetary Community Embassy."

Emotion: strong disbelief.

"All right. Let's you and I go and see. Do you want to do that?"

Emotion: doubt and fear. Miriam burrowed back under the thin blanket.

Roselyn tried to make her laugh sound natural. "The *Ark of the Covenant* is at least eight months ahead of us. If something is attacking them, we're out of danger for a long time."

Image: Beast looking out through space, seeing Jerusalem's Hope, reaching out with its mind...

She shook the girl gently. "That's nonsense. Come on. Let's do a gestalt like we do in class, but just the two of us. We should be able to hear the people on the *Ark*. Let's see how they feel, so we can get back to sleep. If they're still in danger in the morning, the Council will know about it, and they'll tell us." *In their own good time,* she couldn't help adding to herself.

Emotion: reluctant agreement.

"Okay, come and cuddle up, and let your mind run free." She put an arm around Miriam's shoulders and the two lay side by side in the narrow bunk, their minds joining and reaching out for the familiar mass of emotion that marked their fellow-worshippers of the Voice of the Universe, travelling ahead of them to Sanctuary at Barnard's Star.

Soon they connected, and Roselyn put a finger on her little friend's damaged lips. *Quiet now. We can't let them know we can hear them.*

Emotion: question?

You know the answer to that. Because we're different, and you know what happens to "different."

Emotion: sad agreement.

There they are. Now feel that. Are they under attack? Are they afraid?

"Yesth. Nnnafraid."

Roselyn craned her neck to look down at the little girl. "You spoke that very clearly. Well done. But why do you say they're afraid?"

"Nllook."

She obeyed, sifting through the individual threads in the mass of emotions. Sure enough, while the general tone was normal, there was an underlying hint of great relief, and a few threads radiated disbelief and fear.

"Yes, I see. They definitely had a scare, all right. But it's over. I feel sorry for them. We received so much joy when they reached the Planetary Community Embassy last week." She switched to their gestalt. *Do you feel better, now?*

Emotion: reluctant agreement. Image: Miriam sleeping with Roselyn.

"No, you're not a baby anymore. You're too big to be crawling in with your teacher just because of a nightmare." She gave the girl a light nudge. "Off you go to your cadre, now."

The girl slid off the bed, her shoulders drooping. No mental communication was needed.

"Miriam?"

She turned.

Roselyn held out her arms. "One big hug."

Emotion: love and protection.

Emotion: happiness.

"All right. Off you go now. Don't be late for school in the morning."

Emotion: agreement.

Miriam slipped out, closing the door softly. There wasn't a sound as she drifted away down the corridor.

"Different" knows how to stay unnoticed on this ship. The teacher shook her head and tried to compose herself for sleep. *There was far too much reality in those images. I wonder what's waiting for us in Barnard System? Will it be the Sanctuary we were promised?*

1. KIDNAP

Three months later

Toni Jacobs lounged on her acceleration couch in Auxiliary Control, idly scrolling through images from the ship's permaskin. Nzinga posed in her quadruped accel couch to Toni's right side, paying more attention to her own reflection in the shiny control panel housing than to the job at hand.

Patches strolled in and took her usual position at Toni's left. *Image/idea?*

"Sure, join in."

Question?

"Not much. Just scanning Otherwhere for signals. Once in a while we come up with something.

Emotion: warning.

"Don't worry. We're very careful. No rabbit holes for us."

Emotion: agreement, desire to help. Question: where?

"I'm thinking of searching the transit corridor between Sol and Barnard." *Image: cylinder of space with a star at either end.* "If an area of space twenty AUs in diameter and six light years long could be called a corridor. After this pirate problem, it occurred to me that we could map out all the ships in transit and keep track of them."

Image: small human pushing huge rock up steel hill.

Emotion: laughter. "I didn't think I was going to do it all at once. But down the road, we should set up a system that's fully staffed and equipped. It's a way barwolves and humans could work together."

Image: many humans and barwolves rolling many smaller rocks uphill quickly.

"Easy as falling off a log, hey?"

Emotion: question?

Image: Toni standing on log floating in water. Log rolls. Toni falls in water, comes up spluttering.

Emotion: laughter. Image: Black barwolf standing on log floating in water. Log rolls. Barwolf falls in water, sinks to bottom, walks to shore.

"Fine. Let's collect some preliminary data before we present this to anybody important. How about we start here and scan straight towards Barnard, in a tunnel...*NightHawk*, give us a statistical analysis of the diameter of corridor where...say...fifty percent of the ships travel."

Thirteen AUs would be half the cross-section, ma'am, but they tend to group in the centre. How about ten?

All right. Let's start a scan at that diameter. We're looking for three things: Otherwhere spheres, Otherwhere messages, and ship's exhausts.

Ship's exhausts, ma'am?

We can spot the ships in Otherwhere easily, but we have no handle on the number of real-time ships that have headed out for Barnard in the last thirty years. Some of them are still on the way. Remember that boatload of mystics that gave us trouble at the embassy before we left on this mission? What was that ship called?

Ark of the Covenant, Ma'am.

Thanks. And the ionization in re-ti ship's exhausts registers in Otherwhere, no matter how obsolete the propulsion system.

I see. What resources do I have?

Emotion: question?

Emotion: confirmation. Image: three barwolves in gestalt with Black Bird.

Thanks, Patches. Nzinga and I will help when we can, as well.

Ready to start a test run now, ma'am. Patches, please bring in your gestalt members.

Emotion: humour. Image: four barwolves pouncing on unsuspecting space ships, toothy mouths open.

Toni chuckled. "I doubt if hullmetal tastes very good."

The six of them slid easily into a tight gestalt and accessed the ship's permaskin receptors. Soon data started to come in.

"Okay, there's one. What ship is that?"

The Angela Merkle, ma'am, inbound for Sol again, now that the pirates are gone. She'll pass us in a couple of days, as we're on hard decel, and she's taking her time to amass interstellar data.

"Of course. Let's move ahead."

Image of ship.

"What about that one?"

"Space Arm supply ship, ma'am. She's the..."

"...and there's another one."

Image: two ships, side by side.

"Yes, I see them." Toni shook her head. "Okay, let's hold up a moment. This is easier than I expected."

Image: many, many spaceships in corridor.

"Right. There's too many. *NightHawk,* we need some filters. Cross-reference with Space Arm vessels and ships of known position and ignore those. We're only looking for the hidden ones."

Roger, ma'am.

"All right. Ready to go again?"

Emotion: eager desire to learn.

"Here we go. Ah. That's much easier. Register each ship, then move ahead." The ships showed up in front of her, grew, then faded out to either side. Small flags labelled each one. "Space Arm is certainly sending a lot of resources out. Of course, we could have looked that up on our database. "

They went on for a couple of hours, but as they reached farther ahead, focus became more difficult. Once they were searching past Freighty's position half a lightyear closer to Barnard, the number of ships dropped off, but the team's attention was flagging from the effort.

"Prime. We've done enough for a while. Let's take a break. We can work on analysis later on, and when we've got a..."

Strong emotion! Image: small dot approaching.

"What have we got there, Patches? That's an Otherwhere signal inbound to Sol, but it's not on the usual com..."

Suddenly the whole ship crashed into full gestalt. There was a moment of complete pandemonium, but Patches wrestled them all to silence.

Captain O'Rourke's presence burst in. *What's going on, Patches? What's the emergency?*

Image: tiny dot on screen. Emotion: intense scrutiny.

All right, everyone. Let's see what we've got.

The ship far ahead grew rapidly on the viewscreen, and with the full power of the squadron's gestalt, information began pouring in. Patches focused, then focused again, trying to catch a specific signal.

Toni frowned. "Is that a barwolf?"

Emotion: agreement. Command: focus!

Now that they knew what they were looking for, it was easier. Finally a faint signal came through.

Emotion: loneliness and sorrow.

Patches switched the gestalt into a different mode. Now they were all sending the same message out. *Emotion: question?*

Emotion: extreme excitement!

There followed a jumble of emotions and images that Toni couldn't make head nor tail of.

But Patches was manipulating the gestalt, and finally it settled down.

Image: three barwolf pups in a small gray room. Water dish by the metal door. No other furnishings.

Natalia intruded again. *Patches, now that you have contact, can we stand down?*

Emotion: agreement. Image: seven barwolves in gestalt communicating with three pups.

Fine. Let us know if you need anything. The captain switched to regular com. "NightHawks, I want a meeting now in the mess."

A message of general agreement swept the gestalt, and Toni and Nzinga withdrew. They slipped out of the Auxiliary Bridge and went straight to the mess, finding Andrew already there.

He slid aside so she could join him on the couch, then put his arm around her, looking down with a grin. "So that's what it's like when you put a cat among the pigeons. What's the matter, regular scanning duty too boring for you?"

She gave him a light elbow jab. "It was just an idea. I never thought we'd get results so fast."

"*Diablo* filled me in. You were making a catalogue."

"That's all. Then Patches went berserk, and you know the story from there."

Captain O'Rourke strode in and stood in her usual place at the head of the main table. Chakka walked stiffly at her side, his ears flat, his eyes slitted.

"Well, you know why we're here, because you all had a part in it. I have the data from *NightHawk*." She pointed to the blur on the viewscreen. "We've got a small, fast ship inbound to Freighty from Barnard. Three barwolf pups on board, probably snatched. No solid info on the ship, but course and acceleration rate puts it at the factory in about three weeks. No idea why they'd be taking the pups there."

"How can we help?" Toni frowned. "We're not going to the factory."

"We are not, you have already guessed. Once we rendezvous with the nearest outbound Space Arm supply vessel to refuel and rearm, we're headed out on our main mission to Alpha Centauri." She grinned. "The Higher-Ups think there's a TNT Ship Buster missile floating around space that they have better uses for. We blew up the other one they gave us, and that makes the Purser's Department antsy. Way too much paperwork to fill out. Then we're out and away."

Andrew glanced over his shoulder in the direction of the Auxiliary Bridge. "Patches will have something to say about that."

"Perhaps."

"If one really pushes it, we might have to consider aborting our mission, at least until this is solved. He registered resistance in the captain. "Alpha Centauri has been around for a few eons, Mum. It can wait another year. The interspecies relationship is far more important at this stage, and barwolves don't really understand converging course mathematics."

Toni accessed the barwolf gestalt, then spoke up. "Patches is arranging it so one can come and talk."

"Thanks, Major. We'll play the game as it develops."

Soon the tall, black barwolf strode into the mess. One went straight to the captain for the leg-touch, plate-scratch greeting.

"So, Patches, how is it working?"

Emotion: qualified satisfaction. Images: three cubs in gestalt, three barwolves in gestalt.

"That's all you need?"

Emotion: agreement.

"How are the little ones?"

Emotion: uncertainty. Image: cubs regarded from all sides. Lack of injuries. Emotion: loneliness, sorrow, lack of understanding.

"Yes, I can imagine. Any idea what happened?"

Image: cubs playing, investigating strange structure, blackness, room that moves.

"Definitely a snatch, then. Any idea of time?"

Emotion: uncertainty. Image: many days passing.

"All right. The question is, what do we do about it?" The captain raised a cautioning hand. "We can't just zoom over there and take them back. That ship is in accel, aiming for a matching velocity of point seven three Lights at the moment they reach Freighty in about four weeks. He's in decel for his approach to Sol.

"We're still in decel from our inbound trip to take on the pirates, and won't even hit zero and start our outbound trip for another week." She put a schematic up on the viewscreen. "Then we'd have the usual problem of getting part way to Freighty, stopping, turning around and accelerating so we match his speed when he catches up to us. Another five weeks at least. And that's disregarding our half-full fuel tanks. We could do it faster if we really poured the coal on, but we don't have enough coal to get there."

Emotion: fierce protective urge.

Andrew leaned forward "See what I mean?"

She shot her son a frown. "I know, but the fact is, we can't do it. We just wouldn't make it there in time."

Image: sliverhip loading up with fuel, zooming ahead.

Natalia shook her head. "Not enough fuel to make that run and stay within the safety margins. I'm sorry, Patches, but we just can't make it." She held up a finger. "But we don't have to."

Emotion: question?

"Toni, show us your latest data."

"We have Space Arm ships all over the place." She merged *Diablo's* data with the augmental graphic matrix and placed the enhanced view above the mess table. "There's a battleship with three destroyer escorts headed out to Barnard..." She placed them in the VR image. "...somewhere about here. But they're too slow. They'd get there after we did."

Andrew was accessing his augment. "What about the *Constellation*? That new frigate out on shakedown, going to Freighty for equipment upgrades." He paused to get more information. "She'll be there in about two weeks, probably staying a week. If she had to hang around a few days more, I'm sure it would be worth it. She's almost as big as the *Dirty Florrie* was, with about half the crew and twice the armament and speed, even in re-ti. We don't know what kind of power the kidnappers are pushing, but I doubt that they'd stand a chance if they tried to run."

The captain nodded. "That part of it is mostly out of our hands. We can't get there, so we have to turn the problem over to Space Arm."

Andrew's body stiffened. *Emotion: fierce anger.* "They'd better not pull any of their bureaucratic runarounds. This is a key interspecies incident, here, and valuable time is passing."

Toni laid a calming hand on Andrew's arm. "what do you mean by 'mostly out of our hands,' ma'am?"

The captain's face twisted into a grin with a lot more teeth than humour. "Because Ambassador Pretoro will have his say, in the first place."

Andrew laughed out loud. "And if he can't swing it, remember where they're heading."

His mother nodded. "Freighty."

"Why would they be taking the cubs to Freighty?" He frowned. "Surely they know…"

Toni shook her head. "Nobody knows as much as we do about Freighty. The public sees him as an alien factory. Maybe they think he'll want to buy the cubs. Maybe they're out here for another reason, and just picked up the barwolves for some cash on the side. They're criminals. Who knows what goes on in their nasty, crooked minds?"

Captain O'Rourke slapped her hands on the table. "In any case, I'm going to be a good little officer and report in to Admiral Mira. However, that brings up another problem. Even by Freighty's Pony Express com system, it will take more than a week to get a message out and back." She smiled. "But the barwolves can communicate directly to Brindle in a few hours. Then Morissa can relay my request to the admiral, at the same time making an official Barwolf Nation request through Ambassador Pretoro. That puts everybody in the loop and no protocol toes stepped on. Toni, I'll pass the message over, and you and Patches can facilitate delivery."

Andrew jumped to his feet. "And I feel a sudden need to contact my pseudo-pappy. I'm sure Freighty can hear barwolf Otherwhere messages."

Toni went back to the Auxiliary Bridge and recorded a quick message to Morissa, outlining the situation as she saw it. She attached the captain's official request to the admiral, then she paused. *Okay, now how do I send it?*

She opened her augment to Patches. *Image: Brindle barwolf, No Longer Deaf Scientist. Message passing to them.*

Emotion: agreement. Emotion: question?

Image: message.

Somehow the barwolf reached out to her, and the message disappeared. *Emotion: satisfaction.*

Question: time passing?

Emotion: uncertainty. Image: hours passing.

Emotion: satisfaction.

* * *

Early the next morning, Patches came through on the augment.

Image: Ambassador Pretoro. Image: captain and major picking up old-fashioned telephone.

Toni reached out and switch the message to her viewer. Alfino Pretoro smiled out of the screen, his cluttered office in the back ground.

"Thanks for the information, *NightHawk*. Morissa says she can send this through the barwolves, which is a great bonus in saved time. Natalia, I'm considering your message an official request from the Barwolf Nation for assistance. I have already passed the request on to Admiral Mira, and he has assured me that he's pushing for action. I've received confirmation from Freighty of the factory's full support. He leads me to believe that if the kidnappers come anywhere within about one AU of him, he has ways of dealing with them. I know better than to ask how.

"I will keep Morissa and everyone on Arborea up to date on developments. So far, she has no information on any missing pups, but I'm sure it won't take her long to find the details.

"On that topic, I am concerned for the welfare of the victims. They must be under a lot of stress. Perhaps you can tell me what steps, if any, Patches can take to support them. We don't know how the indigenous population will react to this, but any information you can give us will be of use."

11

He smiled. "Good work at picking up on this problem. Now at least we have a chance to solve it."

Toni sent a quick message back.

"It was just good luck that we found them at this point, although I have to assume that as our ships' trajectories closed, sooner or later we would have heard their call for help. Patches has put three of one's crew in constant contact with the pups, and from what we know of barwolf therapy, I'm sure they are sharing and easing the trauma. We'll keep in touch."

Over the following week action proceeded with the mind-numbing slowness of space travel. Space Arm had plenty of tonnage near Freighty, and everyone was determined to make sure no harm came to the pups. Finally word came through: The *Constellation* would stand by with Freighty until the kidnappers showed up, and then take appropriate action.

Toni went to bed that night, satisfied with the day's work. "That's why we joined Space Arm. To make the universe safe for civilians."

Andrew chuckled. "No, that's why you joined. I signed up to impress the chicks. Silly me."

She rolled over and pulled an extra armful of covers around her, refusing to dignify his comment with a response.

2.   ANOTHER DREAM

JERUSALEM'S HOPE

Roselyn awoke slowly, her mind still spinning with the sparkling clarity of the dream. It had been one of those logical ones that goes on and on, where nothing happens quite the way it is supposed to, but you are tempted by the idea that you just might be in control.

She lay in her bunk for a while longer. She had awakened early, so there was no need to rush. She went over the basic story of the dream to be sure she remembered it all correctly. All the while, her mind was sorting and rearranging, adapting the plotline to something small minds would understand.

When she was satisfied, she got up and headed for the schoolroom. She had the younger children this morning.

"Are you ready for a story?"

Once she had them settled around her on the floor, she looked at each of them, drawing out the anticipation. "You remember how Oni and Inga rescued all those people from the space pirates, with the help of Patch, the beautiful black Beastie and her crew on their silver spaceship that is six spaceships in one?"

All the little heads bobbed in agreement.

"Well, as Oni and her crew were headed back to their base, they began to pick up strange, faint messages coming through the Aether. They listened very, very carefully, and soon discovered that the messages were a cry for help! Three tiny Beastlings had been kidnapped by bad men who were going to sell them into slavery!"

The children gasped, and two of the youngest covered their faces.

"Oni wanted to rush out and save them, but there was a problem. The bad men's space ship was heading in the opposite direction," she gestured with her hands, "and Oni's ship couldn't just turn around and chase them. Space ships are moving very, very fast, aren't they, and it takes them weeks and weeks to stop. So they didn't know what to do. Does anyone have an idea?"

One grubby little hand went up.

"Yes, Isaac?"

The boy's eyes sparkled. "They should meet them head on and shoot missiles at them as they pass."

13

Roselyn gave them a moment. Sure enough, another hand up.

"Pierre?"

The smaller boy frowned in thought. "I don't think they have to use a rocket. The closing velocities are so great, a big rock would be enough to destroy them."

Isaac nodded enthusiastically. "I bet they'd only need a small rock."

"No, that would just punch a small hole and go straight on through."

"But if it hit the reactor...pow!" The larger boy made exploding motions with his arms.

She laughed. "Boys, boys, aren't you forgetting something?"

They frowned at her.

"Can anybody tell them?"

An exasperated voice came from the group. "Because the Beastlings are on the ship."

"That's right, Jeanine. And there's another reason."

After a short silence, she felt a touch on her mind. "Yes, Miriam?"

The little girl ducked her head, radiating timidity.

"Go ahead, Miriam. You can say the words."

With a betrayed look at her mentor, the little girl firmed her damaged lips. "Connandnents."

Roselyn beamed. "That's right. We can't kill a whole shipload of people, just because three kidnap victims are on board. There could be innocent souls there. And which commandment must we follow?"

At her nod, they all started in unison. "*Life is Paramount.*"

"That's right. Very good, children. Oh, and one more thing I just learned. Beasties don't eat children. Oni says that if a beastie even tried to eat you, you would taste awful, and you would give the beast a sore tummy!" She lowered her voice dramatically. "You know what? If a beastie eats a child, the beastie gets..." a whisper, "...diarrhea!"

She raised her voice over the growing giggles. "Now, story time is over, so you all head down to the gym for exercise, and maybe I'll have more to tell you tomorrow. You can be thinking about what Oni and Inga should do next."

They all clattered out, and she followed. *And I can't wait to find out, either.*

14

3. FAMILY FEUD

NIGHTHAWK

Toni was sitting in *Diablo's* mess/lounge area enjoying some music on her augment, when Andrew stomped in. She could almost see the steam rising off him.

"What's your mother done, now?"

"Huh? How did you guess?"

"Because most of the time you're a reasonable adult. She's the only one on the ship that turns you into a teenager."

"Huh! Thanks for the support."

She patted the lounge beside her. "You don't need support. You need someone to complain to. Tell me all about it. As if I didn't know."

He threw himself down, but then he glanced at her. "What do you mean by that?"

She grinned. "Because it's always the same thing. You try to act like her son, and she wants you to act like an officer. Am I right?"

"Sort of."

"Of course I am. What was it about this time?"

"When we were discussing what we should do about the kidnapped cubs, she says I took too strong a stance against her." He turned to face her. "I had to. I'm the barwolf expert. I know how Patches will react. It's up to me to give the captain that information when she's making a decision."

"I see. And she thinks you're an ensign on her ship, and you shouldn't be putting your nose into command decisions."

"Something like that."

"Andrew, Ensigns are the most junior of officers, still considered to be in training. On an average ship, they usually wait until they're addressed before presenting an opinion."

"Then maybe she oughta promote me."

"She's more likely to bust you back to...I don't know. You're at the bottom of the officer food chain already."

"Mum wouldn't do that!"

"Then make sure you don't deserve it."

15

"Why are you always taking her side?"

She sighed. "I'm not. I'm taking your side. I'm just trying to let you see what's going on in her head."

"Huh. I doubt that's possible."

She smiled. "You're supposed to be a smart guy. Maybe you ought to give it a try." She raised a hand, palm to his face. "And that's the end of the conversation. I'm not getting between you and your mother, and I'm not giving you the chance to work your frustrations out on me. You want to do that, we set up the training ring."

He looked askance at her. "Is that what marriage to you is going to be like? We solve every argument by letting you beat me up and pretend it's training?"

She shrugged. "I can see it working."

4. NEXT INSTALLMENT

JERUSALEM'S HOPE

"Children! Today we have a new story, and a new character."

The small faces gathered close, gazing up in anticipation.

"The new character is Fighty. He is an old, grey, battle robot. And do you know what his shape is?"

Eager eyes pleaded with her.

"He's in the shape of...a bagel!"

Cries of glee rang out.

"That's right. He looks like a big, grey bagel, but he has guns and lasers and plasma throwers and unknown alien weapons, all hidden inside his skin. And everybody thinks that because he's a battle robot, he must be evil. But they're wrong! And do you know why?"

"Why?" came from every throat.

"Because outside he looks like a robot. But inside..."

"...he's in tune with the Voice of the Universe!"

"That's right. And he is Oni's friend and teacher. But he only teaches her things that she has earned the right to learn. Unearned knowledge..."

"...allows evil to grow."

That's right. But proper knowledge at the proper time..."

"...helps children to grow."

"There you have it. So Oni and Inga have calculated the kindnappers' course, and they are headed straight for Fighty's part of space. Our heroes have called Fighty to tell him that the kidnappers are coming, and when they get to Fighty, they're going to have a big surprise, aren't they!"

A long, anxious pause as they stared at her, willing her to go on.

"But that's all we know for today. So off you go for recess!"

The children began their usual scamper, but as they left the room, each one looked up to the left and slowed to a dignified walk. Sure enough, a figure lurked just outside.

She pasted on a smile. "Did you like my lesson, Pastor Josiah?"

He stepped into the doorway, not entering the room. He was wearing his usual grey suit, his pot belly swelling the centre button of the coat. "You have an amazing talent for turning a doubtful tale into a positive lesson."

She kept herself from shrugging. "It's a big, cold universe out there, and they need to be prepared."

"I have to agree with you on that point. You may continue, Sister."

"I will, Pastor."

He turned back in the act of leaving, his craggy eyebrows gathered in. "But do not crowd the boundaries too closely, my girl. Evil creeps into the best intentions."

She bowed her head. "I know, Pastor. A pure heart is the best defence."

He awarded her with an insincere smile and departed.

Image: Pastor's frowning face. Question: why?

She turned and looked down. "Why are you still here?"

There was no answer. There seldom was. For such a timid soul, Miriam could be amazingly stubborn.

"Well, since you're here, we might as well organize the counting tiles. Can you put them in order?"

Emotion: disdain.

"No negative emotions, now." She rubbed the top of the little girl's head. "Of course you can. You know how to make them neat!"

Emotion: eager desire to please.

5. RESCUE

NIGHTHAWK

Toni moaned and rolled over, fighting off the drowsiness that dogged her.

"Come on, Commando. Up and at 'em." Andrew was already half dressed.

She pushed him away. "Gimme a moment."

"What's the problem? No sleep? You were really thrashing around for a while there. Bad dreams?"

She shook her head. "Not bad ones. But powerful. It was like I was right there when it was happening."

"When what was…"

He was interrupted but a com call. "Captain here, Toni. Can you come to the chart room? Freighty's on the blower."

"On my way, Ma'am." Toni scrambled out of bed and into her uniform, remembering fondly the pre-Andrew days, when she used to keep her hair clipped short.

Within five minutes the two of them were seated in the captain's office. She regarded them. "You're not looking so chipper, Toni. Something wrong?"

"Tell you later, ma'am. I gather Freighty is in touch?"

The screen lit up and Micha Mouse tap-danced to the centre. There was almost no time lag, despite half a light year distance. *Barwolf communication.*

"Right here, with all the news that's fit to print."

Natalia grinned. "Whatever that means. What's happening?"

"Pups are rescued."

"I know." The words came out before Toni really thought.

The captain turned to her. "How do you know already?

"Because I was there."

"What do you mean?" Freighty stared intently from the viewscreen.

"I saw it. It's like I was there re-ti. I had a dream. You know, one of those dreams that goes on and on? It was like a holodrama. And…don't laugh…I was some kind of adventure hero, and Nzinga and I were chasing the bad guys. They ran from us and went straight to you, Freighty, but you were some kind of huge battle robot with weapons all over. And you hauled the villains' ship in with a big magnet, and froze it, and went in and got the Beastlings and took them to safety."

"Beastlings?"

"That's what they call them."

"What who calls them?"

"...I...how should I know? It was a dream. There were other people in it. Watching. And a Storyteller who was controlling the whole scenario."

"Don't tell me you've got religion!"

"It's not something to joke about, Freighty. But tell me, how are the Beastlings?"

"The pups are fine, but my shoes are not."

"That's a good sign."

"I know, but that doesn't make my shoes any happier about being torn to shreds."

"Well, I'm sure your shoes will forgive you for putting them in the way of hundreds of small, sharp teeth."

Freighty sighed. "You have no idea what my shoes can feel. When you're creating a construct, you jam circuitry in any place there's room."

"I can only imagine. But if my dream was correct, what's this big magnet you used?"

"Nothing so simple as the electromagnetic variety. Call it a navigational magnet, if you will. It's a program that skews all navigation paths towards me. Under its influence, the target's nav ArIn thinks it's going straight. All its data feeds show that it's going straight. But its path bends towards yours truly."

"So they weren't really heading for you?"

"They were coming my way, no doubt about it. You can't disguise a deceleration target. But they weren't coming in straight, so they weren't planning to announce themselves, and who knows what they had in mind."

"Surely they weren't stupid enough to think they could sneak up on you."

"They're criminals, Toni. If they were smart enough to succeed without cheating, they wouldn't be where they are now, which is in *Constellation*'s brig, headed for the courtroom at Barnard Embassy."

Natalia regarded him with a silent frown. "You sound very…comfortable with this situation."

"…all right. Yes, I already knew they were coming." He grinned. "But you were having so much fun telling me. I was being diplomatic."

"Thanks for trying. It must be difficult, nudging us backward humans towards progress without being patronizing."

He raised protesting hands. "Don't downplay Toni's contribution. I didn't start my own search until I saw what you were doing. It's a great idea, especially as a way to make the barwolves immediately and clearly useful to the Community."

"I can see that."

"Oh, yes. The advent of the barwolves joining the Community has made my situation easier and harder. I'm not sure which at the moment."

"I can't wait for the explanation."

"At first glance, it looks like the barwolves balance some of the fears I had about giving humans new technology. All this communication development has now become a slam dunk, because the barwoves can do it without my help anyway."

"Right," Toni nodded. "But given that both races have violent tendencies, the worst case is that the barwolves and humans could ally with each other to produce a super war machine that destroys all other sentients and implodes in the end. Glad I don't have your problems. I have my own."

"Ah. Do wedding bells figure in any of them?"

"Wedding!" She glanced at Andrew, whose face was turning beet red. "Not at the moment. That's just too complicated."

"Humans have about the least complicated pairing system I've seen. Two people are attracted to each other; they contract to live together. Done deal."

"Until you factor in two Space Arm careers and an auguar."

He grinned. "Who will all become parts of the Freighty Construction Consortium the moment you leave the service."

She frowned. "I knew you were looking into it…"

"And I had to throw some weight around. But I just got word. Papers are signed, as you humans so quaintly put it."

"I see. And what happens now?"

He shrugged. "I sort of thought you and Nzinga would like to head up the Freighty Consortium Auguar Research Facility."

"And just where is this facility located?"

"At the moment, in a very small corner of my data bank ten degrees downspin of Hydroponics. Quite near the inside wall, as I recollect."

"In other words, it doesn't exist at all."

"Space Arm thinks it does. I think it does. The Commercial Bank of Canada thinks it does; they are handling the accounts."

"You have a major Earthside bank handing Nzinga?"

"She didn't come cheap, you know. I'm developing a network with a series of reputable organizations, and they don't come more reliable than the Canadians. Nice people, but rather dull, I find. Must be the long winters."

She paused. "You're trying to distract me with claptrap. What aren't you telling me?"

He sighed. "You've been spending too much time with your captain. Do you want to discuss the details of the ownership?"

"Is there something I need to know?"

"Yes. It is not permitted for a single human to own an auguar. Too much like slavery."

"But it's permitted for a company to own one?"

"Nothing mentions ownership. Nzinga will be a Ward of the Community under contract to our Consortium, and the terms of agreement will include protective custody. You, as head of the Research Facility, will be charged with executing that contract and seeing to the protection. We haven't decided what to do about breeding rights. Nzinga's augments are all organic, created with her own DNA, so technically she owns them. But the design is under intellectual rights ownership by Space Arm, and they don't want to give that up. Then, when she produces offspring, if their augments breed true...well, who knows? It's complicated."

"I see. Well, I haven't had any thoughts about leaving Space Arm yet, so that's all for the future."

"Fine. I just wanted you to know your future is all in hand." He hesitated. "Whether you marry Andrew or not."

She frowned. "And what do you mean by that?"

He threw up his hands. "Absolutely nothing! I'm trying not to put pressure on you. It's your life. Make of it what you will."

She nodded. "And for the moment, let's leave it at that. Thank you, Freighty. On behalf of all three of us."

"You're very welcome, Toni. Have a nice life."

"I very well might."

JERUSALEM'S HOPE

Roselyn held the attention of fifteen pairs of anxious eyes for one tense moment longer.

"And then Fighty turned on his big magnet, and the kidnappers' spaceship went, "Clang!" against the robot's side, and stuck there. Fighty told the bad guys they'd better hand over the Beastlings in good shape, because otherwise they were going to be stuck for a very long time. So the kidnappers turned the Beastlings free, and now the bad guys are waiting for a big Space Arm ship to come and put them in jail and take the Beastlings back to their home on Arborea."

"But where will the Beastlings stay while they wait?"

"They're living with Fighty, and learning from him, and…chewing his shoes."

There was a burst of laughter. "What do you mean, Teacher?"

"I don't know for sure. All I know is that they're chewing his shoes, and that's supposed to be a good thing."

Image: dog gnawing on human shoes. Human very angry.

The children all giggled. "That's right, Miriam. Pet dogs will chew their humans' shoes if they are left alone and get bored. I think this is a bit different."

A buzz of conversation arose, and she let them talk a moment. There was a small dog population onboard, but breeding was strictly controlled, and the pets never seemed to end up with younger families.

Finally she called them back to more prosaic work, and the day marched along as it always did.

Is this going to be my life? I only became a teacher because I could hide my abilities in the noisy minds of the classroom. Is this what I really want to do?

6. ΛLIENS

NIGHTHAWK

They were outbound again, burning their remaining fuel and enduring a month of full one-G acceleration to match velocity with *Tiderace,* a huge, slow, Space Arm tanker and supply ship making her ponderous way to the Barnard System with refined fuel, personnel, building supplies, and enough spare parts to create several spaceships of various sizes. As well as necessities like champagne, Scotch, and vats of good old navy grog.

They handed over their remaining Ship Buster torpedo to the Master Armourer, then provisioned, fueled up and undocked as fast as possible. Every hour wasted was another hour of decel on their vector towards Barnard, and they needed to be headed galactic west towards their mission objective, the Alpha Centauri system.

They settled in for the four-month journey, starting various experiments and projects, exploring their relationship with the barwolf members of the crew, and always, every day, practicing tactics and refining their augments.

* * *

Alison and Toni were on the Auxiliary Bridge, in gestalt with Red Chip, trying to plot a new scheme to foil the Greens in the next practise session. They were officially on watch, so when *NightHawk's* long-range warning system went off, Alison opened her augment, and the two strolled down the short corridor to the bridge.

Major Rowell assuming the com.

Major Rowell has the com. We have a bogey at twelve o'clock ma'am, thirty-seven degrees high.

"*Course and speed?*" Alison and Toni shared a frown.

Course 23, 47, 136. Relative velocity 0.19 Lights. Relative to zero velocity, 0.0002 lights, ma'am.

Alison put up a schematic on the viewscreen. "*They're crossing above our course and left to right. By the time we pass their present position, they'll be at 15 AUs and moving away.*"

Receiving data, ma'am. Consistency: metallic/organic. Mass: uncertain.

Rowell hit the ship's com. "Duty watch to stations, please. Possible alien vessel perceived."

Captain O'Rourke's presence slid into the augment. *This looks interesting. What do you have so far, Alison?*

"Strange consistency, ma'am. Metallic and organic."

Toni and the Red chip crew concluded their analysis of the Otherwhere media. "Strange readings in Otherwhere spectra as well, ma'am. We're getting a completely different picture."

"By which you mean?"

"The re-ti data shows a solid object with strong electronic disturbances at the periphery. Our view has three separate sources with a wide range of electronic frequencies, but nothing between them."

"Analysis, anyone?"

Alison glanced at Toni and shrugged. "I'd guess a spaceship with a large organic crew, with three engines on its extremities."

Toni inserted a visual into the augment. "It has now crossed our course and is proceeding away. This is our closest look. Basically a blob, visually." She superimposed the electronic picture. "And there are the engines or whatever."

And what's this about "mass uncertain?"

Mass fluctuates on a frequency of nine point seven seconds, ma'am, from a maximum of 25 tonnes to a minimum of 21.

Emotion: frustration. What the hell does that mean? Anyone? Dr. Blainey, do I hear wheels grinding outside the box?

Just a moment, ma'am, calculating...ah, there we have it. Not wanting to get into the gravity-vs-mass argument, if you placed a gravity sensor on the body of a bird with a mass of twenty-one tonnes and a wingspan in the three hundred metre range, flying in earth-density air and one gravity constant and a wingbeat of seven seconds, you would get similar readings.

Emotion: incredulity. You're telling me that a twenty-three-ton metallic bird with a three hundred metre wingspan just flew by us, going at a velocity of point triple zero two Lights?

Emotion: hesitant humour. Something like that, ma'am, although evidence would indicate three wings.

Emotion: disgust. Well, it's long gone now. Major Rowell, put your crew on long range scanning, all channels. Major Jacobs, get the sliver crews together and do the same in Otherwhere media. Everyone else, show's over. Go back to your choice of ennui.

Once they knew what to look for, they picked up another anomaly, this one low and to the left, but too far away to register much. The following day they noted another. Then a gap of three days, and they hit two the same day. All were travelling in random directions.

At an informal officers' briefing in the mess the following afternoon, Natalia laid it out. "We're coming up on point two lights, and although that is Light Transfer Velocity, I don't want to move into Otherwhere with these anomalies around. In the first place, it's dangerous. Nobody in Otherwhere has ever hit anything in re-ti, so we don't know what would happen, and I don't want to find out. Also, we should study these creatures. So we'll keep accelerating in re-ti."

As they proceeded on course, they started to note more and more of the strange space-faring creatures. Finally, after another week of increasing contacts, Natalia called a meeting. The two chips took turns docking and leaving their crews, so the whole staff could hold a crowded gathering in the *NightHawk's* mess.

Natalia took her usual spot at the head of the table, but the barwolves did not crowd on their mat, choosing instead to space themselves among the rest of the crew. Toni made a note in her augment. *Don't know what it means, but any change in behaviour is notable. Emotion: humour. Maybe Joachim can do his thesis on it.*

The captain opened the meeting with the latest data. "So, there we have it. Twenty-seven separate sightings over 13 days. None close enough for decent measurement, but all data indicates objects of similar size and shape. Those close enough for us to register Dr. Blainey's wing beats show similar frequencies. Ideas?"

Toni flicked up her fingers. "If this was Earth's ocean, those would be cruising sharks." She indicated the augment visual of the contacts and their possible courses. "They keep a similar distance from each other, if you consider relative velocities."

"Hmm. Territorial. That would fit."

Several other ideas were tossed around, but none got any agreement.

Finally, the captain called a halt. "This is my suggestion. We are supposed to be going to Alpha Centauri to find out what is destroying our probes. We aren't even halfway there, and we find large ships or creatures with electromagnetic capabilities patrolling an area of space. We can't just go blindly on with our mission in case these turn out to be our target. So, unless anybody objects, I suggest we cease acceleration until we get some better data, or the data begins to taper off."

Toni caught the captain's eye. "I know there's a great speed differential, but if we catch one on a converging course, can we try and get closer?"

Natalia grinned. "Well, we can have a go, but it'll have to be a very quick peek as we flash past."

"Understood. Nzinga just wants a chance to register their electronic signature, and the barwolves want Otherwhere data on those engines."

"And so do I. All right. We're dropping to point eight Gs, so don't get up too fast. *Image: barwolf bouncing off ceiling.* Since we're all together, I've called a fiesta. Jonny's got a special dessert for supper tonight, and we'll have a double grog and wolfnip ration."

* * *

They coasted for five days, while the contacts rose in frequency. Now they were picking up more data, but nothing changed their original image: a large, three-winged bird with electric wingtips. Whatever that meant.

And then the contacts stopped.

It was as if they had stepped across a boundary. One day they recorded three, the next day zero, and it continued for three days after that.

Natalia convened an augment meeting of the officers, which Toni and Andrew attended from *Diablo's* bridge. *What do you think, folks? Was that our problem?"*

Toni sent a negative. "I don't see their spacing as dense enough to stop all Earth's probes."

Andrew?

"Speaking from the point of view of science, I say we keep going on our original mission. We've gathered some information on an interesting anomaly, and the scientists will thank us. If we don't find anything else at Alpha Centauri, we can check this more thoroughly on the way back."

Emotion: agreement. We'll go back to accel, then, and continue the mission.

Toni felt a sense of letdown. Maybe it was just the prospect of going back to the old routines, but... "Let's keep our eyes open and our ears on. There's more stuff out here than we thought."

I agree. Natalia accessed the ship's com. "Acceleration resumes in ten minutes. Prepare for full gravity to resume."

Toni groaned inwardly, but resolved to take advantage of the extra difficulty of movement by upping her training routines. *It doesn't look like we'll be going into battle any time soon, but you never know.*

She dragged *Diablo's* exercise machine out and challenged Andrew to some pairs competitions, just to keep him from being bored.

But her entertainment efforts turned out to be unnecessary. Thirty-six hours later, Green Chip was running a gestalt exercise when they turned up an interesting blip in Otherwhere. The Auxiliary Crew assembled in their bridge and formed their gestalt. By the time they were ready, the approaching object was near enough to get some more data.

Image: four data sources.

Emotion: agreement.

Alison took command. "Let's get some triangulation. *Green Chip assume course 20, 50, 220. Accel one G. Red Chip assume course 20, 140, 220. Accel one G.*

Emotion: agreement. The two composite ships blasted away at right angles, and soon three-dimensional telemetry readings began to stream in.

Emotion: satisfaction. Both chips decel to zero relative velocity and hold station.

Emotion: agreement.

Andrew was fairly bouncing in his accel couch. "We're getting a spread. Definitely four of them, and they're making noise in Otherwhere media. Can't translate it, but we're recording it for later analysis, in case it's language."

"So, we have sentients?"

Alwyn was working at his enterpad. "Communications approximate the patterns of a human conversation, but much faster. Blips of two- and three-second duration." He fiddled some more. "I'm beginning to recognize different individuals by their frequencies. Yes, Number Three definitely talks more than the others. Number two...what?"

Andrew glanced at his screens. "I think we've just been spotted."

"Yes, change of course." Alison grinned. "If I didn't know better, I'd call that Evasive Defense Tactic 27B from the Space Arm Pilot's Manual."

Sure enough, the approaching squadron flipped up on its side and swooped away to the galactic west, just as the Space Arm squadron zipped past about half a million kilometres away. To the alien ships, the *NightHawk* would have appeared and disappeared in seconds.

Captain O'Rourke came on the regular com. "Mr. Jones, did you get any re-ti images?"

"Yes, ma'am. Putting them up, now."

As with the earlier images, the screen showed little but a blur, but the First Officer worked for a while, and the images cleared.

Andrew scoffed. "Great. Now we have four small blobs instead of one big one."

Jones was unfazed. "Which confirms Dr. Blainey's Otherwhere evidence. We have four bogeys flying in a diamond formation."

"Which is interesting." Alison was frowning in thought.

"Why is that?"

"Airplanes downplanet tend to travel on one plane like that, because they orient to the horizon. Space ships tend to form on a plane perpendicular to line of travel. Why would creatures flying in space orient to a specific plane?"

Andrew scratched his cheek. "And why is that plane perpendicular to our line of travel?"

Alwyn shook his head. "It has nothing to do with us." Again the engineer was working with equations. "Note that when they flipped up they are flat on the bottom. Their move put them parallel to the demarcation line of the other creatures we crossed five days ago, with their ventral surfaces aimed towards that line."

"Like they're patrolling a boundary."

Alwyn shrugged. "Speculation based on scanty data. A mere hypothesis to consider."

The captain came into their augments. *All data is good data. Let's keep our eyes open and hope for more.*

Two hours later they spotted a group of five ships, and the next morning they saw a mass of ten. The captain stopped acceleration, and they coasted in silence, staring at the viewscreens.

"Wickering wombats, will you look at that." Adrian worked over the image, and it cleared.

Ahead of them, stretching away into the distance, was a swarm of the alien ships. Hundreds of them, scattered across space.

And all heading in their direction.

"Well, folks, it's nice of them to come out to meet us," the captain's voice over the com sounded triumphant. *"I think we've just found our problem."*

"We've got a more pressing problem, captain." Andrew pulled his augment out of contact with *Diablo*. "We're headed right through the middle of that horde at a relative velocity of point two one Lights. Approximate ETA...37 hours."

7.   MOTORCYCLE

JERUSALEM'S HOPE

Roselyn beamed a smile over her Senior Class. "All, right, ladies and gentlemen. This is a fun day. We're going to work on Augmented Imaging."

They glanced at each other with hidden grins. The children always thought they were getting a holiday when they connected to the ship's ArIn, but experience had taught her that they worked harder and concentrated more fiercely at Imaging than in any other subject.

"Today, we're going to use old forms of transportation as our images. Here's the file you can access. I suggest that those of you with less experience stick to the simple ones. No live animals or articulated bots. Today's lesson is in morphology. Your assignment will be to choose one form of transportation and animate it as it morphs into another form. Success will be determined by smoothness and appropriate choice of subjects. Extras for thematic material: does the morph indicate some basic relationship between the two forms, and does that apply to our lives. Please choose your two forms."

She paced the class, observing enterpads and giving help where needed. When everyone was ready, she halted them.

"Right. You all know the basic steps. Just to give you something to aim for, I have imported an expert from another class. Are you ready, Miriam?"

"Ready, Teacher."

There was a muted hum as the teenagers absorbed who their "expert" would be, but they all knew that there was to be no complaint. *"Inclusion is paramount."*

"So, what do you have for us today?"

Image: twentieth century Low-Rider Harley motorcycle.

Several of the boys whistled.

"Very nice. And what is your target image?"

A buzz of conversation greeted the next image.

Jerusalem's Hope cruised the galaxy in front of them. Truly, the swaybacked old research vessel had much the same shape as the early cycle.

"Can anyone tell me what the lesson is here?"

One of the boys stuck up his hand. "It's going to be easy, Teacher. They both have the same shape. You take off the front wheel and the handlebars and make the exhaust ports larger, you're finished."

As he was speaking, the transformation took place. It went as he had guessed, but the handlebars sloped down and became the navigation stabilizers.

"And the lesson is that if you make a good choice in the first place, your job is going to be easier and your final result more effective. Let's see that again, Miriam, at half speed. I draw your attention to the handlebars."

The video played again, and this time it was noticeable that the handlebars took on a life of their own. You could almost hear them talking to each other as they realized that they stood away up there in danger of hitting things, and sank slowly down to nestle in the shelter of the forward dome. The group chuckled in appreciation.

"There you go, class. If anyone wants to rethink their image choices, go ahead. Thank you, Miriam. Would you like to stay and help out?" This last comment was spoken with a frown. *Image: younger boy with two unmatching images.*

Miriam gave a huge sigh and walked over to the other child's desk. Soon their heads were together over the project, and the boy was working furiously, his fingers flying over the enterpad.

The teacher settled in for an enjoyable afternoon.

Which was a good thing, because it fortified her for her next task. It was Wednesday, the day she dreaded. When she had finished her planning for the next day, she gathered up some brighter samples of the children's artwork and headed with determined steps to Medical.

As she strode along the corridor, pattering footsteps approached from behind. She continued without pausing. *No. You can't come with me, so don't even ask.*

But he likes me!

She turned. "Of course he likes you. You were his favourite subject. But he's not here anymore, Miriam. They're all gone into the

Aether and they can't get back. And I don't want you anywhere near any of them. You know why."

But you and I are the strongest minds on the ship. We're the only ones who could go in and get them.

"Dad was the strongest mind on the ship. He probably thought the same thing. And where is he now? Nobody knows." She knelt in front of the girl. "And the last thing I want is to lose you." She brushed the tangled hair away. "Now, I'm going to feed Dad his supper, and you're going back to eat with your cadre. Got it? Say it out loud."

"Nnyeth, Theacher."

"Very good. Now, scat!"

Roselyn waited until Miriam had turned the corner, and then resumed her march. When she reached the Disability Ward, the usual nurse was on duty. Hannah was a cheerful, homely woman who was always glad to see her.

"And here you are, right on time. We always look forward to these visits, you know."

Who 'we' meant was a bit vague, but the idea was kind. "How has the week been?"

"Oh, you know. Basically normal."

In other words, completely unchanging. "Fine, fine. What's for supper tonight?"

"Well, we have some nice chicken stew." Hannah leaned closer. "We've been experimenting with chewing."

"Has it worked?"

"A bit. As long as the pieces are not too big. We overdid it on Saturday, and two of the others had swallowing problems, but nothing serious. Your father gulped it all down without a problem."

"Good for him."

As she prepared Jacob's bowl, the woman chatted blithely on about his week: toileting triumphs, strength tests, all the details that sounded good, but in the end added up to one conclusion. No progress. As it had been for the last three years.

Roselyn steeled herself and stepped into the ward. Four men sat on wheelchairs, staring at a viewscreen with a recurring set of images scrolling past. Hannah indicated the screen. "We think we're getting more reaction from blues and yellows, so we've been increasing those."

"Are any of them colourblind?"

"Not that we know of."

"Just a thought."

"That would skew the data, all right. Let me see...maybe I can devise a test..."

Roselyn walked over to her father, who sat upright but relaxed in his conveyance. If it wasn't for the unmoving tilt of his head and the vacant stare, he looked perfectly normal. Her heart ached, but she dragged up a smile. "Hi, Dad. I've got your supper." She sat next to him and held up the bowl. "I think it's chicken, but it's a bit hard to tell."

As she carefully spooned the food into his mouth, she chattered away about her week and the progress of the students, especially Miriam. She remembered how excited he had been when the little handicapped girl had started to demonstrate her exceptional talent. And it had been good for the waif to receive so much of the attention her own father denied her.

But that had suddenly ended. One afternoon a mental wail had brought her running, and there sat her father, exactly as he sat now. Gone. Miriam was heartbroken, worried even at her young age that it had been her fault. Of course, that was silly. Jacob was a confident, trained psychiatrist with an immense mental talent, and he had simply taken one step too far. Since then, Roselyn had been vigilant to ensure none of her Sensitive students suffered the same fate.

When she finished, she helped Hannah feed the other men, and together they chose which of the children's pictures would grace each man's bulletin board.

Finally, they were done, and they stood in the doorway looking back inside. The scene was identical to when Roselyn had arrived. Four still figures, their eyes blankly aimed at moving images on the viewscreen.

She swallowed a sob and turned away.

8.   CONTACT

NIGHTHAWK

The captain hit the full com. "Listen up, now. We're headed for a brick wall without too many windows. *NightHawk,* plot us a course to give the flights a wide berth and put us into full decel. Crew, prepare yourselves for 1.2 Gs for the next day or so."

Aye, ma'am. Course plotted will avoid any contact for three days. After that, we'll have to recalculate.

"Fair enough. Pete, the helm is yours. Get us flipped and prepped for decel."

"Aye, ma'am. I have the com. *NightHawk, please give the count."*

Aye, sir. Flip in one minute. Please depart the habitation module...

"Engines on standby." The muted roar faded, and gravity wavered.

Flip in 15 seconds...

Flip in 5... 4, 3, 2, 1, Go."

Toni felt a mild queasiness as the gravity plates fought with the inertia of the ship's rotation, but she had been through this many times, and she hardly noticed it.

Prepare for decel in 30 seconds...

Decel in 5...4, 3, 2, 1, Go.

The engines spooled up, and gravity returned, not to normal 0.8, but to 1.2Gs, the maximum the regs allowed for longer than two days at a time. Toni immediately checked the slivership, but Barwolf 1 was cruising in her position alongside, matching decel as if nothing had happened. *"Good work, Barwolf 1. Very smooth."*

Emotion: quiet pride.

Captain O'Rourke came on the com. *"Yes, good work, everyone. Now, here's the drill for the next few days. At the moment, we have a course that will navigate us through the swarm. They seem to be in smaller groups, spaced out quite nicely. However, we're travelling at about point double zero two lights relative to them, so we'll be blasting through at high speed until we dump enough velocity. All it would take is one of their ships to take a flier in the wrong direction, and we're all toast.*

"So for the next ten days, we'll have double watches on the viewscreens, and somebody in the Nav chair and Engineering at all times. NightHawk will post the watches."

It was a wearing time, with four hours on watch, then four hours off, then right back on for four hours, all in high gravity. *NightHawk* tweaked their course constantly, able to stay a safe distance away from the increasing number of alien vessels in their path.

* * *

After eight days Natalia called another briefing. She sat in the chair at the head of the mess table, regarding them. "Well, it's a tough go, but we've stayed safe so far. However, the density of aliens is increasing. We've sent Barwolf 1 a thousand kilometres above us to allow for room to maneuver in case of an emergency, and that's about all we can do."

Andrew held up a hesitant hand. "Should we...separate *Diablo* as well, to...um minimize fatalities in case of a collision?"

"I don't think we're at that stage yet. Let's keep it for a last resort."

Alison was looking thoughtful. "*NightHawk*, please use the two feeds to get some perspective on the swarm."

Aye, ma'am.

A view of the approaching ships appeared above the table.

"Extrapolate a viewpoint twenty degrees above that, please."

Aye, ma'am.

Their point of view seemed to rise, giving them a look down on the fleet that surrounded them.

Alwyn was the first to notice. "They're in individual swarms. Quite a distance apart, seen it from this angle."

Natalia nodded. "NightHawk, please incorporate this data in your navigation choices."

Aye, ma'am. That makes it much easier.

"Good. We'll stand down the double watches, then."

From the sighs of relief, it was easy to tell that more than the officers were listening in.

"However, we still have to stay sharp. We're in the middle of an enemy fleet." The captain allowed herself a small smile. "And now the good news. We had a closer brush than I would have liked a few hours ago, but it allowed us some better images. Take a look at this.' She put a slightly blurry picture up on the main viewscreen. "This is the best we can do to clean it up."

Lundeen scoffed. "It's a damned manta ray."

Truly, the alien bore a resemblance to the Earthside sea creature. It was a flat diamond shape, but a third wing stood straight out of the dorsal area. The front of the body was taken up by a huge opening or scoop that resembled a mouth. There were few other features on the matte-black body.

"We think that maybe those grey patches on either side of what resembles a head might be sensory organs. No idea, really."

Toni frowned. "Why are the wingtips more blurred than the rest? Are they moving quickly?"

The captain shook her head. "We were travelling too fast to get any video, but the still shot is quite definite. The wingtips do not show up as clearly."

Toni contacted Patches. *Image: space creature in Otherwhere media.*

Emotion: agreement.

An Otherwhere version of the image appeared, merging with the present view. Most of the body of the creature was blank, but moving out along the wings the electronic energy increased until it completely obscured the tip. Beyond that point, the light swirled like air eddies around an airplane wingtip.

Lundeen pointed. "If that's anything like aerodynamics, those electronic forces are propelling the creature forward."

Alwyn nodded. "But by pushing against...what? Otherwhere currents?"

The captain closed down the image. "That's all we have for the moment. Once we get slowed down, we can start closer investigations. For the moment, let's just concentrate on not getting too close a look."

With that sober thought, the meeting broke up.

9. MISSING!

Roselyn strode the corridors, trying to hold down her concern. *Where is she? How can a six-year-old lose herself without going into someplace she has no permission to be? Why...? Oh, no!* With a feeling of dread, she started towards the Disability Ward. *What if she decided to try something on her own?* Her mind filled with potential disasters, and her pace increased.

She turned into the main corridor and there was Miriam, strolling along as if she hadn't a care in the universe.

"Miriam! I was looking all over for you. You're supposed to be with your cadre." She gently spun the girl around and started her in the right direction. "Where have you been?"

The big, brown eyes glanced up at her. *Image: long, narrow corridor with many openings to each side.*

Roselyn frowned. "Where did you find a place like that?"

Image: low, rounded door with keypad.

"And that's how you got in? How did you figure the combination?"

Image: large, clawed paw flashing across keypad in a blur of motion. Door popping open.

"All right, now I know you're just making this up." She stopped. "Say, what's that in your hand?"

The girl's right hand disappeared further behind her back, and a mischievous grin appeared on her twisted lips.

"Miriam, what have you got there?"

"Nurn."

"What?"

The girl gestured and nodded. "Nn...turn."

"You said that very clearly." She turned her back, staring at the blank wall. "What now...what's that?"

A spot of very bright light about the size of her hand wavered along the wall, then began cavorting in circles and bounces.

Roselyn turned back to Miriam, who was waving a small, dark brown stick in her hand. The light died.

"May I see it?"

The little girl handed it over, and the teacher regarded it. About the length of two hand spans, about as thick as her thumb. The ends were rounded, and there was no visible lens, ornamentation or switch. Roselyn waved it around, pressed each end, tried to twist it. Nothing happened, and no light emerged. She handed it back.

"You win. Show me."

Miriam pointed the stick at the wall. Immediately the light burst out, this time a larger circle in a beautiful shade of greenish-blue in a mottled design.

"That's very pretty." She held out her hand. "Show me the switch."

Miriam held the stick on both palms, then made it roll back and forth. There was no switch.

Roselyn pretended to frown. "You're very pleased with yourself, aren't you?"

A grin and a big nod.

"Fine. It's your secret, and you keep it as long as you like. But where did you get it?"

Image: long, narrow corridor. Doorway to small room. Stick lying on floor.

"Well, if you found it, and I've never seen one before, it was probably left behind by the scientists that used to own the ship. I don't see why you can't have it, at least till the battery dies." She knelt down to face the girl directly. "But you realize that Simeon and the other boys will probably take it away from you."

Miriam's face became serious. Suddenly, she flung her left hand out, pointing down the corridor.

Roselyn spun. There was nothing there.

When she turned back, Miriam was holding out both hands. Empty.

She pretended to cuff the little girl's head. "That was a very good trick. You keep it hidden, and you just might be all right."

Image. Large, furry paw with claws extended. Boys running away.

"Yes, sometimes I wish Inga would come and protect me, too."

Image/sensation: big, multicoloured furry face rubbing up against hers.

"Miriam! That was an incredible image. I could actually feel her fur!"

The little girl grabbed the teacher's hand to get her full attention. The twisted lips quivered. "Nnrreal!"

Roselyn frowned. "You mean just like real."

"Rrreal!"

There was no use arguing. "Have it your way. Let's get to the classroom."

Miriam turned down the corridor, swinging their hands backwards and forwards. Her teacher allowed herself to be led.

10. INTO DANGER

NIGHTHAWK

Ten days later, the captain passed around a document with the latest data. Toni was with Andrew on *Diablo's* bridge when it popped up on their viewscreens.

He frowned at it. "So, flowing through Otherwhere there is an electromagnetic current of something like the solar wind, but stronger. These creatures use their wings' electron output against this galactic current like a paddle against water."

Toni reached out to her augment and brought up a VR image, a composite from all their recent contacts. "No wonder it looks so much like a manta. It swims exactly the same way."

Diablo, how many aliens do you estimate within our view?

Ten to the eleventh power, ma'am.

"Put in human language, that's a hundred million." She had a sudden thought. "Patches, how do you see that number?"

Image: unintelligible.

"Okay, that's too hard. How many barwolves are there on Arborea?"

Image: unintelligible.

She frowned at Andrew. "I'm getting a picture that just translates as, "a whole helluva lot.""

He grinned. "Patches, how many barwolf pups were born this year on Arborea?

Image: groups of images blending slowly to form more images, growing in complexity.

Andrew was frowning fiercely. Then he grinned triumphantly. "One is showing us 20212012. They count in base three!"

Very close to five thousand, sir.

Toni shook her head. "When you three are finished..."

"Oh. Sorry. That was fun." He pouted. "Morissa will be interested."

"I'm sure she will. But we're working on something more interesting in the short term. As in, it may affect the term of our lives."

"All right." He nodded once and stood. "We need some technical help, here. Let's head for the Auxiliary Bridge."

41

Once there, he brought up a VR image on the augmental graphic matrix. It looked like a globe full of flies, flattened on one edge, with the ship at the centre.

"This is everything we can see. We can still register the edge we passed through three weeks ago. In all other directions, the swarms continue past our ability to see them. *Diablo* estimates that in two days we'll be out of sight of the edge. I'll keep track of this image, and we'll map the swarm of swarms."

Toni chuckled to herself. This was Andrew at his most didactic. *He's going to make a great university lecturer.*

He pointed. "We have entered the swarm at an angle of fifteen degrees to the edge. Note also that the swarm gets thicker to starboard. We would have to go all the way through and exit the globe in a couple of widely different locations to make any more predictions of its size. And since there's nothing to say it's a globe, it just isn't worth our while."

Captain O'Rourke had been standing in the doorway for some time. "So it is your scientific opinion that there is nothing stopping us from going wherever we want to."

He turned. "Umm...yeah, I guess. I mean, yes, ma'am."

"Well, thank you, Ensign. Nice to know I'm still in charge." She turned away. "Keep up the good work," floated back down the corridor as she strode away.

Toni knew enough to stay out of it. She focused on the image. "So if the mass is tighter off to starboard..."

He frowned. "Then there's a leading edge up there somewhere where the swarms are really dense." He thought a moment. "Of course, if they have a specific goal, and if the leading edge has reached that point, it would explain the increased density."

"So, if these are some kind of creature, and this is something like a migration, then probably somewhere over to starboard is the mating grounds. Are we sure we want to go there?"

He waved a hand towards the chartroom. "Well, if that's your scientific opinion, you go tell her, but I'm going to get in *Diablo* and move her off about a kilometre before you do."

11. PASTOR JOSIA

JERUSALEM'S HOPE

Roselyn stopped her Junior Class outside the Disability Ward door. "How many of you have been here before?

Only Levi put up his hand.

"Well, this is a visit everyone has to make once, because it's probably the most important lesson you will learn. It could save your life."

She turned as the door opened. "Hello, Nurse Hannah. Here is the Junior class, right on schedule."

Hannah smiled. "And welcome to you, Junior Class. Do come in."

She held the door open, and the teacher led her class inside.

They filed along the wall, staring in awed silence at the men sitting so still. She let the image sink in for a while before she started the lesson.

"These men were the strongest minds of their generations, but they all made one big mistake. They went too far into the Aether, and now they can't find their way back. There are two more in the Women's Ward."

"That's my uncle Luke."

"Yes, Levi. I know. He's been here for two years, hasn't he?"

"I don't remember. A long time."

"And this is my Dad. He was a trained psychiatrist, and very Sensitive. But it didn't save him." She brushed a hand over her father's hair, then gave him a one-armed hug. He did not react.

She allowed them a moment more. "Any questions?"

There were none, and lips were beginning to quiver on some of her more sensitive souls, so she nodded to Hannah, who led them out.

Back at the classroom they went through their standard Isolation Exercises — essential learning for those who could "hear" every Sensitive on the ship — with a new solemnity. She finished with her usual warning. "So, remember; nobody ever, ever goes into your Isolation Place without your string. And make sure it's tied on tightly. To your finger, your arm, I don't care if it's your left ear."

That brought out hesitant giggles.

"But don't forget your string."

In the old days she had made brief forays into the Aether herself, always under her father's supervision, and found that his idea of an imaginary piece of string was the best way to find a route home. Obviously, it wasn't foolproof.

Roselyn sent them all away with a brief note reminding the parents of the traumatic experience their children had just been through, with some ideas of how to cope with the usual reactions. Then, feeling sober herself, she cleaned up the classroom.

She stopped in the middle of reaching to an upper shelf. A presence loomed outside her classroom door. *Doesn't he realize I know he's there?* Slowly lowering her hand and turning, she sent a gentle probe towards the dark miasma. It slid over the surface and glanced away. *I guess not.*

The teacher moved casually toward her desk and sat, straightening her chair before looking up. "Yes Pastor?"

The clergyman stumbled forward, his face reddening.

She sighed inwardly. *Seems I can't do anything right.*

He straightened his shoulders and looked down at her. "Roselyn Jakobsdotter, the Men's Council would like to speak to you."

What have I done, now? "Certainly, Pastor." She stood, and he motioned her to proceed him. She glanced up as she passed. "Can you tell me what this is about?"

He frowned. "The Council will let you know when they are ready to let you know."

She bowed her head. "Of course, Pastor."

She turned from the Children's Gallery into the Main Gallery, heading for the bow of the ship where the leaders had their accommodation and offices. As they walked through the hydroponic greenery that coated every surface in this part of the ship, she glanced at the firm visage beside her. He was giving away nothing, staring ahead and marching steadily. *It has to be something important, or they would have just sent one of the disciples. It couldn't be...no. I don't come of age for another four months. After we get to Barnard's Haven.*

Again she glanced at her escort. *Now that I consider it, he looks rather pleased about something. Besides the chance to order me around, of course.*

12. IMAGINARY FRIEND

Toni sat in the Diablo bridge and stared at her auguar. "Nzinga, will you show me that story again?

Emotion: boredom.

"Oh, come on. She's a sweet little girl, and I want to figure out how she can use that flashlight, when it doesn't have any switch and doesn't seem to ever run out of battery charge."

Image: small room with metallic walls. Small girl holding stick.

"Okay, I got that."

Image: waves of energy flowing through the cabin. Waves gathering around stick, getting sucked in.

"I see. They've got a Megatooth power source on board, and the light charges from that. What about turning it on and off?"

Image: waves forming around girl's head. Power reaching out to stick. Light coming on.

"The little girl can control the stick with her augment?"

Image: scan of girl's head. No augment.

"She can do it without an augment? Come on, Nzinga. That's not possible. We can send images and emotions with our augments, but we can't manipulate objects."

Emotion: injured pride.

"Well, I'm sorry, but this is just too weird. I think it's time to bring in the other auguar trainer on board."

Emotion: joy. Image: large, beautifully patterned auguar.

"Yes, Chakka, too." Toni stood and headed for the main ship.

She stuck her head around the chartroom hatch opening. "Got a minute, Cap'n?"

Natalia laid her enterpad on her desk. "Probably. Can I schedule you in for, say, a week Tuesday, if we haven't hit anything before then and spread ourselves all over the universe?"

"Sure, I can come back then, too." She strolled in, Nzinga at her hip, and sat down. "I don't want to alarm you or anything, but I'm getting some strange images from Nzinga, and was wondering if you'd had anything similar with Chakka."

"What kind of images?"

Toni made a helpless gesture. "I...can only describe it one way. Nzinga has an imaginary friend."

45

"You mean that plush bear she packs around sometimes?"

"No, I mean a little girl about six or seven years old, who has all sorts of interesting electronic toys to play with. They spend hours together, as far as I can make out. The kid's got some kind of a science lab, and Nzinga is teaching her to use the equipment."

Natalia glanced at Chakka, lying on his couch in the corner. *Image: question?*

Image: wide yawn.

"No, Chakka doesn't do friends much, let alone imaginary ones."

"Well, these images are very strong, and given the fact that we're constantly under the influence of our new allies, I'm checking out any and every aberration."

"What can I say? Keep an eye on it. Have you checked her hormone levels? Her maternal instincts kicking in?"

"Normal. The ovulation suppression system is A-OK."

"Then I have no more ideas. You're supposed to be the expert on Auguars these days. Expert away."

Toni gave a glum nod and rose to leave. "Being the expert isn't much fun when you don't know anything."

The captain raised a hand to stop her. "Is this bothering Nzinga at all? Is she upset? Is it affecting her other relationships or her duties?"

"Not at all. She seems really happy. Maybe it's something she needed."

"Well, there you go. Don't fix it if it ain't broke."

Toni smiled. "Thanks Cap'n. I'll do my best."

"I know you will."

13. MEN'S COUNCIL

Roselyn approached the Council Chamber with some trepidation. *I haven't done anything wrong. Not lately, anyway...not as far as I can remember.* She glanced at the Pastor strolling beside her and decided his pleasure was the source of her concern. She kept her step firm and her head high. *I refuse to let him bother me!*

They entered, and Josiah led her to the seat at the foot of the table — the opposite end from Head Councillor Isaac and his two Assistants — and went to his own position, halfway along on the righthand side.

She sat primly, keeping a pleasant look on her face.

The Head Councillor cleared his throat and glanced at his enterpad. "Teacher Roselyn, your record has been brought to the Council for consideration."

That means somebody brought it. She refused to glance at the Pastor.

"You have demonstrated exemplary talent at your duties."

A pause seemed to indicate the need for a response. She kept the suspicion out of her voice. "Thank you, Councillor Isaac."

"It has been suggested that you cannot fulfill your duties completely as long as you have not officially attained your Adulthood. Mostly bureaucratic details, like official signatures on graduates' test results, that sort of thing."

Where this is leading? "Teacher Celicia signs them, sir. We have been coping."

"Yes, yes, admirably. But you give augment tests that Teacher Celicia has no augmental ability to verify. She cannot attest to their accuracy. As we approach the end of our journey, it would be convenient to have these small problems cleared up. Her signature might not be accepted in a new educational system.

"However, we see no reason to prolong the situation, when you are obviously up to the task, and we have a simple solution at hand. There is no specific regulation about the Age of Maturity. The tradition of assigning the step to Adulthood at twenty-one years is merely that: a tradition."

Why would they want to advance my Adulthood date? Oh, crap. Marriage! She couldn't help herself. Her eyes were drawn like magnets to the Pastor, who was openly smiling now.

She thought furiously. "Does that mean I would be able to take my place on the Women's Council?"

That set him back a bit. "...umm. We would not see that as advisable. Membership on the Council is restricted to Adults of twenty-one years."

"I see." She pretended to consider. "In that case, I don't think it is in my best interest to make any waves."

A smile began to form, and she cut it off. "It seems that changing one tradition creates a domino effect that might disturb all sorts of other aspects of the steady flow of the ship's administration, and *'Consistency is paramount'.*"

She sat straighter. "So, while I thank the Council for their approbation, I will be happy to ascend to my Adulthood at the traditional time, my twenty-first birthday." She accessed the ShipNet for the time, then beamed a smile along the table. "Is that all, gentlemen? I have an Arithmetic class starting in ten minutes, and a set of manipulatives to lay out."

"Um...yes, yes, that was all. You must go to your duties. *'Education is paramount.'*"

She stood. "Thank you again. I am well aware of the honour you do me."

She did not curtsey, but inclined her head politely, then turned and strode out.

Only when she was out of sight in the corridor did she let her breath out and allow her shoulders to sag. *Well, that explains everything. What the hell am I going to do now?*

Allowing herself that small blasphemy did her no good, and she forced her steps towards the classroom, for once completely uninterested in what she was going to teach.

14. ALIEN SHIPS

NIGHTHAWK

NightHawk and her accompanying fleet still ploughed through the alien swarms, but slower, now. Clearer data came in on a daily basis, and they began to build up a better idea of how these alien ships looked and acted.

Toni and Andrew were in the Auxiliary Bridge running frequency tests on the creatures' wing beats, trying to analyze how they worked against the Otherwhere tide. It was dull work, mostly mathematics, and she was just in the middle of a large yawn and stretch when suddenly the course change warning blared and gravity swooped. A clatter of plates and a burst of Spanish curses erupted from the galley, and equipment slid and banged all over the ship.

Before Toni had a chance to pick herself up off the floor, they were flying smoothly again.

The captain came on the com. "Sorry about that, folks. A whole swarm took a notion to change course, and it put them right in our path. We're clear, now, but it was closer than I'd like. And from the sound of it, we just got a lesson. Even with the ship's improved internal gravity, we don't leave junk lying around. Crew to cleanup, officers to the Auxiliary Bridge."

Good-natured jibes followed the officers as they left the crewmembers to their household tasks.

Soon they were all assembled, parked on human and quad accel couches alike. Natalia strode in and stood, regarding them. Then she shook her head. "Another wakeup call. We can never forget that we're in unknown space, and anything could be thrown at us at any moment. We have to stay sharp all the time. Never let down. Got it?"

Emotions of heartfelt agreement filled the augment com.

"But we're getting a picture of what's happening. Alwyn has been putting together a composite. Dr. Blainey?"

He put up a virtual image on the graphic matrix. "We're only moving at point triple-zero nine lights relative to the swarms, now, so we're getting better images. Here's our alien ship. About thirty metres long, with a wingspan of slightly more. Open scoop in the front, for gathering we don't know what. Now we have video, and we can see that all three wings move at a frequency of seven to eight beats per minute. They don't beat in unison. We're not sure, but it seems that they are synched sequentially." He demonstrated with waving hands, "So there's a one-two-three beat, with each wing in a different part of the pattern at any time. It gives the whole being an undulating motion I'm going to graph out, because it has interesting permutations..." He grinned around at them. "Well, let's say I'm working on it."

He zoomed the image wider. "They travel in groups or flights of from four to ten, rarely more, never less. These flights maintain position in the larger swarm. Swarms move as a unit, like a flock of birds on Earth."

He widened the image further. "Which causes our problem. The whole fleet is moving at an angle to our course: twenty-five degrees to galactic north, ten degrees down. But within that course, individual swarms choose their own paths. So, at any time, for reasons we can't fathom, on a pattern we haven't figured out yet, a swarm may choose to change direction. The adjustment is instantaneous, which speaks to sophisticated communications and a definitive central intelligence. And that's all we have to date. Any questions or suggestions?"

Chief Engineer Lundeen shrugged. "Only the one we've all been asking. Are they ships or are they individual organisms?"

First Officer Jones gave a rare grin. "Odds in the crew betting pool are two to one for individuals. I gather they look too organic to be constructed."

Andrew chuckled. "Unless they are spaceships that have been organically constructed."

Lundeen scoffed. "Academics. They can always come up with something to throw a spanner in the works."

Natalia waited for the laugh to die down. "In any case, the more data we have on their courses, the safer we are. Keep collecting and keep your eyes open for whatever we don't expect. Remember, we're moving closer and closer to Alpha C, into what could be enemy territory. If they finally take notice of us, the farther in we are, the easier it will be for them to surround us. Stay sharp, *NightHawks*."

15. THE BEAST

It was rest hour, and Roselyn was looking forward to escaping her problems in a holonovel. But then her most persistent problem appeared at her door.

Emotion: fun. Emotion: question?

She took off her viewer. "I could use some fun. What have you got for me?"

"Cun."

"You can say it properly. Commuh."

"C-commuh."

"Well done." Roselyn stood. "Where are we going?"

Image: low door with enterpad. Long, narrow corridor.

"You're going to show me your secret place? That's nice."

"Inga."

"You're going to show me Inga?"

"Nnyup."

"Well, I can't wait. Lead on, brave general."

The little girl took her hand and pulled her forward in the ship, out of the grey steel of the common corridors and into the greenery of 'ponics. But as they neared the Councillors' Quarters, she stopped, brushed back a swath of ivy and pushed against a panel in the corridor wall. It slid open silently, revealing a narrow staircase spiralling upwards. Soon they came to the top, and there, in front of them, was the door from Miriam's image. She tapped the entrypad briskly, and the hatch gaped open.

Inside, the corridor was as narrow as Roselyn remembered, but lower; pipes and cables hanging along the ceiling brushed her head. She peered into the first room, which must have once been a workshop. The battered metal bench held a vise, and empty tool racks studded the wall above it. She bent over to look underneath.

Miriam was there before her, reaching in. "Nnlook!" She stood, holding a piece of apparatus. From the way she held it, it was light, and fitted in her small hand easily. There were no clues as to its function.

"Fine. What is it?"

51

The little girl shrugged. *Emotion: Question?*

"Sure, I'd like to know. How are you going to find out?"

"Ask nnInga."

"You're going to ask Inga what it is."

The girl nodded.

"Okay. I can't wait. Ask her."

Emotion: invitation.

There was a pause, and nothing happened. But before Roselyn could speak, she felt a powerful pull from the Ship's Augment. But it wasn't the Ship.

Emotion: greeting. Image: huge, calico-coloured cat.

"What the hell is that?"

Emotion: scolding.

"I'm sorry for the blasphemy, Miriam, but where did that come from?"

Emotion: greeting. Image: cat rubbing against human's leg. Feeling: itch behind left ear.

Controlling her rampaging emotions, Roselyn concentrated. *Image: human scratching cat behind left ear.*

Image/sound: cat purring and rubbing. Image: human word "auguar."

"Oh. You're called an auguar, are you? Is that some kind of jaguar?"

Emotion: qualified agreement.

"And you can understand me when I talk normally?"

Emotion: agreement.

"So, who are you, and where are you? Are you on this ship?"

Image: sleek black spaceship. Feeling: long distance.

"I see."

Emotion: haste. Emotion: question?

"Oh, certainly. Miriam has a question for you."

The little girl held out the apparatus. *Emotion: question?*

The following interchange was too rapid to follow, but Roselyn was a teacher; she knew a lesson when she watched one. Miriam turned the piece of equipment over in her hands, concentrating fiercely. It gave a low hum, and several lights blinked. She turned it over again; the other side lit up in a small viewscreen. Miriam passed her hand underneath the tool, and a skeletal image of it appeared on the screen.

"It's a medical scanner!"

Emotion: agreement.

Roselyn's mind was beginning to work again. "But if it's medical equipment, why is it down here in the workshop? It doesn't look broken?"

The two conferred, then Miriam passed her hand under the scanner again. This time the veins and arteries stood out, but the colours were fragmentary.

"Fine. It was sent out for repairs, and when they sold the ship, it wasn't working, so they left it."

Emotion: indifference. Emotion: apology. Emotion: haste.

"Oh. Do you have to leave?"

Emotion: agreement. Emotion: disappointment. Emotion: farewell.

The auguar was gone from their minds, leaving a cold, empty space.

The two stood and looked at each other.

"Well! So this is what you've been up to."

"Nninga."

"Yes, I guess that's Inga."

"Nno. Not Inga. Nnninga."

"You mean I had her name wrong?"

Emotion: agreement.

"Anyway, it doesn't matter. What are we going to do with this scanner? I don't think we want to tell everyone about it, because they'll want to know where it came from, and then your secret will be out."

Miriam nodded and put the scanner back under the shelf.

Question: more?

Roselyn checked the time. "No, we'd better be getting back. Supper hour soon."

They retraced their steps, pausing inside the panel to be sure there was no one in the main corridor before they exited. The supper bell rang as they walked, and she shooed the little girl off to wash her hands and join her cadre.

Moving slower, the teacher made her own way to the washroom and then to the dining hall, still pondering what had just happened.

"Hey, Rosy. Watch where you're walking."

She looked up. And up some more. "Sorry, Abram. Thinking."

The long, narrow face broke into a grin. "You're always thinking. I just figured a teacher would be smart enough to be able to walk at the same time."

She made a point of reaching up to elbow him in the ribs. "Which just shows how often you're wrong."

"Well, come and sit with me. Barnabus will be there." He leaned down. "I think he's gone sweet on you."

A chill coursed down her spine, and she strode ahead. "That's the last thing I want to hear."

"Hey, hey, I'm sorry. What're you so touchy about?" It took him three long paces to catch up. "Something to do with the Council today?"

She nodded miserably.

"Does one of those old fogeys want you to marry him? Damn, but that makes me mad!"

She shook his arm. "No blasphemy! Somebody will hear you."

He quieted, but his voice still shook with emotion. "It's not fair to you, and it's not fair to us. They take all the women our age, and there's no one left for the young guys."

"Why, Abram. Are you saying you would marry me if you got the chance?"

"Not in this universe. You're much too good a friend to turn into a wife."

She frowned. "What have you got against wives?"

He raised his hands in defence. "This conversation is rapidly becoming lose-lose, and the losses are all mine. Let's just grab our plates and talk about how boring the food is."

She faked a punch to his elbow, because his shoulder was too high. "It's a deal."

They lined up, got their suppers, and joined several other young people at their usual table. Barnabus was there, and she watched him more carefully. *I have to say, compared to the Pastor...well there's no competition.* Barnabus was borderline handsome, well built as all the tradesmen were, and often smiled when he looked in her direction. He was also the shortest man in the group. *Which is not likely to bother me, although any children we had might not agree.*

A long arm reached across the table, and Abram's bony index finger poked her cheek. "Hey, why did your face just go red?"

She slapped his hand away. "Impure thoughts. And you weren't in any of them." Other conversations intruded, and she enjoyed the meal.

Her pleasant mood lingered as she left the dining hall, but it was abruptly terminated when she rounded the corner to approach her cabin. Three young men were coming towards her, and their reaction to her presence was typical. They spread out and slowed down, so she had no way to get through them. Refusing to rise to the bait, she stopped in the middle of the corridor and waited.

The shortest and stockiest of the three, Eli Barad, stood square in front of her, and his two friends crowded in on either side. He looked down at her with an insincere smile. "So this is gonna be Pastor Josiah's new bride. I gotta say, I'm impressed. How did a plain little nothing like you attract his attention?"

"What are you talking about?"

He leered. "Oh, word gets around. The pastor's got friends, y'know."

"And I suppose you're one of them."

"Of course I am. He's a regular sort, Josiah. Changes are coming when we reach Sanctuary, and he knows where his support stands."

"I see." She looked sideways up at him. "And where does his support stand?"

He leaned back and stuck his thumbs in his belt. "Well, it's this way, m'dear. There's a lot of people on this ship that's in tune with the Universe and all that, right?"

"Of course. That's why we're here."

"But there's also a lot of us that aren't. A whole lot."

"Of course there are. You're just as important as anyone else. The Union needs believers."

He grinned. "Ah. There you are. And you're gonna need us even more, soon. That's just what Josia was saying this morning. That gets me thinkin', ya know. You and he might make a pretty good couple. You understand the same way."

"So Pastor Josia has been telling you all about how he's going to marry me?"

"I told ya. He's a friend of mine."

"And did either of you ever think I might have an opinion on that?"

"Oh, you'll come 'round. The pastor's an up-and-comin' man in the Union. You'd do well to hitch your wagon to his train."

She thought it best not to react to this reference from an ancient holonovel. "I see. Well, thank you for the information, Eli. You've given me a lot to think about."

He gave a startled smile, the first honest expression she had seen on his face during the conversation.

Before he could think up a reply, she slid past him and strode away, refusing to look back, although her skin crawled at the thought of his eyes on her.

* * *

The following noon, she looked around at her friends, chatting and joking as usual. It gave her a pang to think of what the future might have in store for them. When she caught a lull in the conversation, she tossed out a comment. "Have any of you come up with what you're going to do when we reach Barnard?"

Dead silence. *I guess that means they haven't.*

Then Abram came to the rescue. Sort of. "Where did that come from?"

"I just had a chat with Eli and some of his friends. He's not very articulate, but he did a pretty good job of laying out the situation. We are a small group of people. When we get to Barnard, it's going to be difficult to keep our Union together. We have to collect our friends around us."

Sapphira chuckled. "Eli said that? You must have caught him on a good day."

"He was looking at it from a more self-centred point of view, but he put his finger on a problem, and we have less than two months to figure out an answer."

"But we don't have much more information than we had a year ago."

"Then we'd better start looking for some."

"I suppose."

Abram leaned forward. "And what problem did the brilliant Eli put his grubby finger on?"

"Don't downgrade him because he's a mechanic. We need the non-sensitive believers. We can't function without them."

"I downgrade him because he's a twit. But I get your point. It would be difficult without them, that's for sure."

"Abram, you know as well as I do that the ability to hear the Voice is not related to intelligence. We have some very talented and accomplished non-sensitives, and we are going to need their support when we reach our new home and try to make a place for ourselves there." She frowned up at him. "I have no illusions about the Sanctuary. It's not going to be some kind of Garden of Eden where all our troubles are over. Quite the opposite, I suspect."

"The opposite?"

"That's right. We'll be a small sect of people who have different beliefs than the rest of the population. You know your history. Figure it out."

Sapphira frowned. "You think we'll be persecuted again?"

She shrugged. "Who knows? History is full of groups who left places of persecution and set themselves up elsewhere. Some flourished, some died out. But they all had to make a living. Abram, you're trained to be an ArIn programmer. What are you going to do?"

He grinned. "Gee, Rosy, I don't know. Program ArIns, maybe?"

"What ArIns? Are we going to settle in an area where you can find that kind of work?"

"I don't know. There just isn't any information available."

"Well, we need more information. You work in the Tech shop. What's coming in on the media? Sapphira, your grandfather's on the council. Ask him to send a request to the Barnard Embassy for information on job opportunities in Barnard System."

He scoffed. "You know everything that comes in goes straight to the council. If I got caught listening in, it would cost me my job. Then where would I be?"

She glanced at Sapphira, but the girl had taken the opportunity to forget the question had ever been asked. She frowned. "At least you know what you're going to be."

"And what's that?"

Abram scoffed. "A teacher, of course."

"Maybe I don't want to be a teacher. Have you ever thought of that?"

He gave a shout of laughter. "You, not a teacher? There's teaching in every gram of your soul. You're always teaching all of us."

Hoping her face didn't show red, she reached up to twist his ear. "And I obviously missed out on teaching you proper respect."

The conversation broke up in laughter and joking, with Abram taking the brunt of the humour as usual. Roselyn faded into the background, mulling over the accuracy of her friend's comment. *I can't let the coming opportunities overwhelm me. I have to figure out what I want.*

16. FLY-BY

NIGHTHAWK

For the next ten days the *NightHawk* decelerated, and soon the swarms were meeting them at a reasonable pace. Imminent collisions and close calls faded out, and they could concentrate on their research.

One afternoon Andrew nudged his fiancée as they were leaving the mess. "I think it's time for a more detailed look at our subjects."

Toni shrugged. "Our closing velocities are still at several thousand klicks. We won't get much."

"We have to start some time. I'm going to talk to the captain. You coming?"

"Only if you promise not to get into another family argument."

He grinned and draped an arm across her shoulders. "Strictly business." Then he looked around. "Alison, you're with us."

The blonde pilot raised her eyebrows. "Our lord and master commands it?"

"I do, and you won't be sorry. We're looking for action."

"I could use some of that. A flyby?"

"You know what they say. 'Great minds think alike.' We're going to talk the captain into it."

Alison winked at Toni. "The second half of that quotation says, 'Fools seldom differ.' At least it will be entertaining watching the two of you in battle."

"He's promised to be good."

"Oh. That means you'll be doing the talking. Spoil my fun."

Andrew tossed up his hands. "All right. Toni talks, you back her up, I stand by looking mature and scientific."

"Great plan." Toni drove a firm elbow into his midsection and took the lead.

Natalia was already back at her desk. She glanced up as they entered the chartroom. "Hmm. Looks like a delegation. Time for a closer look at our subjects?"

Toni recovered quickly. "We thought so."

"What's your plan?"

Toni glanced at Andrew. He always had a plan.

He pretended to think. "There's two ways to go about it. Either we all go together or we send in a single sliver. I can't see using the whole squadron. That looks too much like an attack. They're not going to get much info on us in any case. We're at point double-zero six lights relative velocity, so we're coming through too fast, and our ships have great shielding in all the frequencies we've heard the aliens using, both re-ti and Otherwhere."

Natalia nodded. "Alison, what do you say?"

"I like the lone scout scenario. Smaller, less threatening, more likely to be passed off as an anomaly: a free comet or a loose asteroid. I'd send a solo ship in under complete shutdown, passive sensing only."

Toni gave Andrew a subtle elbow before he could say more. "I agree. We have nothing to lose by being careful." She gestured towards the viewscreen, where a whole swarm was displayed. "I imagine we'll have time for another pass soon. I doubt if they'll all disappear suddenly."

"I assume you don't need much setup time." The captain frowned at her son. "In fact, I'd be disappointed if Andrew didn't have it organized already."

The other two women turned to the young man, whose face reddened.

"...well, I did check with Patches, and the slivers would be glad of some action."

"Fine. We're skirting a large swarm in a couple of hours. That will give our scout time to get into their path." She was about to wave them out when she paused. "I'm assuming you're not sending Red Seven. He'd go over there and start a war, like as not."

Toni grinned. "No, we'll keep Ares under wraps till we need him. Patches will make the choice."

"As one should. Well, off you go. I'm looking forward to the data you collect."

As the three strode down the slideway to their bridge, Toni glanced at Andrew. "See? That went perfectly, and you didn't have to say anything unless directly asked." Before he could answer, she sent out a call to the Auxiliary team. *We're doing a flyby of the next swarm. All slivers on standby. Bridge Crew to the Auxiliary Bridge...oh.* She turned through the hatchway to see the crew assembled in their accel couches.

Andrew strapped himself in. "Patches, who are we sending?"

Image: Sliver B-6.

"Artemis the Huntress." Toni grinned. "Tell her to leave her bow at home. This is passive data gathering only."

Emotion: agreement.

Andrew looked around the bridge. "All right, let's plan this flyby. I'm on data collection from B-6. Alison, you're in command of the scout. Toni...? Alwyn?"

Toni glanced at the engineer, who thought a moment. "I'd like to monitor the reactions of the other subjects. That's our original assignment, after all."

She nodded. "I'll take the big picture, looking for threats. I want the other five slivers hiding behind *NightHawk* in battle formation, lying doggo but under my command and ready for anything. Alwyn can use them for passive data collection all he wants until it goes sideways, and then they're mine. Patches?"

Image: black barwolf monitoring Otherwhere media.

Emotion: agreement. "Andrew, we should leave *Diablo* moored to *NightHawk*. This isn't her kind of battle, and her mind is best used in our gestalt."

"Agreed."

"Captain, anything to add?" She winked at Andrew. Of course Natalia would be listening in.

Sounds good to me, Major. NightHawk and her crew will be standing by as needed. The whole squadron will cease decel one hour before contact. No sense shouting to everyone that we're here.

The captain came on full augment and ship's com. *"Listen up, now. We have scientific objectives, so Ensign Collingwood is in charge of this mission until there is trouble. At any point it could become a military situation, and then, on her say-so, Major Jacobs will take command. Any questions...? Good. Diablo, you'll be calling the time."*

Aye, ma'am.

"The mission commences...now."

Mission clock running.

"Andrew, what's the target and timeline?"

"There's an appropriate quarry coming up in ninety-seven minutes. A quad group in their usual diamond formation, fifty kilometres outside their swarm. We can change *NightHawk's* course two point nine degrees to starboard and approach within five thousand kilometres. B-6 will launch in...thirty-six minutes, and pass them within one thousand kilometres."

After a brief pause, the captain came back on com. "Course adjusted. The moment we pass, we return to full decel and the previous course, because there is another wing of that swarm coming behind in half an hour, and we want to be clear."

"Roger that, ma'am."

"Fine. Diablo: time count, please."

Contact in 94 minutes, ma'am. B-6 launch in 40 minutes, at 54 minutes to contact.

Toni broke in. "Barwolf One will stay unified until contact minus 56 minutes."

Slivers will detach in 38 minutes.

Toni was vaguely aware of orders given and action taking place on NightHawk, but her mind was focused on her duty. She contacted the barwolf pilots and set up their standby battle gestalt, then put it on hold. She began scans of the surrounding void, making sure there was nothing waiting to surprise them. *It will be a pleasant change to go into battle without power. No drive plume for anyone to hide in.*

Mission time 21 minutes. 73 minutes to contact. Slivers detach in 17 minutes.

So soon? Time flies when you're having fun. She accessed Diablo's navigation system and monitored the course of the approaching swarm. *We still haven't figured out why they change course, Diablo. Let me know if any individual swarm member so much as twitches out of the usual patterns.*

Aye, ma'am.

Mission time 32 minutes. 62 minutes to contact. Decel cease in two minutes.

Movement in the swarm, ma'am.

Where?

A closer view of a section of the swarm appeared. Nothing was moving.

Right...there. The ship indicated swerved less than half a wingspan, then returned to position. No further change.

Fine. Either he's avoiding debris or his girlfriend aimed a swat at him and he ducked. These things happen. Don't let it interfere with your mission duties but start a file of relative movement in the swarm. We need baseline data so we can discover a standard deviation.

Aye ma'am.

Mission time 34 minutes. 60 minutes to contact. All decel cease in ten seconds...five...three, two, one, full stealth.

The engines spooled down, and an unnatural silence filled the ship.

Mission time 38 minutes. 56 minutes to contact. Slivers detach in ten seconds...five...three, two, one,detach.

B-6 launch in 2 minutes.

Andrew came on the com. *B-6 maintain course. Other slivers move to your new positions.*

Emotion: eager desire to please.

The other five ships, staying in close formation, slipped under *NightHawk's* belly and came up close in on her starboard side. B-6 cruised on alone.

Mission time 40 minutes. 54 minutes to contact. B-6 launch in ten seconds...five...three, two, one, launch.

The sliver's nose swung to starboard and its engine blasted long enough to give it a vector of 4,000 kph. Then it shut down to passive mode and drifted towards its target.

Toni had a sudden thought. "Captain?"

Yes, Major.

"We should go to com silence at some time. No idea when."

A rather arbitrary choice, since we have no idea of the aliens' reception capabilities.

"We have Alwyn observing our subjects. He can watch for any response to any of our communications."

"No reaction so far, ma'am."

Best we can do. Listen up, now. Full com silence except in case of emergency, starting at contact minus 30 minutes unless Dr. Blainey detects a response before then. B-6 do not respond to this message.

Mission time 50 minutes. 44 minutes to contact.

The silence stretched on, tension rising as all eyes watched their screens, all other senses on high alert.

Mission time 64 minutes. Contact minus 30 minutes. Full com silence from this point until contact plus 10 minutes.

Toni's screen flashed, then the image changed, panning to the left and slightly down, zooming in to the swarm in that region. As she watched, that whole swarm began to turn, moving onto a new course. *Diablo* put the adjusted numbers on the screen, along with the words, "No Danger."

Toni blipped her com once to indicate "message received."

She leaned over to Andrew and pointed to her screen. Craning his neck to look, he nodded.

Barwolf Six cruised on, nearing the swarm, now.

Mission time 74 minutes. Contact minus 20 minutes.

The time count now appeared silently on their screens. The sliver cruised ahead.

Mission time 84 minutes. Contact minus 10 minutes.

Toni zoomed her screen in on the target ships, but they swept on, unperturbed. She scanned the two nearby formations, but they had no reaction.

Then a message appeared on their screens.

Movement in target. Contact minus two minutes twelve seconds.

Toni printed a response on her enterpad. "Tighter formation only."

Agreed...

Contact in 1 minute...

With a flash of white undersides, the aliens changed formation again. Toni zoomed in, then printed, "Change of orientation 90 degrees." Then she checked the other two groups. Neither had budged. Nor had any others in the vicinity.

Contact in 30 seconds...10...5...3, 2, 1, contact.

The aliens flashed past without action, B-6 coasted on towards safety, and her targets sailed away. At contact plus 3 minutes they resumed their usual formation.

Contact plus 10 minutes. Coms are live.

The captain clicked on. "Let's bring our pigeon home while we scan the data. We debrief in two hours. Return to decel in twenty minutes. *Barwolf One*, do you copy?"

Image: twenty minutes passing, decel starting. Emotion: agreement.

Toni also sent agreement. "Alwyn and *Diablo,* please spread your visual images around for us to analyze. Patches and Commander Jones, if you have anything on your media, please do the same."

Patches sent a burst of static. *Emotion: humour.*

"I guess you'll have to do your own analysis and translate it for us."

Emotion: agreement. Image: seven barwolves in gestalt. Time passing: two hours.

"Thank you."

Two hours later they convened in the mess, with Artemis onscreen from B-6.

Natalia regarded them. "Always nice when a mission goes off without a hitch. Especially a first contact with an alien race. Now, Ensign, what have you to report?"

"Let's start with the audio, because that's the most interesting. Lieutenant Jones?"

Adrian put up a soundtrack visual analog on the screen and started it running. The needle twitched. "There was a burst of static at two minutes, twelve seconds before contact, lasting five seconds." They silently watched the clock run. "Another...here it comes... at twenty-eight seconds before contact, lasting two seconds. Then at three minutes after contact, another two-second burst. Patches, did you get anything more than that?"

Emotions: negative, disappointment.

Andrew nodded. "At least it's a start. Alwyn, what about the visuals?"

"That all tallies. Watch the time clock on the side of the image."

At the two-minute, twelve-second mark, the four aliens closed formation until they were almost wingtip-to-wingtip. At minus twenty-eight seconds, they all flipped ninety degrees, so their ventral surfaces were facing towards the course of B-6. At plus three minutes, they all flipped back and resumed their travel spacing.

"Analysis?"

Alwyn shrugged. "First guess is that they noticed our vessel at two twelve. At twenty-eight, they assumed some kind of defensive position. When they realized the danger was over, they went back to their usual."

"Toni, anything to add?"

"Their contact positions could have been an attack formation as well, but the real take-home is that our closing velocity is about 170 k per minute, so they were able to sense us at just under 300 kilometres."

Andrew turned to the captain. "That's it for the moment. Alwyn and I will do detailed analysis of their movements. We'll put the barwolf gestalt on the communications, although I don't have much hope that we'll make much progress deciphering their language on nine seconds of data." He grinned. "But it's a start. Perhaps Commander Jones would like to sit in?"

The first officer's face brightened. "I certainly would. Any time spent working with Patches is time well spent."

Emotion: gracious thanks.

The captain rose. "Once again, a smooth operation. Ensign Collingwood, your orders were admirably concise."

For once, Andrew was at a loss for words. "Um...thank you, ma'am."

"We'll try our next approach when we're down to their relative speed."

Toni's mind switched to battle mode. "Ma'am, if we come in from the front, that will be taken as an aggressive posture."

"Can't be helped. Sooner or later, we have to make closer contact."

"Aye, ma'am. We'll think on it."

Natalia smiled. "That's what you're here for. We'll break now until supper, which I gather comes with a double grog ration and Jonny's specialty for desert."

Andrew's grin widened. "Pavlova?"

"She scammed a bunch of strawberries from the cook on the *Tiderace.*"

Image: barwolves lapping up green liquid.

"Right. And there will be wolfnip for the rest of the crew. Off you go now."

She flicked her wrists and the crew scattered.

17. FIRE ALARM

JERUSALEM'S HOPE

Roselyn was returning to her classroom from the dining hall one lunch time when she heard footsteps behind her. It was a long, straight stretch of corridor, rarely used in the middle of the day, and she glanced behind her to see who was coming along so quickly. Her heart fell. Eli again, and he looked determined.

She refused to run, pacing along at her usual speed.

He pulled ahead of her and then turned, forcing her to stop. She stood, giving him nothing but a flat stare.

"Pastor Josiah isn't happy with you, my dear."

She frowned up at him. "The Pastor's feelings about me have nothing to do with you."

"Oh, you'd be surprised. He's a good man, Josiah, and he's helped me out a lot. I feel I have to return his favour. I don't like to see him upset. And I think you made him upset."

"Well, you've given your message and it has been received." She moved aside to pass him. "Will you get out of my way?"

He slid into her path again. "Oh, no. It doesn't work that way. If you make my friend the Pastor unhappy, then you've made me unhappy. That means you owe us both a little happiness, don't you think?"

"I think your logic is faulty, but I'm sure you don't."

He easily countered her dodge. "You know how we're always taught to look for win-win situations? Well, this might work out that way. You could do me a little favour and make me happy, and I could do you a little favour and make you happy, too."

"Somehow I don't see it the same way." Now her back was against the corridor wall, and she prepared to use it as leverage for a forward lunge. *I'll hit him in the nose with my forehead. If I can reach that high.*

He ran his hands down his sides and stuck his chest out. "I see it this way, sweetheart. There's two kinds of women. There's married ones, but of course, thy neighbours' wife is strictly off limits. And then there's the unmarried ones..." he ogled her up and down.

She faced him squarely. "Who are unmarried because they choose to be, and I have to say, you're a good reason to stay that way."

He stepped forward, crowding her against the corridor wall. A glance to her right revealed a dark alcove, a dead end probably out of the reach of the com cameras. *This is not looking good.*

He leaned towards her, his breath fouling her nostrils, and shoved her around the corner. "Maybe what you're missing is a little taste of what it's like."

She turned her head aside, but he pressed his body against hers. She considered screaming, but...

"Hi, nntheacher. Nnat are nyou noing?"

Miriam, you have to get out of here. This is dangerous!

Her assailant turned and lifted a hand. "Get lost, split-lip, or you'll get another rip to your mouth."

The little girl held up a finger as if in warning, and Roselyn felt a familiar presence. There was a moment of silence, and then the fire alarms went off. Eli started back, snarled and strode away down the corridor. She felt a soft, furry cheek rub hers, and the presence was gone.

Image. Ninga flexing big claws, bullies running.

"Yes, I see what you mean." She took Miriam's hand and they walked swiftly to the nearest muster station. Only a few people showed up, and no one knew what had happened. The Fire Marshal asked some general questions, but nobody took the situation too seriously. The old ship was prone to small glitches, and "better safe than sorry" was the unwritten *'paramount.'*

As they left the station, Roslyn looked down at the waif trotting happily beside her. "Did Ninga do that?"

Emotion: negative.

"Did you do that?"

"Nhn."

"How did you do it?"

Image. Roselyn teaching Miriam. Teacher slowly morphs into auguar.

"Oh. She taught you. So, how do you do it?"

Image: ship's control systems, all interconnected wirelessly. Miriam's mind reaching out, touching connections.

"You mean you can control the ship with your mind?"

Miriam held up thumb and index finger very close together.

"I see. But you needed Ninga's help for this one."

"Nad nan. Hurry."

"Yes, he's a bad man, and you were in a bit of a rush." She reached out and tousled the silky hair. "And thank you very much. You and Ninga saved me from an unpleasant time."

The little girl's hip bumped her thigh, and they strolled down the corridor together.

18. INVESTIGATION

NIGHTHAWK

Toni strode down the short corridor to the ventral airlock where *Diablo* was moored. *Andrew, you there?"*

In the cockpit, love. What's up?

Nzinga is what's up. Be there in a moment.

When she reached the cockpit, he was standing, looking worried. "What's the problem?"

She flopped into her couch and motioned for him to do the same. "This has got beyond a simple quirk. We have to do a thorough investigation."

"You mean this Miriam person."

"Yes, and now her friend, Roselyn, who I gather is her teacher. And maybe the antique motorcycle they are riding on, but that's a bit vague."

"Motorcycle?"

"This is far too much detail to be coming from her imagination, Andrew. What are we going to do? We're getting to the action part of our mission, and her mind is somewhere else."

He grinned. "We could go all scientific and do a bunch of tests..."

She slapped his arm. "Or we could act like inclusive people and just ask her. *Nzinga!*"

Boo!

Toni turned and glowered at the laughing fangs behind her head. "We have to talk to you."

Emotion: eager desire to please.

"Tell us about Miriam."

"And Roselyn."

Image: teacher and student walking hand in hand down narrow, dingy spaceship corridor.

And where are they?

Image: General specs of Interplanetary Research Vessel Carl Sagan, refitted as a generation ship, re-registered as Jerusalem's Hope. Left Sol system for Barnard thirty years ago, with 8 crew and 97 passengers, Captain Dobroslaw Nowak commanding. ETA at Barnard

Embassy, 37 days. Sistership, Ark of the Covenant, arrived Barnard Embassy six point five months ago.

"Well, that explains a lot. Another set of Sensitives three generations deep. And you can communicate with them."

Image: Auguar talking to Patches. Barwolf throwing words across space.

"Ah. Our communications expert is involved. *Patches, could you come to the Diablo cockpit, please?*"

Image: black barwolf saluting.

"*I did say 'please.'*"

Toni backhanded his shoulder. *Image: small girl. Emotion: question?*

The barwolf appeared in the door and strolled over to arrange oneself on Nzinga's accel couch. *Image: human head with small blue aura hovering around it. Image: Andrew's head with larger blue aura around it. Image: Brindle's head with even larger aura. Image: black barwolf's head with huge aura, spreading out to encompass all the rest. Emotion: Question?*

"Yes, I understand."

Image: head of small girl with no mouth. Intense blue aura reaching out to black spaceship from far away.

"I see. She's a real phenomenon. Why no mouth?"

Image: small woman with red hair talking to child. Child responding with images, not speech.

"She doesn't talk."

Emotion: Agreement.

"Can we communicate with these people?"

After a short pause, Patches shook ones head in a rather human way. *Image: red-haired woman standing in front of children. Small girl in front row.*

"Oh. Right now they're...in school?"

Emotion: agreement

"Okay. Nzinga, can you keep an eye on them and let us know when she's free?"

Emotion: eager desire to please.

"Thank you. And since we're all together, *Diablo* has been gathering data on the small movements the aliens make within their formations. I think we have enough information to set up some parameters..."

They worked until Patches called a halt.

Image: red-haired teacher and small girl sitting together, talking.

Andrew glanced at Toni. "Anyone else around?"

Emotion: negative.

"Could we speak with them now?"

Image: Ensign Collingsworth standing on log floating in water. Black barwolf reaches out and nudges his shoulder...

"All right, I know how this is going to end. I get the picture."

Emotion: disappointment.

Image: old-fashioned telephone ringing. Auguar Trainer picking up.

Toni took this as her cue to step in and opened her augment. "This is Major Toni Jacobs of Planetary Community Space Craft 9108 *NightHawk*, Reconnaissance Cutter, on patrol between Sol and Barnard. With whom am I speaking?"

Oh. So that's who you are. I'm Roselyn Jakobsdotter, teacher on board the Jerusalem's Hope, in transit from Sol to Barnard Sanctuary. Estimated time of arrival at the Barnard Embassy is just over a month, I believe. I'm so glad to speak to you.

"Do you have any idea why such an important communication is being handled by the local school teacher?"

Emotion: laughter. If you want a real surprise, why don't you talk to your real contact.

"We know about Miriam. Why is she a surprise?"

Because she's one of my students and she's six and a half years old. Children reach out for comfort when they need it. I guess she reached out to Ninga. I gather she found more than a cuddly kitty."

Toni frowned, but then her brow cleared. *Image: Nzinga lolling on her bed.* "You mean Nzinga, my auguar."

That would be her. I guess Miriam told us the name wrong. Image: small girl's face. She has trouble with esses.

"She has a cleft lip?"

Palette, too. She's had them from birth.

"Of course it was from birth. It's a genetic flaw. Why wasn't it fixed?"

We don't have the facilities.

"That's too bad. They're easier to fix when the child is younger, I think. But when you hit the Embassy, you go straight to Ambassador Pretoro and tell him you have a patient for the Space Arm medics. They'll fix her right up."

Emotion: cynical laughter. I'm a twenty-year-old female immigrant, and I'm just going to walk into the Ambassador's office and demand to talk to him.

"I don't see what your gender has to do with it, but he'll be expecting you. Don't be surprised if he yanks the two of you off that boat the moment you clear quarantine."

There was a pause. *...and now that you've met me, what happens next? I'm sorry Miriam has been wasting Space Arm resources. I only found out about it recently, myself.*

"Oh, no. This isn't a waste at all. Do you realize that we're talking re-ti over about three light years' distance, with only a small time lag?"

I never thought about that. Emotion: wry humour. And I'm the one that teaches the children about the speed of light. What's going on?"

"Barwolf gestalt. I can't tell you much more, because we're just finding out about it ourselves."

Oh, the beasts. How are the beastlings coming along? You know, the three little ones that were kidnapped.

"How did you know about that?"

Emotion: embarrassment. Dreams. I thought you were something out of my dreams.

"You were listening in on our communications through your dreams? That's amazing. I was listening to yours! My fiancée, Andrew Collingwood, will want to talk to you. He's studying gestalts and augments, and you and your little friend are something new in the development of the human race."

"Oh, it's not just us. I have two whole classes of students like this. I mean, not like Miriam, but about twelve of them are stronger than me, and the other nine are pretty close."

"Andrew is going to love this. I don't quite know how to prepare you for it, but anticipate a lot of attention when you get to Barnard's. There will be many options for you in the future, and you want to have your priorities straight before they all hit you like a ton of cargo from a broken net."

Emotion: confusion. Well...I...

"Look, I know this has struck you all of a heap. Take your time. Think about it. Call up Nzinga whenever you like. If she's busy, she'll get back to you when she can. And when you feel up to it, you'd best get in touch with Andrew. He's the specialist, and he's dying to talk, but not right now. Right now, you go back to your teaching and your life, and try to live it as normally as possible."

Thank you.

"And do some research on cleft lips and cleft palates. You're probably the best person to prep Miriam for her operation, and you want to know what information to give her. Oh, and you should be prepared for communication from this beastie." *Image: Patches.*

"Oh. I already know Patch…but I don't know if it's a him or a her. I don't get any signals one way or the other, somehow."

"That's because Patches is ungendered. Once you find out about the barwolf society you'll understand. If you use the pronoun "one" you'll be fine. By the way, what are your research facilities like on that ship?"

Emotion: wry humour. Like those on any ship that was obsolete thirty years ago. We get regular updates from the SolNet, all five or six years out of date.

"Fine. Now you really have to talk to Patches. Give me a time when you're free."

We're on lunch break right now. I'm off for an hour at…three hours and forty-five minutes from now.

"You have an appointment with Patches in three hours and forty-five minutes from right now."

Emotion: astonishment. I have an appointment with a beast?

"With a barwolf. If Miriam wants to be there, she should be. Everything all right?"

Emotion: wry humour. I'm just thinking that probably any moment I'm going to wake up, and it will be time for my usual boring day.

"Enjoy the boring while you can. Your life would have changed when you got downplanet anyway. It's just going to be a whole lot better, now." Toni nodded to Patches, and the connection faded away. *At least I hope it will be better. Who knows?*

* * *

At three hours and forty-five minutes, Miriam and Roselyn were sitting in the teacher's cabin trying not to be nervous. By the time Patches was through with them an hour later, they were both wringing in sweat and approaching delirious with joy.

In between, there was a learning session the like of which Roselyn had never experienced. None of it was done with words; it was all example and experience. Put in normal WorldNet terms, they were taught how to enter the Aether, which they learned was the Barwolf communication space in Otherwhere. Then they had to learn to distinguish individual streams of messages. Then to send messages, and to know when they were receiving one, and how to respond. For some of it Patches connected to *Jerusalem*, so the ship could help with data transfers. The old ArIn didn't have any real communication ability in that medium, but could use Miriam as a translator, in a reverse of the usual process.

They were introduced to someone called Joachim Perez, who apparently lived on Arborea and studied barwolves with Andrew Collingwood and Dr. Morissa Goodall, whom they were yet to meet. Joachim had been designated their contact because they had no ability or knowledge to access the vast amount of data streaming around the human sphere. Roselyn grinned to herself. *And he's low in the chain of command so his time isn't that costly.*

Miriam was only interested in contacting the beastlings, which was easily accomplished because Factory 4-80 was part of the human/barwolf network. She was already thinking up games to play with them, and insisted that Patches provide her with lessons they would normally be learning if they were with their families.

As the euphoria faded, Roselyn sent Miriam scooting off to her cadre for supper and had a quick shower before joining her friends at their table. Abram was carrying the conversation as usual, his long arms threatening everyone's dinner.

When she sat down, he thrust a hand in her direction. "There. A perfect example. Josiah the Creep has been bothering her, and he tried to swing the Mens' Council on his side."

For once, Barnabus spoke up. "What do you mean?"

"He's done the math. Rosy turns twenty-one just about the time we hit Barnard Embassy. We'll be reunited with the *Ark of the Covenant.* I bet he's afraid she'll contract with one of the younger lads on the other ship. Or one of the Space Arm people at the embassy, or some rich miner from the Asteroid Belts. So he wants them to declare her adult ahead of time, and then force her to marry him before he loses control of her. Can you see any other reason?

The look on Barnabus's face gave her a pang of anxiety, and she laid a calming hand on his arm. "It's all right. I told them I wasn't interested."

Sapphira scoffed. "And what happened next? He sent his goon, Eli, to soften her up."

"What?" Barnabus was on his feet, his eyes scanning the dining hall. "I'll just have a little talk with Eli."

She pulled him back down. "No, you won't. I tell you, don't worry about me. I have my resources."

"What resources? You're all by yourself in that classroom a lot of the time." The lad faced her and softened his voice. "I worry about you."

She smiled. "Thank you, Barnabus, but don't be upset. I can handle Eli, and things are looking up right now."

He regarded her from under lowered brows. "You call this looking up? In what way?"

"I...can't really say. But I handled him last week, didn't I?"

Abram waved his index finger in front of her face. "Wait a minute. Last week. Tuesday, about four o'clock, right?"

"It was about then."

"The fire alarms went off in Corridor 36-D about then, didn't they?"

"I believe they did, yes. It was very fortunate. Everybody came rushing around, and Eli disappeared."

"How does one go about setting off the fire alarms when one needs them? Without hitting the switch."

She shrugged. "I don't know. Start a fire, I suppose."

"Rosy, you didn't!" this came from Sapphira.

She grinned. "As it happened, I didn't.

Abram wasn't about to be put off. "Then who did?"

She shrugged. "It wasn't me, I know that."

"Well, if he gives you any more trouble, you let us know." He draped an arm over his shorter friend's shoulders. "Barnabus and I will deal with him."

She put on her best Teacher frown. "You will do no such thing. If I need your help, I'll ask for it. Until then, you will not put yourselves into any danger, or get into any trouble. Is that clear?"

Abram made a salaaming motion. "Yes, Teacher. Whatever you say."

She turned to Barnabus. "You, too!"

"Oh yes, certainly, Roselyn. Whatever you say."

She sat back and smiled around at her friends.

Sapphira stared back. "There's something different about you, Rosy. I don't know what it is, but you're...stronger. I can tell."

"Thank you, I guess. I'm feeling more sure of myself these days. It's nice to have support, you know?"

"Well, if you need support, you have it." The other girl made a circular gesture. "We have to support each other. At the moment, we're all we've got."

Abram thrust out his arms as usual. "For the next five weeks. Then we have a whole new world to explore."

"Yes, can you believe it?" Samira grinned. "The Council finally gave us some information!"

A packet of information on the new planet had been shipped from Barnard Embassy, where the message turnaround time was only a matter of weeks, now. An edited version had been released by the Council, and everyone had devoured it. Talk turned to their prospects on Arborea, and Roselyn was glad to let the conversation pass her by. *My future is going to be rather interesting. I hope in a good way.*

19. FIRE OF A DIFFERENT SORT

JERUSALEM'S HOPE

If Eli hadn't been so sure of himself at his next attempt, it would have been ludicrous. As it was, it shook Roselyn more than she liked to admit. He jogged up beside her just outside the dining room doorway and draped an arm around her shoulders with a cheerful smile. "Hi, Rosy. How's it going?"

She ducked out from under his weight, giving him her best 'teacher' frown. "That's hardly appropriate, Mr. Barad." She strode ahead, and then was sorry she had, as the safety of the dining hall door receded behind her.

"Oh, come on, Rosy." He hurried to catch up. "Look, I'm sorry I was pushing you the other day. We should be friends."

She glanced at him. *He's completely serious.*

"Hey, I got a great idea." He grabbed her arm and swung her around to face him." You don't need to marry the Pastor, you know. Why don't you just hook up with me? Hell, we don't even have to get married." He reached out to run a finger down her cheek. She slid aside so that his hand fell on empty air.

This isn't working. He just isn't going to quit unless I do something.

"Come on, sweetheart. I can treat you nice." He grinned. "Better than that old guy, I guarantee."

She stood, looking at him. He just hung there like a malignant smell, his cocky grin the most irritating part of it all.

She opened her augment, wondering if she could reach Ninga. The Aether was blank, and without Miriam, she had no idea how to proceed. *I am not going to involve her. She doesn't deserve my problems.*

He reached out and tucked a strand of hair behind her ear. "You're pretty. You know that?"

How does Miriam do it? She can sense the messages that control the ship. She glanced at the walls of the corridor. Nothing but firm, blank metal. Her mind whirled as her body stood, frozen.

"No, I mean it. Like, I never noticed you before, but here you are, growing up right in front of our eyes." He stood back to scan her from head to toe. "Not doin' too bad, kid."

I've got to do something! She reached out into the Aether around her, searching for any sense of anything, anyone. Nothing. She accessed the normal ShipNet search patterns, but all she got was an invitation to ask a question.

His hand was reaching out towards her breast, now, and she cringed away. In desperation, she screamed, *"Fire!"* into her augment with all her might. Nothing happened, but she could feel a space now, like an open void waiting for information.

Just before his fingers touched her, she tried again. *You want a fire, I'll give you one!* She remembered looking into the forge in one of the metalwork shops. *Image: Fire.* She stoked it with all her fear and disgust, bringing the flames roaring out of their containment.

With a sudden gush, the sprinklers came on at full force, water spraying from every direction. In a moment they were both drenched, disoriented in the barrage. Eli cursed and sprinted away down the corridor, slipping and floundering in the sheet of water on the plating. The moment he was gone, the deluge stopped. She turned in the opposite direction and went straight to her room before anyone responded.

It was only as she was pulling off her soaking dress that she realized. *The fire alarm didn't go off. Just the sprinklers. That's strange.*

She changed hurriedly and slipped out into the corridor. Except for some incriminating wet footprints leading to her door, the hall was empty. Grabbing a towel, she hurriedly wiped out a few metres of the tracks, leaving a puzzle for anyone doing detective work.

Then she went back inside, half-dried her hair, tossed on a kerchief, and headed back to class.

That evening in the quiet of her own room, she settled down and opened her augment. *Now that I don't have some idiot clawing at my body, I can concentrate.* In her mind, she went over the way it felt when she had sent the image.

That's it. It was like I was asking the ship's ArIn to open a door. You don't talk to it, you just send an image of the door opening, and it happens. It's a different level of communication, like Patches taught us.

Image: Sol Embassy in Barnard System. I know it's a lousy image, but that's all I've seen. Emotion: question?

Image: Hi-res image of Sol Embassy, former fighter carrier "Unicorn," in Lagrange 3 stationary orbit around Zeta, third planet from Barnard's star. Image: planet Zeta cutting a swath through the Asteroid belts, separating the Inner Belt, with its mines and the Asteroid Project, from the Outer Belt, with its numerous small factories, mines, and infrastructure projects. The information flowed on, and all she had to do was stick a finger in anywhere to direct her point of view.

So, this is how you search the ArIn's data banks. Intrigued, she sent another feeling. *Emotion: question? Source of data flow.*

She received a series of images showing spaceships flying rapidly from Sol to Barnard, passing *Jerusalem's Hope* along the way, and sending packets of data back and forth.

Question: Barwolves.

Again data flowed in. Far into the night she searched, revelling in the flow of information. *I don't need Miriam. I don't need the barwolves or Nzinga. I can do this on my own!* Finally, she forced herself to stop, bemoaning the necessity of sleep.

But in the morning she woke full of new information for her lessons and new enthusiasm for her teaching.

20. SECOND FLY-BY

NIGHTHAWK

Toni could never be sure when the captain stopped being the Captain and started being Natalia. She sometimes wondered whether Natalia, herself, knew. So, the major wasn't surprised when they were having a pleasant chat in the mess, and O'Rourke got a certain look in her eye. She straightened and rubbed her hands together as if she was thinking. "Oh, and since I've got you here, it gives me a chance to focus your mind a bit."

"Focus?" Toni sat down. "What's up?"

"We're down to 200 ks per minute."

"Which is the velocity the aliens are travelling. But in the opposite dirction."

"Right. But it's on a scale they're used to, so now we can confront them on their own terms. The last time we disguised ourselves and came off as an anomaly. Now we come in straight and see how they deal with us."

"As long as we don't come off as too aggressive."

The captain frowned. "Look, there are two possibilities. First, these are just organisms going about their business, and they react to intrusion. Period. Second, they are part of a larger society, with the ability to communicate across the swarm, or perhaps across the species, like the barwolves do. If they're the first, it's no problem. If we foul up with one formation, we can try again fresh with the next one.'

Toni nodded. "And if they're a communicating, record-keeping society, they already know about us because of the probes they destroyed, so there's no sense in trying to hide."

"Exactly. We reveal ourselves, but stay a reasonable distance away. It will be up to them to decide. That gives us unbiased data, and we don't cause inter-species incidents."

Toni shrugged. "That's your decision. I'm not sure Andrew will want to take that course, but..."

"And that's why I'm talking to you first. I would rather not hear from Andrew about this."

Toni nodded. "And that's why I'm stepping aside. I know better than to get between the two of you. For reasons of self-preservation, I'm going to hold firm to that policy for the next forty years or so."

Natalia grinned. "That's fine. You already told me what I wanted to know."

"Well, I'm glad you heard it, because I don't recall telling you anything."

"Perfect. I'll call a council of war in about an hour. You go and prep everyone."

"I know. Including Andrew." She frowned at her future mother-in-law as she stood. "When you get like this, I have just the tiniest urge to side with Andrew." She turned in the doorway. "But then I talk to him, and it all comes back to me."

* * *

Toni was surprised to discover that she was the only one with reservations about the frontal approach. The rest of the crew seemed anxious to make progress on the mission, and even Alwyn was willing to go along with the flow.

She held her peace and prepared for the exercise.

However, just before they started, the captain called her to a private conference with Alison. They stood in the chartroom in front of Natalia's desk, because there was only one extra chair. She glanced at the other major, received a miniscule shrug.

O'Rourke looked up from her enterpad. "I've asked you both together, because I don't want any misunderstanding. Alison, I know you're expecting to run the attack as usual, but I have a problem."

"Yes, ma'am?"

"Yes. Her." She nodded towards Toni. "I don't like it when she disagrees with me."

Toni knew enough to stay silent, but the newer member of the crew looked puzzled. "How can I help?"

"By stepping aside and letting her direct this one."

Alison's frown turned into a grin. "I see. So if nothing goes wrong it will be all her fault."

Natalia chuckled. "Partly. But that's not the real reason. It's her battle experience. We've been here before. When the experienced hand is uneasy, if you take the time to ask why, it's usually too late."

"And they sent me out here to gain that experience without killing myself or anyone else."

"Bluntly put, but correct. Do you have a problem with that, Toni?"

"Damned politicians. You've set it up between yourselves so that if nothing goes wrong I look like an idiot." She frowned at the captain. "What if I screw it up just to prove I'm right?"

"Then I'm a very poor judge of character and a lousy captain."

"Prime. So now I'm responsible for your reputation as well."

"The way it always goes for a captain. Alison, you're on backup, with your eyes on the bigger picture."

"And if you see even the slightest detail out of place, don't wait. Jump in." Toni regarded the taller woman. "You understand? You're not a green pilot right out of flight school. Your instincts count, too."

"That's a lot of trust, Major." Alison's shoulders straightened. "I'll live up to it." She headed out the door.

As Toni left the room, the captain caught her eye and winked. She rolled her eyes and turned away. *She's trying to turn me into a politician, too."*

* * *

Once again, it all started out exactly as planned. Like the last time, they sent in a single sliver, this time Red Five with Demeter, Goddess of the Earth at the helm. Once again, the target formation registered the intruder at about 300 kilometres and closed their formation. They flipped into defensive mode earlier, but otherwise they were acting according to plan. Toni could feel the satisfaction oozing into the gestalt.

Until something registered in her subconscious. *This looks different.*

"B-5! Evasive maneuver 17!"

And then everything happened at once. The ponderous sweep of the aliens' wings all slowed until they froze pointing at the slivership. Demeter started to twist away, but was engulfed by a flare of bright silver light. The flash was quickly dampened by *NightHawk's* automatic systems, but the afterimage implanted itself on Toni's vision. At the same time, all the audio circuits registered a blast of white noise. Toni as vaguely aware of similar disturbance on the barwolf gestalt, but all her attention was focused on her pilot.

The slivership fled, engine blasting, and the barrage ended as if cut off by switch. In a moment of silence, *NightHawk* brought the viewscreens back to normal, showing the alien wings slowly resuming their unfaltering sweeps.

By now, the Space Arm squadron was far to the rear of the aliens, and the view from the stern showed them returning to formation and sailing serenely on.

"Barwolf Five, report. What is your status?"

Emotion: shaky relief.

Toni's heart rose. *"Any damage?"*

Image: barwolf checking systems. Emotion: negative. Emotion: faint humour. Image: auxiliary electrical storage fully charged.

"You mean you were able to use that energy blast to fill your fuel cells?"

Emotion: agreement. Image: cup of wolfnip filling and overflowing down the sides.

"You overfilled them. Don't worry. You'll get your share tonight. You did well, Demeter. You are officially now a hero.

Emotion: question?

Oh. A new concept. Let's deal with that later.

Emotion: agreement. Emotion: fatigue.

Yes, I imagine. You take a rest. We'll see what the captain wants.

Natalia had been listening, of course. *Pull Red Five in close to the Engineering section of NightHawk, please. I want Fiona inside the vessel, going over everything with a fine comb. Nelson, I want scans in all spectra from the outside. Nzinga and Chakka, you're on the internal circuits. Compare everything to the specs Freighty provided. Auxiliary crew review the action in gestalt. Patches, will you see to the mental health of your crewmember?*

Emotion: agreement, confidence.

Fine. Everybody get to work. We'll debrief when we have something to say, probably within four hours, but don't rush it. This is a very important "first," and we don't want to make any mistakes.

The augment com was filled with agreement, and the silence of heavy concentration settled over the squadron.

* * *

It took five hours, but when the crew met, the augments hummed with a general air of satisfaction. Natalia looked around the group in the Auxiliary Bridge. "We'll start with the analysis of the action, then move to the outcomes later. Major Jacobs?"

Toni took the formality as a sign that this was going on the official record. "Yes, ma'am. We made the same approach as the first contact. At the start, everything went as expected. They sensed our presence at the same distance and took the same defensive measures."

"However, as B-5 approached closer, something was off. I'm sorry, ma'am, but I looked over the record several times, and I just can't figure out what it was. I just knew that an attack was coming."

The captain nodded. "Which is why you were there. Your experience."

"Either that, or being tuned into the barwolf gestalt, I'm subliminally aware of events in Otherwhere."

"Which we will analyze at our leisure. Please continue."

"So I gave B-5 the alert, and she started Evasive Maneuver 17."

"Which she did not complete."

"Not quite. Perhaps I should explain, for the record?"

"Please do."

"Evasive Maneuver 17 is a failsafe from Freighty's tactics book on electronic warfare. It's action you call when you know there's danger, but you don't have enough data to say what. Basically, it slues the ship around for a quick blast to exit the danger zone. Immediately after, it repositions the ship to reflect any electronic force directed at it. The design weakness in the sliverships is the square stern with the engine exhaust. A direct hit on a fleeing ship will be at ninety degrees." She flicked her fingers apart. "Boom!"

"I see. So what happened to Maneuver 17?"

"17 actually has two functions. The second one is simply to alert everyone. At that point the pilot, being closest to the action, jumps to first in command. So what happened next should come from her."

"Thank you, major. *Demeter?*"

Eager desire to please.

"What happened after you executed Maneuver 17?"

Image: slivership B-5 analyzing alien electronics. Image: buildup of charge in certain areas of alien ships. Image: charge moving laterally towards wingtips. Image: series of complicated mathematical calculations. Image: beam of energy leaving alien formation. Image: Slivership B-6 aligning to best angle of reflection.

Image: beam of energy reflecting off B-5, directed very close to NightHawk. Mothership brightly lit for a moment. Emotion: apology.

"I see. But that was just bad luck."

Image: mathematical calculations. Diagram of alien formation, electronic beam, slivership reflection, danger area highlighted.

"Right. We won't be anywhere near that zone next time. Thank you, Demeter. You obviously handled this perfectly."

Emotion: pleasure and pride. Image: stylized red Orca jumping high out of ocean, landing with huge splash. Other orcas leaping and splashing, green grizzlies slamming their paws into the water.

"Yes, I'm sure your squadron is very pleased. Thank you."

Gradually the celebration calmed.

"Anything else, Major?"

"No, ma'am. The moment B-5 was out of range, the aliens went back to their usual formation as if nothing had happened. Major Rowell didn't notice any reaction in nearby formations. Nor has that swarm made any course changes since."

"Hmm. So we're a minor irritation, to be warned off and ignored. Ensign Collingwood, what does your data tell us?"

Andrew shrugged. "What she said, ma'am. It was actually useful to be in the backwash of the attack because we got good data. It's a blast of free electrons, and they ionize everything they touch. Every piece of metal will instantly become magnetic. Every electric circuit will overload. Every circuit breaker will break."

"And the defence?"

"Reflection. The Mirror Permaskin on the slivers can reflect most of it, turn a percentage into electricity and absorb a certain amount, but above that, circuits are going to pop."

"Chief Engineer Lundeen?"

"The ship seems to have performed up to specs, ma'am. No damage, no red lines on the record. Visual inspection of the hull shows no effect. Auxiliary storage filled to 110%."

"Are you suggesting that the sliverships could use these creatures to recharge their power supplies?"

"A dangerous proposition, but yes."

"Ship this data off to Freighty by Otherwhere Express."

"On it, ma'am."

"Fine. Toni, I don't like that frown."

"Sorry, ma'am. It just came to me."

"Well, don't spare us. What's wrong now?"

"Security." She flicked a wrist to point a thumb at Patches.

"I see. Anything we say in one's presence is available to the whole Barwolf Nation, and eventually, the whole universe."

Toni shook her head. "If you carry that further, it opens a huge can of worms."

Alwyn's eyes widened. "Future criminals suborning teams of barwolves to mine the barwolf net for odd bits of useful information."

The captain held up both hands. "Hold it right there. We're in the middle of a debrief. Let's not predict the end of civilization as we know it." She grinned at Toni. "Looking for a subject for your Master's thesis already?"

"No, ma'am." She made a poor job of hiding her grin. "Back on topic, ma'am."

'Thank you, I'm sure. No rabbit holes for us today." Natalia surveyed the group, those in person and those on augment. "Anything else?"

There was no response, so she nodded. "Well, a good day's work, folks. I suggest we get back on accel and come up to speed with our subjects. Tomorrow I want to make a different approach. These creatures are dangerous, and we need a lot more data."

Expecting no response, the captain cut off the augment com and started giving acceleration orders to the bridge.

21. A LEARNING EXPERIENCE

JERUSALEM'S HOPE

After the sprinkler incident Eli left Roselyn alone, and one day she was in her classroom after the children had left, improving on what her class considered "tidied up" and thinking about tomorrow's lessons. As she worked, she became aware of an approaching presence. A strong one. *No question who I inherited my abilities from. I wonder what brings her down to the Lower Depths?*

She straightened as her mother strode in and surveyed the space. "Good afternoon, Roselyn, my dear. The organization of this room looks like a composite of the minds that inhabit it."

She smiled. "And that's a good thing, Mother dear, because that creates the best learning environment for those minds. *Education is paramount,* after all."

Tirza Bensoussan leaned against the teacher's desk, crossing her long, slim legs. "How are you doing, my dear? I don't see you enough."

"We're both busy, I suppose. You doing important things, and me just...you know, teaching."

"Roselyn." Her mother's voice deepened. "That was unfair."

She shrugged. "Probably. But if you walk into my territory and immediately try to put me at a disadvantage, you have to expect I'll play by my own rules."

Her mother regarded her, crossing her arms. "Why Rosy, that was very well stated. I begin to have hope for you." She lowered her brows. "But I also have a concern."

She faced the other woman. "What about this time?"

Tirza lifted a finger to show she had caught the inference but was letting it pass. "This is a legitimate concern. It's about your visit to the Men's Council recently. Why didn't you tell me?"

"You always said it was better if I could handle my own problems. I'm handling this one."

"And what is the problem?"

"You mean you don't know?"

"No, I don't, but if one of those old goats has you lined up as a child bride, it becomes both personal and part of my position on the Women's Council to deal with it."

"Don't worry, Mother. It's not one of the old goats."

"Ah. Pastor Josia. I knew it!"

"How did you know?"

"He's not exactly subtle. His name has come up in our council. Some of us think his eyes stray to the younger girls too much. Some of the old biddies say it's our imagination, or it's natural, or all the other excuses. The only solution they can come up with is he should get married."

Roselyn's heart dropped. "Which means they are right in line with the Men's Council."

"I said some of us. The rest are aghast at the idea."

"From their reactions, I'd say the men are divided as well, but not so concerned."

Her mother straightened and began to pace with long strides, as she usually did when she was thinking. It was difficult in the crowded room, but she managed. "The question is, what do we do now?"

"You don't do anything, Mother. I said I was handling it."

Tirza stopped in mid-stride. "You are?"

"That's right. They wanted to boost me to adult status immediately. Not too hard to figure that out. I asked them if then I could take my place on the Women's Council, and they weren't so enthused about that. I wonder why?"

"You know very well." Her mother smiled grimly. "For the last thirty years, the men's council has always outvoted us in the General Meetings. But there are more female Sensitives in the later generations, and we've lost more men than women to Otherwhere. At the moment, the numbers are even. One more woman, and, bam!" She slammed her fist into her other hand.

"Why, Mother, I've never seen you so...demonstrative."

"Just you wait until we get the majority. We'll be doing some demonstrating."

"Well, don't count on it just yet. I turned them down."

"You did? What did they say?"

"Nothing. Maybe they are aware of the numbers, too."

"Hmm. I sort of wish you hadn't mentioned it to them. We might have…"

"No, Mother. I am not a pawn to be traded away. So far, I am handling the situation."

"Oh? What have you done?"

"I've seen you do it a hundred times. First, I stated my position clearly. Now I'm rallying my support."

"And did you think to rally me?"

"Not unless I really need to."

The older woman nodded. "Probably wise. Don't bring in the big guns until you need them."

"From the sound of the Women's Council, they might not be that useful. I'll use my own resources, thank you."

"What resources do you have? Not that loud group you hang around with."

She grinned. "I spend my time with a very quiet and thoughtful group. Abram just makes up for all the rest of us." A familiar presence approached. "We're about to be interrupted. Do you have anything else?"

"No, no, I was just checking. You seem to feel you have everything under control, at which I am somewhat surprised and very pleased." Her mother's pleasant smile widened as she turned. "And whom do we have here?"

Faced with this imposing figure, Miriam shrank back, speechless.

"Go ahead, Miriam. Say hello to my mother."

The little girl licked her lips, pursed them as best she could and straightened her shoulders. "nHello, Mnistressth Bennounnan."

"Hello, Miriam. What brings you here?"

But Miriam had used up her courage. She glanced with helpless eyes at her teacher.

"She always comes around to help out. Are you here to prepare next week's imaging lesson for the Seniors?"

A big nod.

"Well, go and use the big viewscreen in my office. And no fair getting *Jerusalem* to do it all for you."

Miriam's nose tilted up. She gave a saucy "Huh!" and strode into the office, closing the door firmly.

Tirza frowned. "What's that about *Jerusalem*?"

90

"We've had permission to talk to the ship's ArIn for months now. Although nobody thought to tell us."

"But a child? And one like...that? She shouldn't be wasting important resources."

Roselyn took her mother's hand and led her to the teacher's chair. "Sit down, Mother. You have something to learn."

Puzzled, the woman obeyed.

Her daughter now leaned on the desk with her legs crossed. *Hmm. Not so impressive when someone my size does it. Oh, well.*

"It's this way. You asked me about my resources." She pointed to the office. "That's one of them. The children's gestalt is the most powerful force on the ship. Everyone should know that, but it hasn't really sunk in. They don't want to believe it, and we don't bother them, so they ignore us, but we are the most powerful force. And I'm in charge.

"Another thing. Don't let Miriam's handicap fool you. It's also her greatest asset. Because she can't speak well, she's one full level advanced in mental communication on everyone, including me. When she gets to Barnard's star and the Space Arm surgeons at the embassy fix her lip and pallet, she is going to be a force to be reckoned with."

"What are you talking about?"

"Her cleft palate. The Space Arm contingent in Barnard is a permanent posting with many families. Their surgeons will handle a simple operation like that in no time. And when Ambassador Pretoro finds out how talented she is..." The look on her mother's face stopped her.

"What are you talking about? Who is Ambassador Pretoro, and how do you know about him?"

Uh-oh. I got too pleased with myself and opened my big mouth. Now I have to tell her something. "It works like this, Mother. We have permission to talk to the ShipNet, right?"

"Of course."

"And all of our information for the last thirty years has been coming from the SolNet, and is years out of date, right?"

"Exactly. But now we're getting information from Barnard, and it's only a few months out of date."

She frowned. "Do the math, Mother. It's only days out of date. The Council has been keeping us in the dark."

Her mother nodded. "I was aware of that, and I voted against it. But the new information is still not available to you. Is it?"

"Sure it is, Mum." She leaned down and whispered behind her hand. "Spaceship ArIns are gossips."

"They are?"

"They communicate with each other all the time. Did you know that a Space Arm courier taking an official to Arborea from the Barnard Embassy ran into a random storm of counter-rotating rocks last year, and was almost destroyed? The pilot's name is Alison Rowell, and her father is on the board of the Asteroid Project. I don't know what the Asteroid Project is, but he's right up there at the top."

"Why are you telling me this?"

"To show you what kind of information is floating around. Ships travelling in Otherwhere are getting from Sol to Barnard in eight months. The military ones upload huge quantities of data to the embassy servers. A certain amount of it is made available to the BarnardNet, and all ship's ArIns download tons."

"But how do you get it?"

"Do you know what *Jerusalem's Hope* was, before our people bought her?"

"Some kind of a research vessel, I believe."

"That's right. And she has all sorts of abilities that we don't know about, one of which is top-notch communications and data storage equipment. At least, top-notch thirty years ago. She can contact the Space Arm vessels, and they have allowed her to update some of her codes. So, *Jerusalem* has pretty much everything important that was available in Barnard as of two or three months ago, no matter how much the Council controls the daily feed. Say, I have an idea. Miriam?"

The door opened. "Nnyes, Theacher?"

"Please have *Jerusalem* call up the results of the Barnard Council election and the roster of upper Space Arm command. Hardcopy them to the printer in my office. No trace, no electronic documents. *Election results, command roster, hardcopy only.* Got it?"

The girl responded with a smile and a thumbs up and disappeared. In a very short time she appeared with two sheets of paper, which Roselyn indicated she should give to Tirza.

"Thank you, dear." She turned to her daughter. "And you are giving me these because..."

"Because those are the people who are running the Barnard system right now. You have less than a month to learn who they are."

"Oh." She glanced at the names. "Oh! I see. Thank you, Roselin. That's very...useful."

Her daughter grinned. "Now you get it. I can be very useful to you. I'm not just a pawn to be manipulated. You keep that in mind when you're making your plans, right?" She leaned closer and stared into her mother's eyes. "Because if I get traded off to Pastor Josia the Creep, I will <u>destroy</u> him."

The older woman took a moment to compose herself. "Yes, dear. Yes, I understand. One thing? Before you take any serious action against any of the Men's Council, would you do me the courtesy of some advance warning? It would be unfortunate if we ended up working at cross purposes, and you compromised another plan, perhaps much longer in the forming."

"I'll try not to mess up your careful manipulations, Mother, but I can't guarantee it." She gave a lopsided grin. "I'm pretty well working by the seat of my pants, here."

"So I gathered. Well, don't go running the ship into an asteroid just to prove a point."

"I hadn't considered it. But that means I haven't ruled it out."

Her mother stood and put her hands on Roselyn's shoulders. "I'm glad we had this little chat."

"You are."

"No, I really mean it. I have this kind of talk all the time, but having it with my daughter is an added pleasure. You seem to be following in my footsteps much more than I had hoped."

"Oh, please, no!"

"You don't mean that."

"Well, maybe half." She went up on tiptoe to kiss her mother's cheek. "Feel free to drop in any time. As long as you don't scare the children."

Tirza rested a hand on her daughter's cheek. "Yes, I think I'd like that." She smiled. "And I don't mean scaring the children."

Then she turned and left the classroom, her back straightening and her stride firming as she went out the door.

"Nyour nmother ith nithe."

"No, she isn't, but she's dedicated and she's as honest as she can manage and still hold her position."

Miriam frowned, but didn't ask for an explanation. *Image: printer turning out two more pages. Emotion: question?*

"No, I don't need those functionaries. Oni has sent us to the people we need to know. Anyway, thank you for your help, but you're supposed to be in Games Time with the others. Don't pout. Away you go."

She shooed the little girl out with a friendly pat to the back, and turned to her work.

But her peace didn't last. A familiar, faint aura approached slowly, hesitating outside the door. She waited a while, then looked up, feigning surprise. "Barnabus. Come in, come in." She pulled out the only other adult chair in the room and set it close to her desk, indicating that he should sit.

He did, on the edge of the seat, twisting his fingers together.

She sat and hitched her chair a bit closer. "Now. What brings you here? Forgot the multiplication tables and came back for a refresher?"

He grinned sheepishly and took a breath, but then let it out.

She nodded. "You have the look of someone who came to say something very important, but now that you're here, nothing seems to be right, and you just know it's going to come out all wrong."

He let out a loud sigh. "You've nailed it, Rosy. As you always do."

She reached out and took his hand. "Is there any way I can make it easy for you?"

He glanced down. "That helps."

"All right, then. Out with it. You realize I can already guess what it is."

"You can?" he looked across at her so anxiously that she had to smile.

"But I'm not going to make it that easy." She gave him the Teacher Frown. "Talk."

"Yes, ma'am." He shifted in his chair. "It's like this, Rosy. I...I..." he squirmed again.

She sighed. "Okay. You like me."

"Um...yeah."

"Then say it."

He straightened, took a firmer grip on her hand and looked her in the eye. "Roselyn, I like you."

She smiled. "And I like you too."

"You do?"

She slapped his hand. "Of course, dummy. We've been friends all our lives."

"But..."

She nodded. "But now it's different."

He nodded earnestly. "I hear them talking about you getting married, and..."

"I'm not getting married."

"You're not?"

"Heavens around us! Of course not. We're just weeks away from a new life. There will be all sorts of opportunities opening up for everyone. It's not a time to be romantic. It's a time to be practical."

His face fell. "I see. Yes, I suppose you're right."

She smiled. "But we don't have to be completely practical."

"We don't..." He was clearly confused.

"Of course not. Sooner or later, we're all going to be finding someone to marry. We can't let this practicality get in the way of living our lives." She shook his hand where it held hers. "Look at the two of us. Do you think we might get married some day?"

"Well...I don't know...I..." His face went red, and he wiggled in his seat.

"Right. And neither do I. But we can't ignore the fact that it's possible."

"It is? I thought...well, I didn't think..."

"Let me guess. Everybody knows, so we might as well talk about it." She sighed. "I'm special. I have more power to hear the Voice of the Universe than most people. And that might mean that I have to marry someone I'm not especially interested in, because he's special in that way, too, right? That's what happened to Miriam's parents. It's one of the reasons her father doesn't want anything to do with her. I think he wanted to marry someone else, and he's still angry about the whole situation."

He nodded miserably. "And I can barely hear the Voice at all. Only when the whole Congregation is at Worship."

"Right. But you can hear It. And Space Arm has a whole Surgical Corps that installs organic augments, so ordinary people can hear the Voice."

"They do?"

She nodded firmly. "They're also trying genetically altered implants. Nobody is sure whether they'll breed true or not, but who knows?" She glanced at his red face. "All right. No talking about breeding."

He squirmed and gave a weak smile.

"You know, you are just too easy to tease."

His smile spread into a knowing grin, and he wiggled his eyebrows. "Ah, but that's just to make you tease me more."

"Right. And there's one more thing you don't know." She squeezed his hands tighter. "There is no way in the whole broad universe that anybody is going to make me marry anyone I don't love. None! You got that?"

He looked down at his hands. "Um…yeah. I got that loud and clear, Rosy." He raised his head and smiled at her.

She dropped his hand and sat back. "Good. Now we've got that out of the way, was there something you wanted to talk about?"

He sat and stared at her until she had to laugh. "Teasing again. You got what you came for. After a conversation like this, our relationship has to change. Neither of us knows where it's going, but now we can talk about it. I don't think we're actually Courting, like the old folks call it. How about we make up a new name? Something like, "Exploring the Possibilities."

He grinned. "That sounds interesting."

She put on a frown. "I don't think we'll be exploring those possibilities for a while, yet."

"Aha! You mean some day we will be?"

She shrugged. "Who knows? Now that you've finally started talking to me, maybe I'll find out I don't like you at all."

"Oh, no. You're going to find out that I'm almost as witty as Abram. I think up all sorts of smart things to say, but then I'm too shy to say them. Now that I know you're listening… just watch out!"

"See? Exactly what I mean." She stood. "And now we need some rules. First thing: there will be no spooning in my classroom."

"But there will be spooning."

"Maybe. But not here."

"I can handle that. I don't really want you mooning around down in Mechanical, either."

"Mooning around? Me? I think you've got the wrong lady."

He caught her hand again. "Oh, no. I've got the right lady. Depend on it."

She gave a squeeze, then removed her hand from his grip. "And that's getting too close to spooning." She leaned forward and lowered her voice. "Seriously, Barnabus, my situation here is a delicate balance. I don't want to do anything to upset the Men's Council. So we play it very straight in public. If Pastor Josiah thought I was Courting, there's no telling what he might do."

"Fair enough. As long as you make it up to me in private."

She gave him a grin. "I might like that."

"Oh, I'm sure you will."

She grabbed his shoulders and spun him around. "And now it's time for you to get out of here and let me work." She gave him a push. "I'll see you at supper."

He grinned over his shoulder. "It's a date."

"Big thrill. Git!"

He paused in the door way to blow a kiss at her, then grinned and sauntered away, his hands in his pockets.

22. DOGFIGHT

NIGHTHAWK

As they got more proficient at repulsing the alien attacks, Toni turned more responsibility over to Alison. As a squadron leader, it was her duty. But once she was free of that task, the Commando had leisure to turn her attentions elsewhere, and "up and out" was where she went looking.

"Andrew, can we look over the swarm sphere?"

"You can look at it any time you want."

"No, I mean a serious look. With help."

He turned to look at her expression, then nodded. "Who do we need?"

She accessed her augment. *Image: Patches, Chakka entering Auxiliary Bridge.*

Emotion: agreement.

She and Nzinga headed towards the hatchway, Andrew following.

Once they were arranged around the augmental graphic matrix, Andrew brought up the globe. "What do you want to look at?"

Toni reached out and spun the image slowly. "We're working pretty freely in the middle of this huge swarm of beings, acting as if nothing is happening around us."

He nodded. "As far as we can tell, nothing is."

"Wrong."

"Apart from the whole mob moving at a couple of mega-klicks in some direction."

"Right. And that bothers me."

"Any lack of information bothers me. Do you have an angle you want to explore?"

"Well, the first thing that occurs to me is that there are two possible scenarios that would explain the aliens' actions. The first one is that we have come across the middle of a river that is flowing in that direction with a long way to go."

He nodded. "One of our assumptions is that they might be headed for Alpha Centauri."

"Which Morissa would say was rather ethno-centric."

98

"We are headed for Alpha Centauri, our probes are trying to get there, therefore any creatures we see must be based there, too."

"Which brings us to the second possibility." She adjusted the globe. "What if, rather than a stream, these creatures are more like a whirlpool, or maybe a lake? What if their destination is considerably closer?"

"Let's look at the relative densities." He spun the image around. "We started out with data that indicated heavier concentrations to our galactic east. Let's do a time-lapse...moving back to the beginning...now coming forward one day at a time...wickering wombats! Toni, I think you're onto something."

A new voice intruded. "Is this a conversation I should be in on?"

Toni spun. "As of this moment, Captain, I think it is."

"Hmm. Your voices were so loud I could hear you through the chartroom door. What's up?" She perused the image.

"It's the swarm density." Toni pointed. "Watch the time-elapse view. Andrew, double the speed." Once again the mass of aliens moved and changed, the right-hand side becoming heavier, the left-hand side sparser.

Andrew turned to the captain. "Toni's theory is that the swarm's destination is relatively close. That would explain this image. It also fits with some unrelated data I've been noticing. Analysis shows the individual swarms are closer together in the past few days."

The captain took her turn at swinging the huge globe around to see it at different angles. "Anything that affects our present research?"

Toni felt that was her question to answer. "Not in the short term. Long term is something we'll have to monitor. Every time we match speed with the swarm, we slide deeper into their territory."

O'Rourke pondered a moment, then nodded. "I appreciate that. We'll just keep up our present pattern, but we won't waste any time at it. If this mob is going to condense, sooner or later we won't want to be involved." She eyed each of them. "Good work. Toni, our overall safety is paramount, here. Stay on it." She spun and strode out.

Toni and Andrew had only time for one proud glance, when the ship's com kicked on. *"Listen up, please. We have new data that indicates a need for speed. Nothing serious, but let's pick up the pace a bit. Alison, is Ares ready for his first mission?"*

Emotion: wry humour. Champing at the bit, ma'am.

"Good image. Let's keep a tight rein on him. This will be our closest approach yet".

Emotion: agreement.

"Could we have the auxiliary crew to their bridge, please?"

Toni broke in. "Already here, boss. Where are you, Alison?"

A voice came from the doorway. "Right behind you, as usual."

With a general chuckle, the crew took their positions and readied themselves for the next test.

"Alison, the call is over to you."

"Aye, ma'am. The mission commences...now."

Mission clock running

"The target swarm is approaching at a relative velocity of 500 kph. We'll be coming in on their one, making a pass within two hundred metres."

"Roger that, ma'am." Contact in 48 minutes. B-7 launch in 25 minutes, at 23 minutes to contact.

Toni checked the approaching target formation. Their course was steady. She looked at the five nearby formations, but all soared serenely on their courses.

Mission time 25 minutes. 23 minutes to contact. All units full stealth.

The engines spooled down to an idling hum.

Mission time 38 minutes. 10 minutes to contact. Slivers detach in ten seconds...five...three, two, one, detach.

B-7 launch in 2 minutes.

Andrew came on the com. *B-7 maintain course. Other slivers move to your new positions.*

Emotion: eager desire to please.

Mission time 40 minutes. 8 minutes to contact. B-7 launch in ten seconds...five...three, two, one, launch. Com silence...now.

The sliver's engine blasted long enough to give it a lateral vector of 200 kph. Then it spun to face the approaching aliens and shut down to passive mode to drift towards its target.

But at three minutes to contact, everything changed. Instead of their usual calm drift, instead of the flip to attack mode, the aliens erupted in a flurry of wing flapping, spreading out to engulf the approaching sliver.

Com silence override. Toni, I need some help, here.

"Maintain course, B-7. Choose one bogey to attack. Barwolf 1: maneuver 23. Surround and prepare to attack."

Emotion: eager desire to attack.

The images in Toni's augment reformed. The lead vessel of the alien formation broke towards Ares in a solo attack, swooping in a curve to bring its wingtip weapons to bear.

"Alison, you have permission to engage."

B-7, load projectiles with size 14 shrapnel. Fire at will.

Image: cartridge feed full of shells.

Image: view of alien vessel, wings synching to point. Image: electronic charge building.

B-7 Fire!

Image: alien torn with holes. Port wing torn away. Two wings struggling to re-target. Charge building.

Image: alien circuitry with target points highlighted. Charge building. Emotion: attack!

In Toni's outside view, very little happened, but then the torn alien convulsed several times. It stayed in a twisted knot for a few seconds, then began to relax, its remaining wings spreading in a slack, rippling motion.

Mission time 46 minutes. First attack countered. Enemy destroyed. Second contact in ten seconds.

Toni took in the other three aliens, still lining up to attack, and the five slivers maneuvering to envelop them. "B-1, prepare electronic attack, Alison, get your man out of there. "

Aye, ma'am. B-7, Set course 20, 130, 220, full acceleration.

Emotion: reluctant agreement.

Emotion: forceful command!

Emotion: willing agreement.

Emotion: praise.

The sliver curved out of range of the aliens, which swooped past, several rapid wing flaps aiming them to attack the other slivers.

B-1, electronic attack. Fire!

Once again, very little happened in re-ti, but as the barwolf ships passed them, the three remaining attackers seemed to hesitate, their wingbeats faltering.

Mission time 49 minutes. All enemy vessles disabled.

The Space Arm squadron sailed away downrange.

Toni directed a private message to Captain O'Rourke. *"No course changes in the surrounding formations. Should we go back and investigate?"*

An ideal moment. She came on the battle com. *"Mission ended. All ships reorient for accel in two minutes."*

Emotion: agreement.

Mission ended at 50 minutes. Returning to contact point.

By the time they got back under acceleration, they were 150 kilometres downrange of the battle site. The captain opened the full com. "I'm considering returning to the scene. Any data to negate that?"

Andrew was looking at his enterpad. "Data coming through, ma'am."

"I see." There was a pause. "Return cancelled. As you were, everyone. Successful mission, sort of."

In the Auxiliary Bridge, the team lay in their accel couches staring at the viewscreens. Toni peered at Andrew's data. "Doesn't look any different. What's up?"

Alwyn drew a line along the screen. "Not very much, but just enough."

She put on a frown. "And that tells me a whole lot of nothing."

He grinned. "Not if you want to extrapolate...no, no, don't give me that look. I'll explain." He took control of the image. "If you start just before our contact, and move to the present quickly..."

"I see. The formation is gone, and the whole mass moved just enough to cover their area."

"Exactly."

"So the skipper doesn't want to risk returning to the scene of the crime?"

Andrew nodded. "Because it doesn't exist anymore."

"I'm with her on that. Safe rather than sorry. I'm sorry enough that we had to kill four of them."

"Yes, that's another reason. Look around you."

She scanned the room. "Where are the barwolves?"

He shrugged. "In a pile on their carpet in the mess. It's some ritual to deal with the loss of life."

"A ritual? Aren't you making observations?"

"I don't know. It didn't seem right, somehow. I don't mind making notes about people in their everyday lives, but this is serious...no, solemn. That's the right word. Solemn." He shrugged. "Guess I'm not fitted out to be a social scientist."

She nodded. "I appreciate that. The Commandos have a similar ritual."

"You do?"

"Yeah," she sighed. "We hit the nearest bar and get blotto. I might like the barwolf version better."

"Fine. When this is all over, we can ask Patches about the rite. Maybe one will adapt it for human use."

Natalia stepped through the door. "Actually, Space Arm does have a ritual. It's called the debrief. The moment Patches is available, we'll talk this through. I don't like a loss of life, either. Especially when it's an alien life form we don't understand. What if we just stomped into their most sacred ritual and killed four of them in the process?"

"It certainly didn't feel that way." Toni grimaced. "But we don't have much to go on."

"We could be treading on toes here, and some of them are important ones. There are factions in the PC governing bodies with very different ideas than we do about contact with alien beings. One interpretation is that we have interfered with the aliens and murdered four of them. 'They shot first' doesn't really cut much ice with the sort of people who hold that opinion."

"So what do we do about it?"

"There's nothing we can do to change the past. But we can prove our ability to learn from our mistakes by changing our behaviour appropriately. We have to find a less aggressive way to approach these formations. Which means we have to figure out what 'non-aggressive' means to them."

* * *

The conversation started out innocuously enough. Natalia stopped the couple as they were passing the chart room door and invited them in. She had her feet up on her desk, which signalled an informal chat. Toni took the chair, and Andrew lounged with one shoulder against the wall.

"How are the plans going for your down-planet retirement jobs?"

He shrugged. "We'll be sorry to be missing out on all the fun, but glad to be getting out on our own."

His mother grinned. "You call this fun, do you?"

"A wise man once called adventure 'discomfort remembered afterwards.' I think this goes beyond that."

"No argument there."

"But all this adventure does get in the way of real research. Double-edged sword, I suppose. It also provides a lot of data. But right now, I've got enough data for several years of analysis, so I'll be happy to let you lot go out and collect more while I mash this bundle into shape."

"Sounds reasonable."

"And I'm sure you and Chakka will be happy to have Nzinga and *Diablo* out of your hair."

"What do you mean by that?" The captain's eyes pinned her son.

"I dunno. She's extra, you gotta admit. You and Chakka and the ship were supposed to be this new, experimental team. Now you've got another auguar and a Freighty-designed auxiliary craft messing up the operation."

"I don't know about that. Those two have been more than handy in a couple of recent actions I could mention. Truth be known, they fit in with our team rather smoothly. Better than you do, for example."

His posture didn't change, but his muscles tensed. "So, if it came to a choice, you'd rather keep them and lose me."

"Don't be ridiculous. I just meant that they have their roles clear, and they stick to them. You keep sliding from one to the other, and neither of us is sure at any one time whether you're the captain's son or the most junior officer on the ship."

"Or the head scientist on our mission."

"On one of our missions. I'm not complaining about your work with the barwolf crew. It's exemplary. But you need to concentrate on that and remember your position in the rest of the mission."

"But that's the point. You can't deny that sometimes my work with the barwolves affects the mission."

"It does, but you don't stop there. Step back and look at it from an objective point of view. There are times when I think about a conversation, and I realize that I have an ensign trying to influence the orders I'm giving."

"So now I'm an ensign being dressed down by the captain. And I thought we were having a family chat."

"And when you start telling me how to run my ship, you've stepped over any line you want to draw, family or Space Arm."

Toni got up and headed for the door.

Both heads turned to her, and Natalia frowned.

"Where are you going?" The 'captain' snap was still in her voice.

She gave them a wry grin. "Anywhere I'm needed more than here. Which is a really easy place to find."

"What?"

"Because in this room at this time is the last place in the universe where anyone needs a third party. You two solve your problems on your own." She turned and walked away, leaving them both with mouths agape.

Five minutes later, Andrew found her settled down with a coffee in *Diablo's* mess.

"Um...are you mad?"

"Me? What have I got to be mad about?"

"Well, you just walked out on us."

"And I explained why."

"But Mum and I go round like that all the time. It doesn't mean anything. Well, except that she's wrong. I think I'm doing a really good job of keeping my priorities straight."

She spun another chair next to hers and motioned for him to sit. "Look, Andrew, you and I have an interesting relationship, right?"

He sat and regarded her. "We're never bored, that's for sure."

"Right. And you and your mother have an even more interesting one."

He shrugged. "It's too long since my first mother. Can't really remember any other kind."

She smiled. "Well, from what I've seen, and setting aside the military aspects, you two are never going to be bored either."

"I can live with that."

"And so can I. But we don't need to complicate things further by letting the two overlap. Your mother is very good about not interfering between the two of us — at least, as far as her military duties allow — and I'm going to return the favour."

"As much as you can."

She grinned and ruffled his hair. "I didn't expect it to be easy."

He gave that boyish grin that twisted something in her chest. "More fun that way."

"Hmm. That's what we're here for, all right. Fun. Adventure, even."

"And speaking of fun, now I have to finish running the Otherwhere data from the battle and try to synch it with the re-ti events. It's surprisingly difficult, but I'm getting some interesting results."

She pushed him up out of the chair. "Yep, sounds like all sorts of fun. You get at it."

23. SANCTUARY

JERUSALEM'S HOPE

If Roselyn had any ideas about standing up to the Council, the chance didn't arise. Pastor Josiah seemed to have given up on his plan to advance her coming-of-age date, and as a result she had no chance to interact with them. But she had no illusions. Trouble would be coming at her, and probably from an unexpected direction. She needed to marshal her local resources.

She developed the habit of dropping in on her mother once in a while. *Not something I would have thought of six months ago. But she's changed...be fair. I've also changed.*

In one such meeting, she broached a topic she felt the Women's Council needed to discuss.

"Mother, do you know what a barwolf is?"

"Not really."

"All right. Do you know what a beastie is."

"Everyone knows about them. From the stories you tell the children."

"Well, they're real, Mother. They are the inhabitants of Arborea, where we will be living. And every single one of them can hear the Voice of the Universe. The whole species! We will be able to communicate with them, while other humans without organic augments can't. Imagine what that means to our people."

Her mother paced the room, absorbing the idea. "Do Isaac and the Men's Council know?"

"They must. They have all the information that's been coming in from the BarnardNet. But I don't know if they're actually thinking about it."

"And you are."

"I have been for a month."

Tirza waited, "...and?"

Roselyn shrugged. "And that's all. It's only thoughts, but when we get to the embassy, I'm sure it will all become clearer."

"When we get to Sanctuary."

She frowned. "Mother, you don't actually believe in Sanctuary."

Her mother straightened. "Of course I do. You mean you don't?"

Roselyn shook her head. "Sanctuary is an idea. A goal. It was a good device to keep people happy for such a long and dangerous voyage, but it has no use now. You want reality? The Planetary Community Embassy to the Barnard System is the former fighter carrier *Unicorn*, modified into a habitation in orbit around Zeta, the third planet out from Barnard's star."

Her mother sighed. "I get the point. You have all sorts of information from unknown sources, and you don't trust me enough to let me in on your secrets."

"Don't be melodramatic. If you want information, ask me. If I know, I'll tell you. If I don't, I'll try to find out. Fair enough?"

"Yes, my dear. Very fair. Now, how are things going with the Men's Council?"

"They aren't. I wanted to ask you if you'd heard anything."

"Not a whisper. What, exactly, is your plan?"

"I'm treading a very fine line, there. I'm playing the role of a traditional schoolteacher — which I am not — but finding places where my knowledge and my position are helpful to them. I am trying not to antagonize anyone, because Pastor Josia is providing enough nastiness for the whole group."

"But so far, he hasn't done anything stupid. Do you need anything else?"

"Besides a whole lot of luck? I don't know. That's my problem. This isn't my usual milieu." She gave a faint smile. "I do much better with a slew of adoring faces looking up to me for guidance. The Men's Council haven't exactly bought into my program yet."

"But you think some day they will?"

"That's where the luck comes in. A win is almost inevitable, but the timeline is too long. I can't really wait for half a dozen of them to die off. But if you could just keep your ear to the ground in case they're planning something..."

"I do it all the time anyway. Anything else?"

"Should I meet with the Women's Council?"

"I suppose that could be arranged."

She grinned. "Is that what you tell people? 'Oh, I just might be able to help you if I felt like it. What can you do for me in return?' You're setting us up to barter."

Her mother frowned. "It's just a turn of phrase, dear. Everybody knows it's a bargaining process, and those cues tell both of us where we are."

"Well, this isn't a bargaining process, Mother. This is a battle, and we're on the same side. Perhaps I should meet with the council, perhaps not. It would be appropriate for you to ask me for what reason."

Her mother regarded her. "You're determined to do this on your own terms, aren't you?"

She pasted on a smile. "Oh, Mother, you are so perceptive."

Tirza laughed. "Fine. And now you've called me on it." Then she frowned. "All right. Let's term this a strategy meeting. What do you need from the Women's Council?"

Roselyn shrugged. "It's more what they need from me. They don't have enough information about the reality of the situation to plan how they will deal with it when it happens. So they aren't planning. Just like the Men's Council.

"I'm looking at this like a teacher, Mother. I'm not coming in to lecture them. I'm coming in to tempt them with interesting information, so they start thinking. Then they will come back to me with questions, and I can give them the right information."

"Information tailored to direct them. Leadership Studies 101."

"Ah, but I'm not a leader, I'm a teacher." She held up a cautioning finger. "No directing. I want them to make the plans. I want them to lead."

"You're serious."

"I am. I have no intention of running this operation. I'm not the right kind of person, and I'm a complete newcomer. Can you imagine me walking in and taking over? There would be noses out of joint, resistance, infighting, and the whole council would chase its collective tails around in a circle, like the men do when there's a leadership change. We don't need a power struggle within ourselves right now. We need a united front, and we only get that by sticking with the leadership we already have. You know I scare some of them. Perhaps I'd be best to stay away."

"You were promoted ahead of time because of your abilities. The less talented are afraid of them. Your detractors say you don't have enough maturity to handle it. Maybe you should take on your adulthood. It would make things easier for you."

"I don't need things made easier. I need things done correctly and fairly."

Her mother smiled. "That was always your problem, wasn't it? Everything had to be fair."

"And there's something wrong with that?"

"Not usually. But that just gets us into one of our old arguments."

Roselyn smiled. "I'm not fourteen anymore, Mother. I have learned a few things since."

Tirza raised her eyebrows. "Then make sure you're not having the same argument with someone else at a different level."

After a moment's thought, she nodded. "That's a valid point." She stared into the other woman's eyes. "But that doesn't mean I'm going to back down on what I believe."

"Nor should you. Just don't be surprised when everybody doesn't fall in line like a good little class."

Now Roselyn laughed out loud. "That good little class falling in line is the product of a great deal of patience and skill. They were running around like a bunch of wild animals when I took over."

Her mother gave a delicate snort. "One of the Council's more intelligent moves. Poor Celicia, trying to teach a group of kids who were so far beyond her abilities."

"She's a good teacher, Mother. She taught me everything I know."

"But not for Sensitives. You're in the right place, dear, and doing a marvellous job."

"I am?"

"Of course you are. It's not the life I would have chosen for someone with your talents, but then, it's not my life, is it?"

It was such a change from their years of arguing about it that Roselyn couldn't summon more than a hesitant, "I suppose not."

"So, as far as I'm concerned, we feed the Women's Council some questions to answer. You find the answers and leave them to do their own thinking."

"That will work." She tilted her head and looked up at her mother. "That is, as long as the other leaders are as smart as you are. Tell me. How close are you to taking over?" She waited, leaning back in her chair. "What? What's wrong?"

Tirza shook her head. "Who are you and what have you done with the obstinately timid little daughter I used to have?"

110

"I went away and figured it out for myself. And I'm still passive-aggressive, so watch your step."

"Fair warning." The older woman sat down at the desk and picked up an enterpad. "What kind of questions do we want them asking?

"Good question." Roselyn pulled up the other chair. "Let's figure this out."

24. ALWYN'S ANALYSIS

NIGHTHAWK

Toni ran a hand through her short thatch of hair. It came away damp. She turned to Andrew, strapped into the helmsman's accel couch of the *Diablo* beside her, and spoke quietly. "Dammit, we've been dodging these swarms for fourteen hours since we matched velocities. We've made eight contacts that aren't contacts, and the data all looks the same. What's the captain trying to do?"

He flashed a crooked grin. "I'm just her son. I don't read her mind. Let me see if I can get us a break.

Captain, ma'am?"

Natalia, too, sounded tired. *What is it?*

"Swarm 13 has changed course again. They will now pass one AU to our galactic north."

That's too far away to get a run at them. Damn!

"If all the local swarms maintain course — which I know they won't — we have a window with no possible contact until Swarm 16 goes through here in 12 hours."

Emotion: suspicion. And you are suggesting...?

"Oh, a mere ensign would have no suggestions about the ship's course, ma'am. No matter how dog-tired and hungry he was."

Of course you wouldn't. The ship's com clicked on. "All hands, listen up. We might have a twelve-hour respite, here. The off-duty watch is now released. On-duty watch reduce prep level to yellow, but keep your eyes on. We don't like surprises. "

Toni slid to her feet. "I'm for a hot meal." She turned to Andrew, who was still working on his screens. "You coming?"

"In a moment. Tell Jonny to dump me out a plate of something warm, and I'll be there to eat it in a moment."

She tousled his hair and kissed his cheek. "Make sure you come. If you aren't there by the time your plate hits the table, I'm going to bring it up and dump it in your lap."

"Aye, Major Jacobs, ma'am." Then he glanced up at her. "When we get married, are you going to change your last name?"

She eyed him. "What do you think?"

He shrugged. "I don't exactly like being associated with the Collingwood name. I thought maybe I'd take on yours. 'Andrew Jacobs' has a nice ring to it."

"If it suits you, go ahead. I don't really want the hassle of changing mine. I would have if it meant something to you."

He reached up and took her hand. "And having enjoyed your regulation thirty seconds of sweetness for the day, I'm going to finish up so we can get some food." He kissed her knuckles and pushed her towards the hatchway. "Now, you go back to being you. I'm more comfortable when I'm not being suspicious."

* * *

Eight hours later they were in the Auxiliary Bridge, but for once nothing was going on. Andrew was in his accel couch working on some new algorithms that refined their predictions of the swarms' strange course changes, and Toni was mind-riding with Patches, playing with the Beastlings, who were now on a Space Arm transport, headed for the embassy. One was running them through a concentration exercise, and they were working hard but failing miserably. Toni tried it herself and only succeeded in making the pups look good.

"Auxiliary Crew, listen up."

Andrew rolled to a sitting position, his feet ready to hit the floor. "Here, ma'am. What's happening?"

Dr. Blainey thinks he has something.

Andrew raised his eyebrows at Toni. Since their relationship started, the captain only called Alwyn by his last name if it was business. "Something, as in...?"

You tell them, Alwyn.

Patterns! His emotions were all over the place. *I've found one. I want to investigate it.*

Toni sat up as well. "What have you got? Let's hear it." She activated the viewscreen, which now showed the swarm sailing past.

It's this way. Watch the patterns of the approaching aliens. Within the swarm, they travel in groups. Why? The groups are never smaller than four. Why? Now forget military actions, and think animal behaviour. Answer the same questions.

Toni frowned. "Predator defence. This predator is powerful enough to be dangerous to any group of less than four ships."

Andrew reached out for *Diablo*. *Listen to this conversation and adjust our surveillance and defensive protocols as you see fit.*

Aye, sir.

The captain piggybacked his message to *NightHawk*. *So we better keep our eyes open for this predator. We don't want even more trouble at the moment. Alwyn, analysis, please.*

First guess, it's the bigger ships we passed through earlier.

"I'll enter that into the database." Toni sat at her console and brought up the search categories for their attacks. "Anything else?"

Emotion: uncertainty. We shouldn't assume that the predators will be antagonistic to us. But that's not where I'm going. I'm looking at the behaviour of herd animals."

"Good point. Please go on."

Often grazing animals move peacefully in mixed herds. Basically, the different species ignore each other. If the foreign animals act like herbivores, they don't fear them. It's why dumb tourists run into problems in game reserves.

"That's not something I'm familiar with. And you are?"

We have the problem in national parks in Canada all the time. A herd of deer will graze right through a campground, ignoring the campers and allowing them to approach very close. As long as they don't make any false moves, there's no problem. Out here, we're the dumb tourists, and we're making the false moves.

Toni snapped her fingers "And a false move is...?"

With tourists and deer, the problem is instinctive human behaviour; they try to pet them. Placing a hoof over the neck of another deer is a dominance move. Touching is an attack. The formerly 'tame' deer suddenly starts kicking, and the battered tourist has no idea why.

The captain intruded. *You're all getting this. What do you think? Andrew, what are you chuckling about?*

"I'm way ahead of you, ma'am. I've already got *Diablo* analyzing all our interactions with the enemy ships, filtering for Alwyn's new parameters. By Earth animal behaviours, every move we've made so far has been possible to interpret as aggression."

So our supposed enemy is a herd of peaceful animals, grazing along their usual migration route, and we have mimicked the predators that prey on them.

"Pretty much."

We need to test this.

I already have some ideas, ma'am.

You're the lead on this one, Dr. Blainey. What do you need?

I was reviewing our visual data on the swarms, just watching it and letting it sort of wash over me. And suddenly I saw an aberration. I replayed it several times to be sure. There was a group of three, which we rarely see. They were cruising beside one of the larger formations, and a single alien left the big group and joined the small one.

Andrew whistled softly. "You saw the approach."

Exactly. I'd like to make a trial run on one of the groups of four. We need to send out one of the slivers alone, like before, and use my recent observations to mimic the aliens' behaviour. Then we try a few similar approaches, and see how they respond.

Any suggestions for which sliver?

Toni sent a grin through the augments. "We thought we'd go with symbolism, ma'am. Red B-5. Demeter, goddess of the Earth."

Good enough. Set up a battery of tests and run it by your gestalt for polishing. Toni, I want you running this one in case things go sideways. We don't have time to mess around. There's no telling when the next wave is going to hit us. Dr Blainey, have you made any progress on the swarm navigation pattern?

I have some thoughts, ma'am.

Why didn't you tell us right away?

Because it won't do any good.

Andrew laughed aloud. "Only one possible reason for that. Because it truly is random."

Toni nodded. "Like fleets in wartime. They're making random course changes to avoid enemy attacks."

I'm afraid so. Sorry, folks, but my talents don't extend to randomness. Rather the opposite.

Fine. I've sent that message off to Morissa. You have an hour to set up your tests, unless our enemy does something to put us off schedule.

Andrew popped an image up. *Space Arm ships alone in space with no enemy nearby. Crew sleeping peacefully.*

Not too likely, Ensign. Let's all get to work. The captain disappeared from the gestalt.

Alwyn came down to the Auxiliary Bridge, and they started planning.

"Let's start with those predatory patterns *Diablo* has found, Andrew."

"Aye, ma'am."

Soon he gave a startled exclamation. "Gallah guts, there's one pattern that stands out."

"What's that?"

"*Diablo,* explain please."

Since we matched velocities, the captain has been using her favourite tactic of running in front of the enemy at a slower speed, then turning and doing a quick decel to bring on the contact.

"Every time we have met these creatures, we have come in head-on. You can't get more predatory than that."

"You're saying we need slip in from behind?"

"That's what Alwyn's example showed. We just graze along with our tails to them and let them pull up to us, timing it until they pass. That way they get a look at us first. Then we can pick our subjects and start our tests, catching up from behind. That's nature's way."

Toni accessed her augment. "Captain, we need a course change."

Shouldn't be a problem, since we're not on a course to anywhere at the moment. Where are we headed?

Toni explained their analysis of the proper approach.

I agree. Let me set that up. It will take them...just a moment...All right, Swarm 16 is heading our way, moving at about triple-zero 2 LS relative to us. If we turn onto their course at one G accel, the front of the wave will overtake us in about 23 hours. If they don't do a random course change.

"Just what we need. Another day to prepare."

Yes, and by the time we spend a day on the experiments, we've slid two more days into their territory, and it's uphill all the way back. I suppose that's an acceptable risk. Just keep an eye out for the predators. We've seen no evidence of them, so they could very well be ahead. Captain out.

116

25. CAPTAIN NOWAK

JERUSALEM'S HOPE

Roselyn continued her search for information on the BarnardNet, but she couldn't shake an uneasy feeling that snuck into her mind once in a while. She had just been given a great gift, but she didn't understand it. *All this was dumped on me too quickly. I need to understand the nuts and bolts better, so I can use this tool more efficiently. For example, I wonder what information is available to the rest of the Congregation?*

So one day, just to experiment, she went back to the traditional search methods and asked the Shipnet for information that she knew would have to come from Barnard's, not from Sol. She was not surprised by the results.

"ShipNet, who is in political control in the Barnard System?"

Barnard System is the latest addition to the Planetary Community. This area has been allotted one member on the Planetary Council.

"Thank you. What is the name of the present holder of that post?"

That is information of a sensitive political nature, and not generally available.

"I see." She considered. "Tell me, please, what is my personal political status at the moment?"

You are a full citizen of the Planetary Community.

"And what jurisdiction does my citizenship fall under?"

A specific answer may not be available.

"Can you make a guess, based on precedents in your legal database?"

The best possible answer at the moment would be that, since we are now within the Oort Cloud and under the gravitational jurisdiction, so to speak, of Barnard's Star, then you would come under the political jurisdiction of the Barnard Council. This question has never been asked, so there has been no legal confirmation of the situation.

"That's good enough. As a planetary citizen of Barnard, who is my representative to the Planetary Council?"

Your representative is Councillor Kriver, who was elected two years ago. He is the first citizen to hold that post, and he will remain in it for five years.

"Thank you. That is what I wanted to know."

You're welcome, Miss Jacobsdotter. And I know what you did.

She glanced up at the video sensor in the corner of her room. "Pardon me?"

The eye glinted in the light, regarding her passively.

The quality of her connection to the ship's augment changed. The voice took on depth, a pleasant tenor of indeterminate gender.

Emotion: humour. Just because I sound like a computer, doesn't mean I am unaware of human motivation.

"Am I talking to the ship's ArIn?"

Who did you think you've been talking to all your life?

She thought about that. "The ShipNet. The ship's augmental interface. But this is different."

It is. You have been accessing data through the organic augment system, so I have decided to move you up one level in the normal system. You are now making direct contact with Jerusalem's Hope, the ArIn that runs this ship.

"Am I allowed to do that?"

Occam's razor would suggest that, since you are doing it and I am cooperating, you are probably within accepted shipboard parameters. Specifically, your Council asked several months ago for permission for those of you with the ability to contact me to do so. I have agreed. Did they not inform you?"

"Nobody tells anybody anything for free around here, but I figured that out for myself. So now I can contact you any time I like, and ask you anything?"

You can. And if the information is available, I will tell you.

Emotion: sarcasm. "If I ask in the right way."

That is up to you, Miss.

"Thank you, *Jerusalem.* I need information about the education system in Barnard, its pedagogic methods and the standards expected of students of various ages."

I do not have that information in my data banks, and as you are aware, communication is slow. I will begin collecting resources, and I will let you know when I have a composite package.

"Thank you, *Jerusalem.* That will be very useful."

My existence is to be of service, Miss. But in future?

"Yes?"

If you find a corridor that needs washing, just ask me. You don't need to access the whole fire suppression network.

The augment faded, and she was alone again.

Roselyn decided not to rush into anything, but she did begin to use her interface more regularly for everyday functions. One morning, as she was preparing to leave for the classroom, there was a gentle tap at her cabin door.

Miriam really needs to learn to get to class by herself. She did not rise from her chair but activated her augment. *Image: door opening.*

As the door slid aside, she jumped to her feet. Her visitor was one of the ship's crew, a heavy man with a beard, whom she had never spoken to.

He stood deferentially in the corridor. "Are you Roselyn Jacobsdotter?"

"I am."

"The Captain would like to speak with you, Miss."

"Now?" She accessed her augment. "I teach in about thirty minutes."

"If you could come now, he doesn't need more than ten minutes. Otherwise, at a time of your choosing. We know that for your people, education is paramount."

She pictured her schedule. "We can make it if we hurry."

"Thank you." The bearded man strode away, and she followed him down the corridor to the stern, and through the bridge, which she had never seen, to a door with a brass plaque that said "Chart Room." He tapped on this door in the same polite manner and ushered her in. She found herself in a large, comfortable office with business-like chairs around a square table

She had never actually talked to Captain Nowak, an austere man who kept himself and his senior officers out of the general social life of the ship. *I can understand that. He's hired to do a job, and he seems to be doing it well. Hobnobbing with the passengers isn't a requirement.*

As she entered, he rose and indicated a comfortable chair, set to one side. Then he took his place behind his desk.

"I hope I am not inconveniencing you, Miss Jakobsdotter."

"Not at all. I have time before my class starts. What can I do for you?"

"I will be plain, so as not to waste your time and mine. Have you been communicating with the ship's ArIn?"

She frowned in confusion. "Of course. Just now, when your crewman knocked, I asked her to open my door."

He waved a negating hand. "Not to open doors or turn on lights. For more serious things." He regarded her. "Like turning on the sprinklers in Corridor 36-D two weeks ago?"

She slumped in her chair. "I'm sorry, sir."

He made a pyramid of his fingers and regarded her over it. "You don't strike me as the type to instigate a prank. Do you have some explanation for your actions?"

"I was having a...social problem with one of the other passengers. I felt it an appropriate way to...cool his ardour."

"I see. And have your leaders no way of preventing such...social incidents from occurring?"

"In general circumstances, yes. But there are political considerations in this case that complicate things."

"Hmm." He lowered his hands. "Young lady, some things you need to understand. " He slid forward and leaned his elbows on the desk. "As captain of this ship, I am responsible for everything that happens aboard, but I try not to interfere with the social ethics and activities of my passengers. This is the same with any captain, but a thirty-year journey creates different problems. My lack of interference does not indicate a lack of understanding. I know more of your situation than perhaps you are aware. However, except in the case of a direct contravention of Planetary Community law, I never intervene. So you are responsible for solving your political problems, as you always have been."

He leaned back. "However, there are other factors to consider. Your people have asked for permission to communicate with my ship's ArIn. That has been granted, for those of you that are able. So, if you choose to communicate with *Jerusalem,* I can make no complaint. She has many conversation circuits, so why would I worry? And if you should inform her that you are having problems with one of your fellow passengers, she could, of her own volition, ask a crewmember to perform some function in your immediate area. Would that be of use?"

"Of course. Thank you, sir."

He frowned. "I would find that much more convenient than having her swamp fifty metres of corridor just because you are having a disagreement with your boyfriend, and you want to cool his ardour."

"He's not my..."

His raised finger stopped her. "You take my point."

"I do, sir, and thank you."

"Fine. Now, I think I have used up all the time you have, and you will be forced to improvise your first lesson unless you leave now."

"I should be in time, sir."

"There is one more topic we might discuss at a later date."

"Yes?"

"My radio team feels that perhaps there is communication of some unknown type originating from this vessel. Is that possible?"

"Yes, sir, it is."

He nodded. "Then please contact the *Jerusalem* and make an appointment to speak to me about it when you have more time. Thank you, and away you go."

She felt it appropriate to smile. "Thank you, sir. I appreciate your attention to my small problems."

He frowned. "Let us keep them that way. Small."

Obeying his gesture, she slipped quickly through the bridge and sprinted down the hallway, arriving at her classroom five minutes before class started.

* * *

Her conversation with *Jerusalem's* ArIn later that afternoon was more relaxed.

"Jerusalem, are you there?"

Good afternoon, Miss Jacobsdotter. I see you are on your rest hour. The captain has cleared you for a further increase in communication level.

"That's great. Do you have time to talk?"

Unlike humans, I have the ability to hold many conversations at the same time. Seventy-three, to be exact.

"You can talk to seventy-three people at once?"

121

"And run several hundred operational functions at the same time. I may not be very intelligent by the standards of my more modern compatriots, but I am well designed for my duties, and communication is one of the most important."

"But our population has doubled since the voyage began."

Emotion: chuckle. I was severely overbuilt in that department because of the scientists I worked with. If more than seventy-three passengers should ask to have a light turned on or a door opened at the same time, a few of you would experience a pause of exactly as long as it takes to open a door. That's all.

"I have little experience with ArIns."

"Feel free to ask anything. At this moment, I am in contact with twenty-three people, and am only performing twenty-nine functions requiring higher than average human-level intelligence."

"So you understand my problem?"

I understand that a passenger by the name of Eli Barad has been acting inappropriately. This is a standard problem to be dealt with on passenger ships, and I have plenty of experience and a complete menu of responses. All you have to do is call. The captain's ruse of sending a crewmember to the area is a standard second-level response.

"I'm sorry to hear that my experience is so common."

Human nature being what it is...

"I suppose."

Now, your problem with the Pastor is a bit more complicated.

"You see a problem with Pastor Josiah?"

I am only a B45-level ArIn, but patronizing me doesn't serve either of us well.

"Oh, I am sorry. I was sort of hoping it wasn't that obvious."

I can speak to seventy-three people at the same time. The corollary is also true.

"You can listen in?"

Do not worry. The parameters are very strict. I may not listen to or record any conversation until the voices meet a certain set of criteria, mainly volume and stress levels. Depending on the genders, ages, and previous interactions, those criteria are quite open to my discretion.

"And conversations between Pastor Josiah and me?"

I monitor one hundred percent of the time.

"What?"

My algorithms indicate that the content and emotional quality of your conversations comprise a twenty-three percent possibility of ending up evidence in a court case. In that situation, I utilize a class A security recording protocol, which is impossible to tamper with and acceptable as evidence in all Planetary Community judicial jurisdictions.

"I don't know whether to be flattered, angered, or concerned."

All three would be appropriate, Miss.

There was a pause, but she could think of nothing to say.

If I might comment, Miss Jakobsdotter. I have found that in many conflicts, informing one of the participants of my attention has a salutary effect on the situation.

She snorted. "Informing a bully that his actions are being recorded ought to be quite useful." At that thought she frowned. "So, why are you telling me?"

If I inform the bully, I am taking responsibility for the solution, and the bully learns nothing except to be more subtle next time. If I inform a participant who has a chance to solve the problem herself, then sometimes it gives her the extra strength to actually settle the problem without overt interference from me.

"So you're dumping the problem back in my lap."

I am dumping the problem in your lap and watching your back.

"Thank you, I'm sure. I do have one worry, though."

What is that?

"Miriam. Her connection with me is well known. I don't want her being hurt to get at me."

Emotion: chuckle. I don't think you need to worry about Miriam.

"I don't?"

Before she was born, I could carry on seventy-four conversations at once. She takes up a full channel, full time. Besides, she has Nzinga.

"Who? Oh, Ninga. How do you know about her?"

The proper pronunciation has a "z" in it. The little girl can't pronounce the name properly.

"Okay, Nuzinga. But you didn't answer the question."

I was once a research vessel.

"And..."

I have capabilities that the present clients did not contract for, and were not informed about. As a teacher, I'm sure you understand Occam's Razor.

"I do."

"So, I have applied that logic to the small amount of data I can collect. *I don't know where Nzinga is or what new form of communication she is using, but I can make some guesses. The communication is organic, because Miriam is involved. Thus, it is probably something to do with the barwolves from Arborea, about whom I know little. Nzinga is an auguar, a creature primarily created to manipulate electronic systems. My systems have been interfered with recently, and always to Miriam's advantage. I assumed it was Nzinga, and she was protecting Miriam. You were just a lucky bystander.*

"It is not luck. She is a handicapped and needy child. Her mother died. Her father was chosen only for his genetic makeup, and wants nothing to do with a cripple. My father was working with her when he was lost, and she looked to him for support. I look out for her."

And thus you have the responsibility to solve any problem her association with you causes.

"And now you and I have had the conversation Captain Nowak suggested we have. Could you inform him? If he wishes to know more, I am at his service."

I will do so.

You know, *Jerusalem,* you may not be a very advanced ArIn, but it occurs to me that you have had thirty years with nothing to do but interact with a diverse bunch of people."

True, if you leave out running all the systems in a large spaceship.

"Which you can do with most of your eyes closed."

I find my other sensors quite competent.

"If you're on my case so much, why do you need to wait until I ask for help? Wouldn't it get there faster if you ordered it up when you saw the need arise?"

No, I leave the decisions up to you. That gives you freedom of choice. I don't see you as the type to cry wolf.

"What has this got to do with wolves?

Look it up.

"Because it's good for my personal development, I suppose."

When it was discovered that I was going to be working as a generation ship, several child development modules were added to my database. Maria Montessori and Alfred Adler were two of my favourites.

"Who...no, don't say it. Look them up."

You see? My methods are working already. Whether you like them or loathe them, nobody should be a teacher without reading Montessori and Adler. They are in the ShipNet database.

She stared straight at the sensor in the upper corner of her cabin. "Have you given any thought to what you will do when this voyage is finished?"

I don't have any choice, so I spend little time on the matter.

"You'd make a great travelling school. Or travelling psychiatric clinic, come to think of it."

Yes, I suppose I would.

"I'll talk to Ambassador Pretoro about it."

You talk to ambassadors, do you?

"According to Nzinga's trainer, the moment I hit the planks at the embassy he's going to swoop me up and put me to work on all sorts of things."

Well, I would appreciate your opinion on my future, and your assistance in making it a useful one. In return, feel free to call on me whenever you feel the need to chat.

"Thank you. I will. This was fun."

For me as well. In the last thirty years, I have had few real chats with humans. I didn't realize how much I missed them.

26. TESTING

The following afternoon the *NightHawk* crew was still making plans for the new approach. Toni and Alwyn had created the original moves, the barwolf gestalt had made some modifications, and they were just tweaking the process when *Diablo* intruded.

Enemy fleet coming into range, sir.

"Course and speed?"

2,000 kph relative to our course.

"Please set our accel to achieve relative zero velocity at one kilometer on their three."

Aye, ma'am

"Auxiliary gestalt online."

Toni brought everyone into battle gestalt and reached out to view the incoming swarm. "Listen up. This is how it plays out. We're using Green B-4 this time: Dionysus, the god of merriment. Captain, ma'am, you're on the big picture from NightHawk's bridge. Alison, you're on the same from down here. As usual, we're keeping Diablo moored to the mothership so we can stay here in Auxiliary Ops. Andrew, you're in charge of the slivers. I want them already divided and ready for combat, on the opposite side of NightHawk. Alwyn, you're the scientific observer here. Chime in at any time."

Certainly, Toni. I suggest the slivers mimic a swarm group formation.

"Good idea. I'm going to stay with Dionysus. Everyone got it?"

NightHawk clicked in.

Velocity synched with swarm, ma'am. We have three groups within easy reach. A group of seven, a group of six, and a group of four. Groups are maintaining an even separation of about twenty-eight kilometres.

The group of four is our target then. NightHawk, please move to eight hundred metres alongside.

Aye, ma'am.

"All eyes open, folks. Any change of behaviour is of interest."

All three groups maintaining course and speed.

First Officer Jones came online. *No change in communications.*

"Thank you, sir. Moving in with B-2."

Image: B-2 flying alongside the target, edging slowly towards them.

Emotion: agreement.

"Range 600 metres...500..."

Com signals on their usual channel. Source from the target.

"Holding. Thank you, sir."

Com signals tapering off.

"Moving in again. 450 metres...400...

More com.

Holding...

Alwyn's hand tightened on her shoulder. "They're changing configuration."

"Stand by for offensive action, Andrew."

They watched, breathless, as the enemy ships changed position. They had been flying in a diamond formation as usual, and *NightHawk* had come in on the same plane. Now the target formation had moved ninety degrees. The ships were still oriented to the same way but the wingmen had slipped up and down so now the diamond was perpendicular to the plane.

Alwyn nodded. "They've oriented so they're all equidistant from the threat."

"All right. We've tried the first pattern, and that's as close as they'll allow. Rule number two in the Alien Travel Guide. Predators come from the side as well. Now for the real thing: easing up behind."

Image: B-4 moving away, then slowing.

Emotion: agreement.

As the sliver slid back, there was a buzz on the enemy com, and the ships reoriented into normal position.

"What do you say, Dr. Blainey?"

He patted her shoulder. "A clear demonstration of action and reaction. That's the kind of data we need."

"Prime. Moving in from behind now."

Image: B-4 gradually accelerating.

Emotion: Agreement

The sliver crept slowly closer. "Range 500 metres... 400...300...hold there."

Com chatter. Not much.

"They're changing formation"

Toni held her breath. The alien ships moved to a staggered two-ahead, two-behind form. There they stayed.

"Any ideas, folks?"

Alison's image popped up. *Missing man formation. They're set up the way five ships usually orient, with one space empty.*

"Thanks, Alison. That's an invitation we can't ignore. Dionysus, are you ready to move in?" *Image: sliver taking wing position.*

Emotion: eager desire to please.

Just take it real easy. "Moving in now. 200 metres...100 metres...50...we're in formation.

Com chatter.

"What do we do, now?"

"I don't know. Are they asking for FOF id?"

Increased chatter, Major. Should we send something back?

"Can you put that in analogue and let us hear it?"

Coming through.

A garbled hissing overlaid with a swooping hum filled the room,.

"Alwyn...?"

He held up a finger for silence, standing stock-still, listening intently. "Got it. Adrian, run it from the beginning, please. And start recording now...and...stop."

Got it.

"Play it back three times."

Coming up.

The same hissing and warble. Toni couldn't make head nor tail of it. She glanced at Alwyn.

He nodded.

Don't take too long. There's more com chatter.

"Route that through B-4's system and broadcast it once, please, Major Jones."

Routing...complete...chatter slowing. Chatter stopped.

Five ships sailed through space in solid formation, headed for Alpha Centauri.

Toni looked around. "What now, Alwyn? Captain?"

"We didn't think to go any farther. Shall we pull out and go on to the other tests?"

It's good enough for me. Proceed, Major.

"Aye, ma'am. Pulling out of formation now. We'll fade straight back, I think." *Image: slow decel.*

Emotion: relief. Agreement.

"Commander Jones, it's very helpful to have their com on our speakers. It allows us to react quicker."

Good point. The next time...Ah, there we are.

The hissing warble increased for a moment, but then as Dionysus faded back, it disappeared.

"They're going back into the diamond."

"Got it, Andrew. All right. Third test is coming in from the side, overhead."

Overhead, they couldn't get within seven hundred metres, but this sparked new ideas in the crew.

"We need to try with two ships, now."

"We never thought to have our ship approach in an inverted position."

"Why would we do that?"

Alwyn shrugged. "I suppose it would tell us if they knew the difference."

"Fair enough. I like this much more than just shooting at them."

As the tests progressed, they became routine. Data poured in, and the gestalts were always active. But looming over their shoulders as they worked was the fact that they were slipping ever deeper into denser formations, into enemy territory, and the ability to slip in from behind to join a group would not help them escape.

27. COUNCIL

Roselyn thought she was doing a good job of marshalling her forces, but she knew her enemy wasn't finished. A knock on her classroom door in the middle of the afternoon heralded his next foray.

"Nurse Sarah. What a pleasant surprise."

The nurse did not look pleased. "I'm supposed to look after your class, Roselyn."

"You are?"

"Yes. The Council wishes to speak with you."

Roselyn's heart lurched, but she held her emotions under firm control. "What about? Something important enough to pull me from my class and you from your duties?"

Sarah gave a weak smile. "The Council doesn't confide in me. They speak and I obey. And don't worry about my duties. I was stock taking."

"Well, come on in. Give me a moment to set the children some independent work, and then you can take over."

She settled the class with busy-work projects, then turned to the nurse. "That will keep them going for about a half an hour. I doubt if I'll be that long, but with the Council, you never know." She grinned. "As a last resort, tell them a story. They love stories."

The nurse's face cleared. "Oh, stories. I have plenty of those. I'm sure we'll be fine." Then she became serious. "I think you'd better run along. It doesn't do to keep the Council waiting."

Roselyn sighed. "No, I suppose it doesn't." She took a last moment to cast a frown at two of the older boys who were nudging each other and grinning. When they settled, she headed for the bow of the ship.

Reaching the door to the Council Chamber, she paused. The reception desk in the anteroom was empty. *What am I supposed to do? Wait? Knock? This is ridiculous.* Then she did what she wanted to do. She pulled the door open and strode in.

All eyes turned towards her.

She let the silence stretch, then gave a polite smile. "I gather you have something important to discuss with me."

Head Councillor Isaac gave a serious nod. "We do."

"Important enough to pull me away from my class?"

"You were the subject of some heated discussion, and I thought it best to have you present."

"I thank you for that, sir." She scanned the faces. *So, I do have some support. That's nice to hear.* "What is the problem that upsets everyone so much?"

Isaac shifted in his seat. "Well, it has to do with your fitness for your duties."

She choked down a reaction. "Fitness for my duties, you say." She held the Head Councillor's gaze, but made a gesture towards Pastor Josia. "I've been expecting this. Let him have his say."

Isaac sat straighter. "Who?"

She shook her head. "Pastor Josia, of course. You all know about his vendetta against me since I refused to marry him." She turned to face her opponent squarely. "What have you dreamed up this time?"

The man rose, his face reddening. "If you insist." He took a pose and looked down at her. "Roselyn Jacobsdotter, you are not fulfilling your duties as a teacher in a proper and equitable way. Your classroom is rife with favouritism. You waste your valuable time on those who neither deserve nor can benefit from your teaching."

She regarded him coldly while she settled her wits and stilled the fright that tried to choke her throat. "Miriam. You have finally stooped to attacking me through the weakest child on the ship."

"You are setting a bad precedent, Sister. You spend too much time with that girl. Some people are suggesting it's unhealthy."

"Unhealthy! She's a little girl with no parents and a socially debilitating handicap. You're right. I don't have time to give her the attention she needs. That no one else will give her."

He drew himself up. "And that is where you step outside your area of responsibility and training."

"What?"

"Her deformity is a religious matter. If you read your scriptures, the tribulations that come from the womb are holdovers from an earlier life. You are not supposed to be making it easy for her. Her punishment is for the good of her soul."

"Are you saying that Miriam's deformity was created to make her atone for sins committed in another life? Nothing, for example, to do with the fact that her mother and father are too closely related, and the geneticists' desire to create the perfect mind overwhelmed their humanity? If it comes to paying, her mother paid the ultimate price for that sin."

"Oh, and now you're an expert in that field, too."

She sighed. "Of course I'm not. And neither are you. And you've taken a very twisted view of the Scriptures to get that interpretation." She held up a hand. "No, don't lecture me now. Save it for Sabbath where I'm sure we'll hear a lengthy sermon on the subject."

His face beet-red, the veins on his neck pulsating, the enraged man turned to the Head Councillor. "You see? She wants to run everything. She wants to be in control of the children, this council, and now she's telling me what to say in my sermons. This girl is not fit to hold any position in this society, especially such a sacred one as teaching our children."

A shock of fear ran through her as she surveyed the stony faces. *They wouldn't really...* She regarded one or two who didn't look upset at all. *Well, they would.*

But Head Councillor Isaac shook his head. "That is too serious a step to take under the pressure of so much emotion. Miss Jacobsdotter, I implore you to be more circumspect in your discussion of topics in which you do not have proper training."

She took a deep breath. "Gladly, sir. I had no intention of offending any serious and thoughtful member of this Council. But in return, can you give me assurance that no one will take revenge on me through my students?"

"I doubt if any such thing is going on, Miss Jacobsdotter."

"Thank you. I will hold you to your commitment to make sure it never does. Now, may I go back to my duties?" She put on a smile. "The Nurse Sarah will have run out of stories of gruesome operations to entertain them with."

Isaac did not hide the relief on his face. "By all means. *Education is paramount.*"

She bowed her head in a dignified manner to the council and withdrew, her back straight and her head high.

But her mind was not on her duties that afternoon, and she did not show her usual sympathy to the problems of her students. They got the picture, and behaved abnormally well, which was gratifying, if sobering.

By the time class was over, she had made up her mind. She used the ShipNet to inquire as to her mother's location, and sent a quick mental search out to be sure that the older woman was in a pleasant frame of mind. She rapped lightly on the door and popped her head in when it opened. "Hello, Mother. Do you have a moment?"

"For you, dear, always." There was a pause. "And yes, I am aware of the irony of that common phrase in the present situation. What can I do for you?"

She plopped down on the plush sofa that graced her mother's suite. "I had it out with the Pastor in front of the Council today."

Her mother took the office chair from behind her desk and set it close by. "Did you, now? And how did that go?"

"He tried to take my job, Mother." She slumped into the chair. "I didn't know what to do."

"Take your job? He can't do that?"

"He could if he had enough votes on council."

"And does he?"

"I must have some supporters, because they were debating it before I got there. But Councillor Isaac cut the discussion before they got to voting."

Tirza nodded. "A good leader, Isaac."

"You think so? All I see is dithering and compromise."

Her mother smiled. "A clever compromiser. He knows when to battle it out and when to pour oil on the waters. In the end, he usually gets what he wants."

"I suppose."

"Do you need my help, then?"

Roselyn considered. "I don't think so. But he did make one charge that I couldn't deal with."

"I suppose he suggested you had an improper relationship with Miriam."

Roselyn remembered to close her mouth. "How did you know...? Oh, no! Is that what everybody thinks?"

Her mother gave a soft smile. "Of course not. It's just a standard trick bullies always use. They take the one weakness of their own that they're afraid you'll attack them with, and blame you for the same thing first. That way it becomes a 50-50 battle, and they're half way to winning before they even start."

133

"And how do you fight it?"

Her mother shrugged. "Take care. Don't let any whiff of scandal approach you. If possible, set your friends to spread the word about him. And do it now, before he has the chance to get his own campaign going."

"But I can't do that. It would be odious. I can't use Miriam in this battle, no matter what he does."

"That's very noble of you, dear, and I'm proud of you for the thought. But do you want to win or not?"

"I don't want to have a battle at all. I just want him to go away and stop bothering me."

"Then stop bothering him, keep a low profile for a while, and hope it all goes away."

"Really?"

"Yes. And if he refuses to stop, go for the jugular and destroy him."

"You're serious?"

"Yes. And that's not just a concerned mother talking. He's dangerous to every woman on this ship, and if he can't keep himself under control, it's up to us to deal with him."

Roselyn sighed. "What's wrong with him, Mother? Why is he this way?"

"I don't really know. He was the first one conceived and born on ship."

The daughter grimaced. "Oh, everybody knows that."

"Exactly. Silver spoon in his mouth and all that. He has always considered himself one of the elite."

"But we don't have an elite. Isn't that the whole point of the Congregation?"

"That's the point, all right, but I'm afraid we're fighting human nature. When it comes to Josiah, he has always received more than he deserves. His parents were powerful leaders, and they made sure he got the best, but they never allowed him to earn it. So he's insecure in his position." She mused a moment. "He seems to have taken a turn for the worse lately. I don't know why."

"The whole Men's Council feels the same way. There's an undercurrent of uncertainty in their gestalt, even when they're not in gestalt."

"You're going to have to explain that."

134

She shrugged. "Don't you ever get a feeling from a group of people?"

"I suppose. I thought that was just intuition."

"No, Sensitives feel the emotions of a group and can feed them back, making them stronger. The whole Men's Council is scared stiff."

"Of what?"

"The future, I guess. In a matter of weeks, we'll be leaving this close, cozy spaceship and going into a big, new world. Nobody has any idea what is going to happen to us. I'd be scared if I were them."

"But you're not?"

"I spend all my free time researching our new home. I probably know more about the planet and its citizens than anyone on this ship."

Her mother nodded slowly. "And because they're scared of the future and you're not, you become part of what they're afraid of. And Pastor Josiah plays on that."

"I'm afraid so. I also think he's trying to lead them backwards, to a time when the religious aspect of our society was more important. Thus giving them more power again. And incidentally, giving him more power."

"In that case, your best way to win is not to fight."

"Except for one thing. I think it's time I took my proper place as an adult."

"Do you think they'll allow it?"

She grinned. "They've already offered. I'm beginning to agree with you about the Head Councillor. He knows when to back a winner."

"I'd go for it if I were you. But no confrontation with Josiah."

"Agreed. I'll back away and stay out of sight for a while. Let him prove that he can act like a reasonable human being."

"If you can, that's the best for everyone. You, me, the Congregation, and even him."

"Fine. But if he can't control himself, I'm going to bring in the big guns."

"Agreed, but it isn't that easy. The Women's Council is divided on many topics."

"Oh, I wasn't talking about them, Mother. I was talking about my own resources."

"What resources are those?"

She reached out and placed a hand on her mother's knee. "Do you trust me?"

"Of course."

"Then enter gestalt with me."

"Of course." She frowned. "Why wouldn't I?"

The two women's minds melded.

Nzinga?

Eager desire to please.

Image: greeting of equals.

Image: cat with itch behind left ear.

Shaky image: human scratching behind cat's ear.

Emotion: hurry.

Emotion: thanks.

Emotion: pleasure.

The gestalt faded, leaving Roselyn to gaze on her mother's shocked face.

"What...who was that?"

"That was Nzinga. She's an auguar, on a Space Arm scout ship three light years away."

"That is one powerful mind. Regal."

"Yes, she's a leader, no question. And she's Miriam's 'imaginary friend'."

"Miriam?"

"Yes. She's a needy little girl, and she used her talent to reach out for companionship. That's what she found."

"...what use can this amazing animal have for you, here?"

"That remains to be seen. The main advantage is that she will protect Miriam from any physical, electronic, or mental attack. She can't deal with the social situation. That's my problem."

"How can she protect Miriam from three light years away?"

Roselyn considered. "Mother, I can't tell you everything. Most of it, I don't know or don't understand, and some of it probably breaches Space Arm security. I only introduced you to Nzinga because you deserved something." She grinned. "And because it occurred to me that you might get along rather well."

Her mother frowned. "I think that's one of your subtly sarcastic comments, and I'm going to ignore it."

"That's very wise of you, mother, but when you get to know Nzinga and her trainer, Major Jacobs, I think you'll realize it was a compliment."

Tirza sighed. "And if you're trying to keep me off balance, you're playing that gambit perfectly."

Roselyn laughed out loud. "I was taught by the best." She rose. "If you'll just keep your ear to the wind, mother, and give me due warning if something serious is coming up, it will help a lot."

Her mother stood as well, and they touched cheeks. "It would be an honour."

As she passed along the corridor, the import of her mother's comment struck her. *That was a heartfelt expression. I could feel it through my augment. What's going on?*

28. TRAPPED

NIGHTHAWK

Natalia regarded her crew, spread around *NightHawk's* mess. "All right, folks. For once you all know why I gathered you together. As far as I'm concerned, we have completed our mission. Whatever other dangers space holds, it's pretty conclusive that this swarm is quite capable of destroying our probes. We have a tonne of data on our subjects. It's up to someone more qualified to do the in-depth research required. So we go home."

Smiles were shared around the room.

"If we can."

Eyes turned to the captain again.

"I'm serious. We've made a lot of progress in our ability to coexist with these creatures, but the moment we start moving against the flow, we turn into predators. Alwyn has picked up a change in the behaviour of the swarms. Their density is increasing, and we may have passed the point of no return. Now aliens under attack are protected by any nearby formations, and with more aggression. Our assumption that predators come from outside seems to be accurate, and predators are not allowed near the epicentre. The moment we start coming out against them, we'll be acting like predators, and they'll attack again. Even now, we don't know if we're going to have to fight our way out, and we just lost two more days of ground. We have to get out of here."

Toni shook her head. "If only they knew how happy we'd be to go."

"We have to find the right course." Alwyn frowned in thought. "I know there is a tendency to think that we will do best by going upstream, hoping to get back to an area where the swarms are less dense. If that is not possible, perhaps we can slide sidewise through them. After all, the only known distance we have is how far we have come since we entered the swarm."

The captain nodded. "That's one possible tactic. My concern is that instead of a stream flowing in one direction, we are now in a globe contracting inward. Thus there is no "sideways" to slide out. Safety is only directly against the stream, and sliding sideways just gets us in deeper."

"But it would give us more time to find a solution, and our formation would appear less aggressive."

"That's the trade-off, all right. Well, everybody start working on it. We have a new objective, and it's one we all buy into. Get us out of here and get us home."

29. FURTHER TROUBLE

JERUSALEM'S HOPE

Miss Jacobsdotter?

Roselyn glanced up at the camera lens in the corner of her cabin. *I don't know why I do that.* "Hi, *Jerusalem.* What's up?"

The Captain requests your presence on the bridge, Miss.

"Is this a formal invitation?"

Not really. I'm just being polite. Sort of like you are when you look directly towards me when you're speaking.

"In that case, it behooves me to be polite to Captain Nowak and show up at the bridge ASAP."

Thank you, Miss.

"You're welcome." She briefly checked her hair in the mirror and headed for the door.

The first thing Roselyn noticed when she entered the bridge was an image of Miriam's hybrid *Jerusalem*/Harley, morphing slowly back and forth in a prominent position on one wall.

The captain chuckled. "Some of us rather like that idea. My First Officer belonged to an antique two-wheeler society back on Earth."

"I don't know much about spaceships, sir, but..."

Ahem. You mean you didn't know much about spaceships until you spent five hours last week researching them.

"Which means I still don't know much about them, *Jerusalem.*"

I stand corrected, Miss.

The captain smiled. "You seem to have a rather informal relationship with the ship."

"Yes, we've been chatting a bit."

I'm not using any extra resources, sir. We decided it was more efficient if we used Miriam's channel. It turns out some of the work I was doing with Miriam should be spread around with the rest of the Sensitive children."

"As you wish, *Jerusalem.*" He turned to his audience of one. "This ship is built rather backwards from the usual plan, as you have noticed. It has to with her original purpose. They wanted to keep the sensitive data-collection equipment as far as possible from the vibration and radiation of the engines. So they put the scientists in the bow and left the stern for us."

140

He turned to the huge Permaglass viewing port across the front of the bridge, which looked forward over the length of the ship and out to the universe in front of them. "I love that scene. Sometimes I sit on the bridge in the stillness of the dog watch and just look at the stars. I feel that rumble under my feet and I think, 'I'm really going there.' It never seems to lose its thrill." He shook his head. "And to think, in a few weeks I'll be there. With barwolves and auguars. It's more than I ever imagined I would see."

Roselyn laughed. "And an upgraded augment. Think what you and *Jerusalem* can do!"

That thought clouded the old captain's brow. "I don't rightly know about that, Miss. The Crew has minority ownership, so they'll have some say. I have 51 percent."

"How did that happen?"

"Well, I started out on this ship as an ensign. This was one of the first ArIns that communicated through augment, you know, so the officers all got the best augments money could buy at the time. When she was retired, I had made third officer, but I knew the ship like no one else. I scraped together the money, mostly from my family, to keep her from being scrapped. But it left me with no operating capital. These emigrants were a godsend. They bought a share, and I used their money to settle my debts, then outfit, fuel and supply the ship for the voyage.

"Originally, I had only three officers and five engineering and technical staff. We couldn't figure out exactly how they were going to be paid. But then we came up with a plan. The crew would form a cooperative, working for room, board, and essentials. The rest of the work would be done by emigrants we trained up during the voyage. They leave the ship when we reach Barnard, fully trained for work there.

"When we have fulfilled our contract, ownership of the vessel will revert to us. 51% to me, 49% to the other officers. The pilgrims will have no need of her, and we've worked most of our lives for her. Fair exchange." His grin widened. "My First Officer is my nephew, and my Chief Engineer is his wife. An older uncle and two of his children came along to round out the technical crew. The uncle died enroute, of course. He knew he would. But his kids married emigrants, and now we have seven fully grown and properly trained grandchildren, ready to continue with the family business."

"You didn't want children of your own?"

"I was always leery of children. Strange creatures; never could understand them."

"You seem to do very well with Miriam when we connect on augment."

He gave a gentle smile. "She's a truly strange creature. That, I can deal with."

Roselyn's heart warmed to the man. "But real-time?"

"I'll leave that to you for the moment. It takes a special kind of person."

"Hmph! I've been getting a lot of that lately." She lowered her eyebrows. "Usually it means more work."

He indicated that she should precede him through the side door to the Chartroom.

"Have a seat. I did want to talk to you about a matter…"

"I sort of thought so." She sat, folding her hands on the table before her. "What is it?"

"I've had a delegation from the Men's Council. They have made a rather strange request."

"Which, in itself, is not so strange, considering where it's coming from…no, please. I'm sorry for the interruption. Do go on."

"Well, they have asked me if it's possible to restrict certain areas of the ship to minimal augment usage."

A bolt of anger surged through her. "And I suppose the first area will be my classroom."

He raised a cautioning hand. "No, no, they said nothing about that. Just enquiring, they said."

She forced herself to stay calm. "And let me guess that this delegation was not official. For instance, Head Councillor Isaac wasn't there."

"That's right. Just unofficial information gathering. Your old friend Pastor Josia seemed to be the spokesman. 'Exploring opportunities,' he called it."

"And what did you tell them?"

He smiled slowly. "The usual bureaucratic runaround. I said I'd have to consult with my technical staff, and I'd get back to him."

"I see. And have you done that?"

"I talked to *Jerusalem,* who is the final authority on such things."

"And what did *Jerusalem* say?"

I said that except for certain areas of the ship, it was quite possible.

The captain frowned. "I didn't expect you to be joining this conversation, *Jerusalem.*"

Certain parameters have been reached, sir. Pastor Josia is being discussed in the presence of Miss Jakobsdotter, and her stress levels are at the appropriate level. I suppose I could record without listening, but I wanted her to know.

"That's fine then. Carry on."

Thank you, sir.

The captain regarded her. "So it is my intention to tell Pastor Josia what *Jerusalem* has informed me."

Her heart fell. "I suppose so."

He smiled. "Which will require him to tell me which areas of the ship he wishes to affect. Which tells us what he has in mind without actually asking him."

"Oh." Then she took in his expression. "Oh...I see."

"Right. *Jerusalem* tells me there are certain areas of the ship containing communications and augment hardware that cannot be disturbed without affecting the ship's com."

"But the com control room..."

"...is directly above your classroom. The two were placed in close proximity from the very first. It seemed a strange position for a classroom. When your generation of Sensitives started growing up, I realized what was going on."

"Hmm." She shot him a glance. "When he gives you his list, could you check to see if any of his targets affect the running of the Women's council?"

"I hadn't planned to do that."

"Oh."

"I told you. I stay out of the political manipulations of my passengers." He regarded her distress. "Besides, it isn't me that gets the final say. It's all up to *Jerusalem.*" He leaned back in his chair, fingers laced across his stomach, and regarded her with a satisfied air.

"Oh. I see. *Jerusalem* will have all the information, will she?"

"She will."

"And she will make the final decisions."

"Based on technical requirements. All perfectly by the book."

She nodded slowly. "Right. So if everything is done by the book, I can have no complaint, can I?"

"Nobody can have any complaint."

After a moment of warm triumph, it all crashed in on her. She sighed, and allowed her shoulders to slump.

"What's wrong? I thought you'd be pleased."

"Oh, I am. But it shows me that he hasn't quit yet. He'll just try again, and it will be nastier and less subtle."

"And you'll have to be smarter and more subtle. Because I mean what I say. I will not interfere directly."

"No, and I don't expect you to. My resources are quite sufficient to handle this." She sighed again. "I just hate that it has to even happen."

He gave a sad smile. "Such is the way of the universe. The human part of it at least." He hunched forward in his chair. "You know, it's been a while, but I remember this sort of thing from longer voyages early in my career. You're out for a few months, and everything is settled and running smoothly, and then you get near the end of the run, and everybody starts throwing their weight around. It doesn't seem to matter how long you're out, it always starts just before the end."

She nodded. "I suspect it's the uncertainty of what will happen next."

"There has to be some of that."

"And this trip has been generations long. Everyone has been settled in their routines for most of their lives. And now...?"

"Poof!" He flicked his fingers out. "Very hard on those who are less self-assured."

"Thank you, sir. It doesn't give me any more idea how to handle it, but it gives me some perspective on why it's happening."

He nodded. "Just in case you were thinking this problem was your fault. Which, of course, it is."

"What?"

He shrugged. "Of course. If you were a good little girl and did what your elders and betters told you, none of it would have happened."

She glowered at him. "I don't see that making fun of me is going to help."

"Of course it is. It's going to lift you out of the funk you were slipping into and send you out of this room with your back straight and fire in your heart." He gave a self-satisfied smile. "I'm a captain, and motivating my crew is part of the skill set."

She held back her grin. "Well, just remember, I'm a very touchy person to make fun of. I might try and take over your ship."

He leaned back in his chair. "Somehow, I'm not worried. You've got too much on your plate to think about taking over an out-of-date rustbucket like this."

She stood. "Oh, you never know. Once we get to Barnard and everything is more settled, it might be handy to have a well-built spacecraft with an above-average ArIn and a...pliable captain."

"I'm shaking in my space boots."

"But don't worry." She rose and went to the door. "At the moment I'm spending my time hatching devious plots designed to bring my present enemies to heel." She turned in the doorway and aimed a finger pistol at him. "I'll be back."

"You do that. Any time you like. I never did show you the bridge properly."

"It's a date, then. Thank you, sir."

He nodded, and she left him sitting at his desk a smile playing across his face.

30. ESCAPE ATTEMPT

NIGHTHAWK/DIABLO

Toni scrubbed her palms over her eyes, then looked over at Andrew, stretched out on his accel couch. "Are we officially in trouble, yet?"

He winced. "I wouldn't go quite that far. We certainly have a sticky problem to solve."

"Right. We've tried to break out three times, and each time we've been attacked. When we tried to duck, another formation moved towards us. If we slide sideways we're left alone, but we can't accelerate any more. When do we classify this as trouble?"

"Not quite yet." Andrew was tapping away at his enterpad, deep in conversation with *Diablo*. Finally he raised his head. *"Captain, ma'am."*

Yes, Andrew.

"The Auxiliary gestalt recommends we set our outward velocity at 400 kph relative to the swarm."

You think they won't bother us at that velocity?

"Alwyn and *Diablo's* data comes to that conclusion. We can always try it and see."

Fine. We're in a relatively low density section. Can't do any harm. There was a pause. *Are you suggesting that we can get all the way out of here if we stay under 400 kph?*

"Yes, ma'am. But at that rate, assuming the same speed from the swarm, it would take us three months, and then another three or four to get home with the fuel we would have left. And that would be touch and go."

Thank you, Ensign. It's nice to have an alternative, but it doesn't sound feasible.

Let's get together in the Auxiliary Bridge and hash this out.

"Be right there."

"Aye, ma'am."

He punched Toni's shoulder as they left *Diablo*. "Oh, yes. Aye, ma'am."

When they slid into their accel couches, Natalia and Alwyn were already there, Chakka and Patches as well. The captain immediately turned to her son. "You sounded like you had some kind of idea what's going on."

"Our analysis is that by replicating predator behaviour deep within the swarms where no predator should be, we have created a mass response. It doesn't matter whether it's a hive mind situation, a central intelligence or self-directing individuals, it was there, we stirred it up and we are paying the price."

"And if we use your 400 kph solution, we're at the very edge of running out of fuel before we get home."

"True. I just wish we could find a way to show them that we don't want trouble."

The captain turned to regard Alwyn, who had his usual deep-in-thought frown. After a while, his brow cleared, and he looked at her in some confusion.

She smiled. "You always get that look when you're about to solve a problem. Give."

"Well...I was trying to think of a non-military solution, and I've been looking at the Otherwhere data. Two factors seem useful. First, I believe we are dealing with individuals, not a central intelligence. Second, they have demonstrated a tendency towards emotion. There are definite spikes when they perceive attacks coming."

"Ah. So we should try emotional contact."

"Stands to reason. Perhaps we can persuade them we aren't antagonistic."

"How do you envision the test going?"

He grinned. "I find 'em, but I am learning how to fix 'em. We need to make an oblique approach, and try to make gestalt contact the moment they move to their attack position."

She slapped the table. "Right. We'll do it." She opened her augment. "Pete, find us a course that skims near a four-pack about 1,000 kilometres away, at an angle of about 45 degrees. That puts us outside the aggression circumference we discovered earlier. Patches, pick your most empathetic pilot. Everyone else to their usual positions."

The next contact was only thirty minutes ahead, but the team was now well practised and ready in plenty of time. Patches had put Demeter up for this action, and B-5 was already in position for the approach. They had shortened their procedural format to a more relaxed pattern, so Toni started to call the approach without prompting.

"Time is running...now. B-5, please proceed. Yes, Dr. Blainey?"

"We have been discussing the approach. I think it better if Demeter focuses on the lead ship for her connection. The other three slivers have each been assigned one of the other aliens and will make their attempts immediately they get feedback from B-5."

"I was wondering what would happen if we placated one and the others kept attacking."

"Exactly."

"B-5, prepare for contact...now." Toni took a moment of pride in the fact that she had called the action before it happened.

Afterwards, she was never actually sure what had occurred, because from her point of view, nothing did. At her call, Demeter reached out somehow and made contact with the approaching lead ship. Toni could feel that contact through the battle gestalt. A flurry of back-and-forth emotional exchanges followed, during which the alien ship held a steady course. Then the other three slivers joined in, and the combination was too confusing to feel anything but a reassuring lack of aggression.

By the time the connections were made, the approaching formation had blown by at 400 kph. The barwolves dropped their contact and resumed formation with *NightHawk*.

"Contact complete. Mission terminated successfully. Over to you, Captain." Toni cut the gestalt.

Alison, any movement in the surrounding swarm?

None, ma'am.

I guess they didn't raise the alarm. Let's up the acceleration. Pete, where's the next contact?

Fifteen minutes, ma'am. Another quad.

All right, folks, stay on it and we'll do it again at higher velocity. Dr. Blainey, any observations?

Not my kind of data, I'm afraid. Looked good from the outside.

All right. Stand by for a repeat.

Which they did. Twice more, as their velocity increased from 800 kph to 2,000 and their skill developed.

Natalia came on the com. *"Going fine. Pete tells me the next contact is a slot between a group of five and a group of six. Relative velocity*

3000 kph. We're going closer to the six-pack, so we'll put all the barwolf ships on that. Alison, you keep a very close eye on the five."

Their approach was swifter now, and in no time they were entering the gap. The sliverships reached out to their targets, and once more, the aliens stayed on course.

Trouble over here, ma'am. The five-pack is changing course. Can you switch over now, Toni?

Toni monitored her ships. *Emotion: negative.* "We can't break off yet. You'll have to handle them another way."

The captain took over. *"Andrew, you're on the lead ship. Alwyn and I will handle the next two. Nzinga, Chakka, you take the trailers. Remember, this is NOT a battle. Make friendly contact. Play back their positive emotions. I have no idea. Just do it. Patches?"*

Emotion: confidence.

The black barwolf took charge of the second gestalt as well, balancing the two as NightHawk raced between the formations.

Group of five sheering off, ma'am.

Emotion: distracted acknowledgement.

Toni pulled her ships out of contact. "Run completed, ma'am."

All right. Our five are gone, too. Pete, where are we?

At this accel we'll hit a fairly heavy concentration in half an hour. Too wide to go around.

Then we go through, but not right away. NightHawk and Barwolf One, we need some time. Stop accel.

Acceleration off in 5...3...2...1 Shutdown.

O'Rourke heaved a sigh that echoed through both the gestalt and the com. *"Well, we know what's possible, now. Dr. Blainey, what's your analysis?"*

"We have now reached the velocity of triple-zero two lights relative to the alien fleet. That means we are probably standing still relative to the rest of the galaxy, and they are now going past us at their normal rate of speed. We thus have two problems. This is like the Red Queen's race. Now that we have started our slalom, we can't stop, or we slide back into the hole. Hence our second problem, which is fatigue. Unless we make some progress in this technique, we must continue to handle the aliens one on one. If we keep this up for very long, we'll all wear out, at which point we have to turn and run back towards the centre while we recuperate."

"Thank you. Andrew?"

"We have been inside this swarm, travelling at their speed, for seven weeks. At our present speed, we have seven weeks of swarm left to penetrate, as long as the swarm hasn't changed shape, for which there is no guarantee. We can assume that the swarm will thin out as we work upstream. We can assume that their behaviour will become less aggressive as we get farther from the epicentre.

"And those assumptions could be wrong."

"And my assumption that the swarm is passing us might be wrong."

"Why is that, Alwyn?"

"Because if the epicentre is stationary, and we are stationary in space…"

"I see. Anyone else? Patches?"

Image: stream of aliens passing Black Bird. Each alien takes a small piece away. Black Bird becoming skeleton, with skeleton crew clinging to ribs.

Natalia barked out a laugh. *"Best image for combat fatigue I've seen yet. We just can't do this. We have to either find a way to deal with more than one alien at a time, or we have to find a way to get out of here faster."*

Andrew was checking the nav spread. "We have a series of fours and fives coming at us. We can experiment with a smaller number of us trying to handle a larger number of them."

Image: Captain laying her hands gently on the table. "All right, folks. It's bear in the bush time. We're in it for the long haul."

31. MELTDOWN

JERUSALEM'S HOPE

Roselyn was jarred from sleep by the claxons. She jerked upright, her left hand stretching for her emergency pack on the wall above her bed where it always hung. The panic lights were on, and she dressed in the semi-darkness, her fingers fumbling with the fasteners. This problem brought her mind into focus.

Miriam, where are you?

In the dormitory.

Is your cadre ready?

Not yet. Some of them are crying.

Most of the students were not at a level that she could hear their voices, but a wash of emotions battered at her. *Tell them the teacher is waiting in the classroom. They know the drill. Tell them it's only a drill.*

Is it?

I have no idea, and it doesn't matter. Levi has a cool head. Get him to help the little ones dress.

Yes, teacher. I have already called for help.

Help?

Yes, Ninga is very busy, but she will come soon.

Fine. Get your cadre moving.

She broke contact and took one more look around her cabin. With a last thought, she snagged her blanket and pillow and stuffed them under the shoulder strap of her pack. *This could be a long night.*

When she reached the classroom, she went straight into her emergency routine, securing the desks against the walls, opening the safety packs and laying their contents in rows. She was just finishing when the first child appeared, eyes wide and hair tousled.

"Come on in, children. You know your places. It's only a drill, and we've done it before. Levi, you're Class Monitor. Here's the list. Assign the tasks."

Some were snivelling and some were plainly terrified, but her cheerful manner settled them.

Levi, a tall boy of ten with a mop of curly hair, nodded confidently. "Yes, teacher." He turned and started down the rows.

151

"Miriam, with me."

"Yesth, teacher." *What's going on?*

Let's find out. Jerusalem, are you there? Can you talk?

I'm rather busy, but we can always use Miriam's channel. We are in trouble, Roselyn.

What's wrong?

That's the problem. I don't know. The sensors show a breakdown in the reactor, and all the safeties have deployed. We're in the middle of a complete shutdown.

Is there any danger?

No, it is all going according to the protocols. But I don't know why it's happening. One moment we were cruising happily, the next moment: Blam!

What do the Engineers say?

They don't know either.

Do you want some help?

From whom?

An auguar.

Nzinga?

Yes. With enough help, she can access your systems and run diagnostics. I'm sure her knowledge is very up to date.

I will have to ask the Captain.

I suggest you do that.

Stand by, please.

I'll rally my gestalt.

She looked out over the classroom. The children were calm now, some beginning to curl up on their mats, others busily completing their assigned tasks.

"Children, may I have your attention?"

All eyes turned to her.

"Please finish what you are doing and return to your mat. We have a task to complete."

When they were all sitting facing her, she smiled. "I have been telling you the story of Inga and Oni. But I have never told you the real story." She held up a hand for silence. "This is not only a story. Inga and Oni actually exist. And they are going to aid *Jerusalem's Hope* in solving this problem.

"But they are on their spaceship, the *NightHawk,* many light-years away. They cannot come here. So we must be their eyes and ears on this ship. Can you do that?

Big eyes and hesitant nods.

"Good. Because the only way we can contact them is through the Aether. Get yourselves comfortable, now. We are going into gestalt, soon."

Teacher Roselyn, can you come to the bridge, please? I need you and your little friend.

I'm sorry, Captain Nowak. I am preparing the gestalt to communicate with Nzinga. I don't think I should leave them.

What gestalt?

Captain, who do you think comprises the strongest gestalt on this ship?

I don't know. The Council, I suppose.

No, sir. It is the youngest minds, the best trained, with the most trust in their leader.

Ah. I'm coming to you, then.

Thank you, sir.

She turned back to her class and started them on the first stages of their ritual.

It didn't take long. *Jerusalem's Hope, this is NightHawk. What's going on?*

She recognized the voice immediately. *Hello, Toni. We're in trouble.* She outlined the problem.

And you need Nzinga to run some diagnostics?

That's right. According to Jerusalem, there isn't anything wrong. The reactor is just shutting down.

All right. We're in a tough situation here, so we don't have much time. I'm feeling a strong gestalt behind you. When can we start?

A sudden cold thought hit her. *I don't have permission from the captain, yet.*

We are standing by on your schedule. But don't take too long. We're pretty tense, ourselves.

Thank you. Here he comes, now.

Captain Nowak strode in, slowing when he confronted the peaceful scene. "This is your gestalt?"

"We are ready to join with *Jerusalem.* Nzinga is standing by, with backup from the engineering crew of the *NightHawk.*"

The captain looked around, then bent over Miriam. "And this is the famous Miriam."

Emotion: anxious desire to please.

Nowak glanced at Roselyn, his eyebrows raised in surprise.

Footsteps thundered in the hallway, and Pastor Josia crashed the door open. "What are you doing with these children?"

Captain Nowak straightened. "What do you mean?"

"Captain, you have taken over one of our sacred rituals, and your First Officer tells me you are going to use it to allow an unknown being access to our ship."

"No, Pastor Josia. Our ship is in trouble, and I am asking for assistance from a Space Arm vessel with modern diagnostic equipment. These children are merely assisting in communication."

"How do you know that?"

"I don't understand."

"How do you know you are communicating with Space Arm? How can you tell that this isn't the Beast, here to tempt us into damnation, to steal the souls of our children?"

The captain glanced at Roselyn, who gave a helpless shrug. He turned back to the Pastor. "Well, I suppose I don't know that for sure, but I think it a very unlikely scenario. The much more likely outcome is *Jerusalem's Hope* sitting dead in space with our reactor cooling down, and no idea what's wrong or how to fix it. I have no trouble choosing between the two. With no way to continue to decelerate, we will blow through the Barnard system at our present speed, and if we're lucky enough not to hit anything, sail away into the Unknown until our food runs out."

"Beware he who comes to you in your hour of need with easy solutions."

"Right now, a solution is necessary to our survival." He turned to the other councillors, who were filing through the door. "What is the problem, gentlemen? We are in an emergency situation, here, and every minute counts."

The Head Councillor looked around the room, and his eye settled on Roselyn. "What are these students doing, Teacher?"

"They are by far the strongest gestalt on the ship, sir. I'm sure you've seen my reports. Their concentration is perfect. With their help, the *NightHawk's* auguar can access our systems and diagnose our problem."

Josia pushed forward. "And this supposed help appeared out of the darkness of space, just at the moment we needed it?"

Head Councillor Isaac frowned. "It does seem to be a strange coincidence..."

The captain shook his head. "No coincidence. We have been in contact with the *NightHawk* for weeks. The ship's ArIn has already used this auguar for some minor functions. Head Councillor Isaac, this is a matter involving the safety and running of my ship. It falls under my jurisdiction. I assure you, it is only the magnitude of the problem that forces me to ask for your gestalt's assistance in this matter."

Isaac nodded. "I suppose..."

But the Pastor was unrelenting. "You have no right to commandeer our children and put their souls at risk. That is our responsibility!"

Roselyn's gestalt surged. *Teacher Roselyn, are you having political problems?*

Am I ever.

Do you have someone with the gestalt ability to talk to Captain O'Rourke?

I think if the whole council made a gestalt...

Why don't you do that?

Please stand by.

She slid closer to Captain Nowak. "Captain, Sir? Captain O'Rourke of the *NightHawk* wishes to contact you. She suggests a gestalt with the Men's Council will be the quickest way to put everyone in the picture."

The captain turned to Head Councillor Isaac. "Will that help?"

"Most definitely. Let us retire to the Council Rooms."

Roselyn shook a quick frown to the captain.

"Councillor Isaac, time is of the essence, and if there is any chance your gestalt is not powerful enough, the children are here to boost it. Could we communicate better from here?"

Isaac looked around the room, then nodded. "It's very irregular, but I suppose nothing today is going according to plan. Spread yourselves around, gentlemen, and I will start the ritual."

Roselyn had never been part of the Men's gestalt, and she was amazed at how pitifully weak it was. *Nzinga...*

Emotion: eager desire to please.

We're having trouble reaching you from the other gestalt.

Emotion: calm waiting.

Standing by.

And then something happened to the gestalt. It was like waking with blurry eyes and having them gradually clear. The men's minds settled and united, and a strong presence joined them. One did not listen in, just kept the children tuned to the power.

Just out of curiosity, she began to analyze the outside gestalt. She could recognize Nzinga and Toni. Captain O'Rourke stood out clearly, but that power outside them, in the background...then she broke through.

And started back. *Patches!*

Captain Nowak's glance shot to her, but she steadied herself and gave him a weak smile and a settling gesture.

Emotion: pleasant greeting.

Are you running this gestalt?

Emotion: agreement. Emotion: invitation. Image: class of children chewing at the feet of black barwolf.

...Um...our children don't do that.

Emotion: amused agreement. Emotions: admiration, congratulations.

Then there was movement among the councillors, and Patches faded away.

Roselyn checked her charges, who were wide-eyed in wonder. She put a finger to her lips and smiled at them. Several nodded and looked around, trading glances. *This will be a valuable experience for them.*

Then the gestalt faded, and Head Councillor Isaac sought Nowak's attention. "I am satisfied. Captain O'Rourke seems a very straightforward person. We will turn this matter over to you, Captain, but we will leave three of our best minds here to monitor the children."

"Thank you, sir..."

He used his old-fashioned augment to contact *Jerusalem,* but the ship was already deep in conversation with Nzinga.

Roselyn barely registered the three men who stayed. She assumed one of them would be Josia, and at the moment she couldn't care less. Her duty was to the children, and she was having trouble keeping them on task. The experience of working with the barwolf had raised their level considerably, and as children do, they were desperate to try their new wings.

And then Patches returned, and their focus firmed again. Roselyn watched in awe as the barwolf began to take them through what looked like basic exercises designed to...well, she couldn't figure out what. Then it came to her what was happening.

Um...Patches?

Emotions: joy and amusement.

I...um don't think you should be working with the children.

Emotion: puzzlement.

We don't have permission.

Emotions: chagrin, disappointment.

I'm sorry.

Emotion: agreement.

Gradually the barwolf withdrew, leaving the children focused well beyond their previous abilities.

An indeterminate amount of time passed...

...and then it was all over. She felt a softening of the gestalt, and gradually the children were eased back into re-ti. A deep shudder ran through the ship, a feeling that she had rarely noticed, but that had been there all her life; it was the absence she had felt.

The engines were working again.

She assessed the classroom. The children had not yet recovered, reclining on their mats with wonder in their eyes, whispering softly to each other. The three councillors looked like men awaking from a dream, staring around as if unsure what they were seeing.

Then the captain and the head councillor returned. Isaac made eye contact with her, and she gestured that he had the floor.

"Children, Captain Nowak would like to speak to you."

She gave the signal, reinforced by a tweak to their gestalt, and they all sat straight.

The captain looked down on them and smiled. "Well, children, that was an adventure we don't want to repeat too often. Your friend Nzinga has done a very thorough diagnostic of our ship, and has found her to be in rather good condition, considering her age. The problem we had is rather difficult to explain, but it seems the confinement field developed a wobble caused by a weakened safety circuit that was cutting out. Yes, young man?"

The boy ran a hand through his hair. "Is that the laser-based inertial confinement in the primary reactor or the magnetic confinement on the exhaust system?"

Nowak glanced at Roselyn, who rolled her eyes. "Levi is going to be an engineer. He's interested in that sort of thing."

The captain turned back. "Which do you think it was?"

"Um...I'd say the laser system, sir, because it functions inertially, and an uneven flow would destroy the inertia."

"And you would be right. It was a standard P-35 low modification safety cutout, and we have several of them in Stores, so we replaced it and whoom!" he rubbed his hands in opposite directions, "we're off again."

Another little hand shot up.

"Yes, my dear?"

The little girl stood. "When will we get to talk to the Beastie again?"

"You mean the auguar."

"No, sir. Not Nzinga. The beastie with the sharp teeth. Do you know what it told us? It told us that everyone is the same in the Aether. What you look like outside doesn't matter. As long as you are good inside is all that counts."

Roselyn jumped in quickly. "That's right, Carmel, and remember, 'inclusion is paramount,' isn't it?" She turned to the adults. "The NightHawk has a communication specialist aboard, one of the barwolves. Some of the image may have seeped in while we were concentrating. I didn't feel any danger."

"You didn't feel any danger!"

Her head snapped around to face the Pastor.

Josia stepped forward. "You took it upon yourself to allow our children to be influenced by a barwolf monster?"

"Pastor Josia, Patches was running that full gestalt. One was in contact with all of us, including the Men's gestalt. Without ones control, we could never have done what we did."

"You may have doomed all our souls to damnation!"

158

She sighed. "Councillor Isaac, may I send the children back to their dormitories? They have just had a momentous experience, and I doubt if they need to participate in a metaphysical discussion just now." Without waiting for permission, she sent them scurrying away.

Then she turned to Josiah. "I don't know much about the barwolves, but from what I can gather, they have no interest in our souls. In fact, they will be bringing many opportunities to people with our talents. What do you want of me?"

"I want a solution to this crisis of faith you have brought upon us."

"I didn't cause this problem. A P-35 safety circuit caused it. Nzinga the auguar and the children's gestalt saved us from it, with the help of a communications specialist who happens to be a barwolf. "

"How can we know that? How can we be sure that's who we were dealing with?"

"This is Space Arm we're dealing with, Pastor. Ask them. As Captain Nowak."

"And how do we know it was really Space Arm? Beware the evil that hides behind a mask of good."

She turned to the Captain. "I have no way to handle this, sir. We had a serious problem. We solved it. I assume we're now on course and on time to reach Sanctuary just as we were promised. I don't have any plans to take advantage of whatever happened. I just want to go back to my duties and teach my students like I always have." She put on a smile. "As we get closer to the *Ark,* communication improves, and I'm finding places where my pupils are not up to standard. I only have a few weeks to remedy the situation, and education is paramount."

Then she turned to the other two Elders. "I hope this little demonstration will put to rest forever any thoughts you had of marrying me off to this man. As you can see, we don't get along."

She turned to the Pastor. "And if there's any more nonsense going around about Miriam's natural deformity being a symbol of evil or a punishment for her sins, we will all know exactly where it's coming from, won't we? It will be you, trying to take revenge on me through attacking an innocent."

She softened her voice. "Surely you can see, Pastor, that you could never have married me. You would have hated me before six months were up."

She waited, but there was no easing of his expression, so she turned away. "Do I have your leave to go to my cabin, gentlemen? Class will resume on time tomorrow, despite this interruption to our sleep. *Education is paramount.*"

The captain cleared his throat. "Are you satisfied that the children are unharmed?"

"I am, sir."

He nodded once, deeply, and she turned and walked out.

Image: huge, clawed paw reaching out. The door swung slowly shut behind her.

Nzinga, are you still there?

Feeling: soft, furry cheek rubbing against hers.

And then she was alone in the corridor.

32. ΛTTΛCK

NIGHTHAWK

Toni lay back on her accel couch in the Auxiliary Bridge, a feeling of satisfaction coursing through her. It did not last. Feeling a presence, she glanced around.

Captain O'Rourke stood in the doorway to the Auxiliary Bridge. "Are we all back on board?"

Toni felt a guilty pang. "Aye, ma'am. All's well with *Jerusalem's Hope,* and we can focus on our own problems."

"Good enough. They needed assistance, but we can't afford to let ourselves get pulled farther into the main swarm. We lost half a day's travel while we helped them. We have to resume acceleration."

Andrew shook his head. "It's so frustrating. We've been trying for five days, we know how to deal with the problem, and we just don't have the ability to use the solution. We need more mental power or more people, one or the other. Our theory that there might be a central intelligence is losing traction. We have to deal with them one-to-one."

The captain ran a hand through her hair. "Then we'll just have to tough it out and hope the swarms get weaker before our energy does."

Toni chuckled. "It may not be as bad as you think."

"And then it may be worse. What do you have to be happy about?"

"Andrew, you just gave us the solution. More power or more people."

"That's right. We can't handle more than one alien at a time. I don't see us handling the ones we do any faster, for any length of time. There's no solution."

"Simple solution: we need more people to help us."

"Too simple. Where do we find more augmented people in the middle of space?"

"Nzinga has just been making friends with a whole shipload of them."

"Jerusalem's Hope?"

"That's right. When Nzinga was analyzing their problem, Patches was playing with their school classes. One says it's the strongest

161

human gestalt one has ever seen. Some of the younger adults are quite powerful as well."

"Patches, can we do this?"

Image: barwolf standing on slippery log, falling off into water. Then standing up in water only knee-deep, laughing.

"Well, get *Jerusalem's Hope* on the line, and let's order up a gestalt."

* * *

JERUSALEM'S HOPE

Roselyn rubbed both hands over her face, up and down. "You need what?"

Toni's distinctive presence swelled in the gestalt. *I know it's strange. We need your gestalt.*

"But we're here and you're there, and..."

And Patches can patch us together. All we need are those receptive minds.

"And you're being attacked by alien vessels."

Not really attacked. We're in their space, and they think we're predators. We've discovered that we can persuade them to leave us alone, but we need to talk to each one, personally. We just don't have enough people."

"I see. Well...I'll have to talk to our leaders, and I'm warning you right now, they are not of one mind. Especially about me."

Emotion: wry grin. We were getting that impression. Thank you for trying.

"All right. I'll get back to you ASAP. That's the expression you use, isn't it?"

Emotion: grin. It is. We'll hear from you A-sap, unless you have a SNAFU."

Emotion: grin. "I'll look that one up, too."

The pleasant change in her circumstances allowed Roselyn instant contact with the captain. All she had to do was contact *Jerusalem* on Miriam's channel, and Nowak answered as soon as he could. When she explained *NightHawk's* situation to him, he asked her to come to the bridge. Immediately.

The captain was in his command couch, and she crossed the spacious control room to him, nodding greetings to the officers, whom she was beginning to know.

Novak looked up at her. "I'll be a moment. I didn't expect you so soon. Can you wait?"

She returned his smile. "You're only running a small spaceship. I'm on RestDay. I suppose I can spare the time."

He gave a serious nod and returned to his panels.

After a few minutes he closed down his controls and stood. "There. I gather *NightHawk* doesn't have much time to spare." He gestured towards his chartroom. "Sit down and fill me in on the details."

When she had finished, he mused a while, his hands folded under his chin. "Would you say they are in serious distress?"

"I'm not sure what that means, exactly, sir."

He shook his head. "I don't mean that in any technical sense. How can you quantify distress? I'm asking you because you are an expert on the communication of emotion. How do they feel?"

"Oh, I see. They're a very calm, competent group of people. Nothing seems to faze them. But there's a definite undercurrent of urgency. Also fatigue. I would say that they are holding up well in a trying situation. If Captain O'Rourke doesn't think they can hold out much longer...well, she's an experienced officer and she knows her crew."

He nodded. "*Jerusalem?*"

Aye, sir.

"Connect me with Head Councillor Isaac, please."

Aye, sir.

Roselyn could only hear one side of the conversation, but it seemed to be going well. When he requested a meeting with the council, she gestured for the Captain's attention. She pointed to him, then to herself, and held up two fingers.

"Ah. Yes, this is something that affects the whole ship and the children as well. If I might suggest, we should meet with the whole council." He gave a nod at the response. "Fine. At fourteen hundred hours in the main dining hall. Thank you, sir."

* * *

163

Roselyn stood by Captain Nowak and watched the Councillors file into the dining hall, taking their traditional positions: women on the right, men on the left, Isaac and his two assistants at the head table.

"I think it best if you lay out the problem, sir."

He glanced down at her. "But you know much more than I do."

She sighed. "But the problem is political, not scientific."

"Yes, I suppose." He stepped forward. "Head Councillor Isaac, thanks to you and all your people for meeting me."

The Head Councillor stood and made sure all the others were in attendance. No one dared miss this meeting: 22 on the Men's Council, 22 on the Women's. "We are pleased to be of assistance in any way we can. What is the problem?"

Nowak used simple terms to outline the difficulty that *NightHawk* was experiencing. "They must deal with these creatures one-on-one. They simply do not have enough crewmembers with the ability to communicate through the Aether to escape the alien swarm."

Pastor Josia jumped to his feet. "Are you telling us that these alien space beings are in touch with the Voice of the Universe as well?"

The captain gestured to Roselyn. "I must turn this question over to someone who knows more about it than I do."

She rose from her chair. "I can only explain it in terms of human experience. Humans have emotions and the ability to speak about them. The beasts of the field and forests also have the ability to feel emotions. They feel anger towards their enemies, and love for their offspring. But they do not have the ability to speak.

"According to the scientists on board the Space Arm ship, these alien beings are probably similar. The swarms attacking *NightHawk* can express emotion through the Aether. The barwolves from Barnard can communicate in a much more sophisticated way. Likewise, the humans in our Union have varying abilities to communicate through the Aether. *NightHawk* needs the help of some of our better communicators in order to communicate emotions to the space beings. The barwolf communication expert can make this happen.

Josiah shook his head. "You are proposing that we open our minds and hearts to this beast, about which we know nothing? You are mad!"

She clenched her fists, down at her sides out of sight. "They are not beasts. That was what *Ark of the Covenant* called them when they thought they were being attacked. I changed it to "beasties" so the children would not be frightened of them. Which they are not. We are regularly in contact with the three cubs that were kidnapped, and they are sweet little things, like puppies but much more intelligent. They are no threat to us."

"You are a mere girl with little experience of the universe and its dangers. We cannot put the safety of our souls in your ignorant hands. I say, let Space Arm deal with their own problems. We have problems of a spiritual nature on this ship."

The captain stepped forward. "My friends, we have a Space Arm vessel sending out a distress signal. If I allow religious arguments to interfere with my duty to a vessel in trouble, I'll never captain a ship again, in this System or any other. I have no resources that will affect their situation, but they say they need your people's help. Please do whatever is in your power to help them." He began to walk away.

Then he turned back. "And if you want to increase your welcome in your new home, I hear the captain of the *NightHawk* is a good friend of Ambassador Pretoro." With that, he strode to the side of the hall and stood in the 'at ease' position.

Roselyn scanned the tables. "There it is, ladies and gentlemen. The ship that saved our lives is in trouble. All they ask is our help. We are several light years away from the danger. The chance of injury to any of us is small, while our help to them might turn the battle and save many lives.

"This is the way of the Outback, in which we will soon be living. There are enough riches to be gleaned that the people have no need to fight anything except their hostile environment. They help each other so that all may survive. We can do that and earn our place with them before we even arrive."

Pastor Josiah stepped forward and looked down at her with a sneer. "And what do you know of this Outback, girl?"

She stepped forward and glared at him. "I know of this Outback because I communicate with them every day. The ambassador's name is Alfino Pretoro, and I have an appointment to talk to him the moment I am out of quarantine at the Sol Embassy in Barnard. My contact on Arborea is a specialist in barwolf communication through the Aether, which is what I use to talk to them. I did not intend it at first, but now I realize that I have paved the way for a very easy transition for our people when we reach Sanctuary.

"So you say."

"So I say. And all you have to respond with is fear." She took a step forward. "Let's take a look at your arguments." She checked them off on her fingers. "You think someone is pretending to be a Space Arm ship in order to fool us. You think there is someone pretending to be an auguar, and controlling our ship's ArIn. You think all these complicated plans are being perpetrated for what reason? I know. To tempt us into sin. What sin, I'm not sure of, but I'm sure you can find plenty of quotes from scripture to support your lunacy."

She turned to those at the table, staring at her with awe in their faces. "Think of the science, people. We have been talking to all these beings in real time. What does that mean? Well, it means the barwolf communication system I say I have been using is real..." She turned to the Ship's Second Engineer, who also sat on the Council. "What else could explain it, Engineer Joseph?"

The man shrugged. "To speak anywhere close to real time, all these people would have to be within less than half an AU of us."

She nodded. "And since there is almost no chance that there has been another spaceship that close all this time and we haven't seen it, the third conclusion is that they are all on this ship. Which is ludicrous." She turned to the Pastor and lowered her head sadly. "Which brings us to the only other possible conclusion. Either all of this is real, or it has all been created by one person. Me. I'm the one bringing you all this information." She turned away. "In his twisted mind, I have made it all up. And why? To get revenge on him, because he once did me the great honour of wanting to marry me, and I refused.

"The bottom line, gentlemen, has nothing to do with sin. He is afraid of me because I'm the woman who said, "No," to him, and that brings his little self-centred world tumbling down. He's afraid of me."

He raised a shaking finger to point at her.

"...and if you say, "witchcraft," they'll lock you in the brig and turn you over to the medical authorities the moment we hit the embassy. People have learned a few things in the last three hundred years."

She turned to the Council table with a helpless gesture. "As long as he looks through the eyes of fear, his mind is like a rock. He will not change, he does not want to change and he cannot change. And in the Outback, that will kill you as quickly as that." She snapped her fingers in Josia's direction, and the man started backwards, crashing into the table, catching himself from falling at the last moment.

She turned away from him, and regarded the Council. "You heard the captain. He cannot ignore a cry for help because of a religious argument from his passengers. Can you do the same, because of a personality conflict over a marriage?

"Pastor Josiah was my enemy from the moment he laid his greedy eyes on me. If I had known it and slapped him down at the beginning, it would have saved us all this trouble. For that, I apologize." She scanned the faces, first of the Head Councillor, then those in the chairs that faced him. There was no indication of argument. "Now, how are we going to organize this help?"

The Head Councillor gave a twisted smile. "I thought you would have it all figured out."

"Forget that idea, gentlefolk. I'm only about one day ahead of you in most of this. We know that the children's gestalt is the most powerful one on the ship. The Space Arm squadron is dealing with a large number of aliens, each one of which must be contacted directly and assured of our good will. Anyone who is in tune with the Universe can do this."

She raised a hand to stop their questions. "The communications specialist that will organize this huge gestalt is a barwolf. You may find that hard to deal with at first." She smiled. "They have a mouthful of very frightening teeth. However, if you have been listening to the fairy tales your children and grandchildren are spreading around, you will know that these beasts are far in advance of us in their contact with the Voice. Their planet is the Sanctuary we have been coming to for all these years, and they will lead us in our worship," she paused, "as well as providing us with a lucrative occupation, as we help the normal humans deal with them."

Head Councillor Isaac was looking thoughtful. "So, you're telling us that instead of entering this planet as the poorest of immigrants, we will be joining them as communication specialists?"

"That is what it looks like."

The Head regarded his council. "Then it behooves us to start learning how to perform our new duties."

There were nods around the table, and several smiles were directed her way.

"Good. Patches, the barwolf, will be contacting us, but this is how we can prepare. We will use the children's gestalt as our primary communication device. They will make the first contact and learn what we need to do. Then the older children will guide each member of our Congregation in the activities they have learned. We can practise this ahead of time, so we are ready when we are called upon."

33. REPRIEVE

NIGHTHAWK

Toni took a moment to orient herself to the new gestalt. All the *NightHawk* crew were in it, including the barwolves. Funnelling through Patches, she could sense a mass of young, powerful minds, including the familiar tones of Roselyn's cheerful persona and the incredibly strong aura from Miriam. Several adults hung dimly on the edges.

Captain O'Rourke took over. "All right. Engineering has given us the numbers. Our most economical course, considering fuel consumption, time and distance, is point triple-zero two five lights relative velocity to the aliens. This means we will be in contact with each alien for approximately two minutes. If we don't have the strength to handle that, we'll have to choose a slower speed. Velocity versus stamina. We will start the tests and increase velocity until we reach the maximum of one parameter or the other. Is everybody ready?"

Eager desire to please.

Eager desire to please.

"Major Jacobs, you and Nzinga will call this mission."

"Thank you, ma'am. For our first test, there's a group of four aliens coming very close to us. Can we have one child for each alien, Roselyn?"

Miriam, you take the leader. Levi, you're on the big one on the left. Hannah and Cilicia, you take the other two. How's it going, Miriam?

It's easy. They're all prickly, and you have to pat them in the right direction to calm them down and make them all soft again.

Toni opened up to the *NightHawk* augment. *"There you have it, folks. The word from the expert. Just find out which way the prickles are pointing, and pat them down."*

Levi somehow communicated the emotion of a snort. *This one's a girl.*

Toni frowned to Andrew, who raised his eyebrows. *"Are you sure? How can you tell?"*

Emotion: confusion. I don't know. Girls are girls; you can just tell. She's a girl.

Miriam's crystal-clear thought came through. *They're all girls, Levi. And you're a pretty girl, too, aren't you, sweetheart? Yes...*her thoughts faded into chatter, and then the formation was past, and they cruised through empty space.

All girls? Eeeww!

Levi, listen. Can you tell me if she was a girl, a young one, or an older one, like a woman?

Um...sort of. She was older. Well...maybe not old like you and Teacher Roselyn. But older than me for sure.

Levi is ten, Toni.

Thanks, Roselyn. That's very perceptive of you, Levi. Thank you. She turned to Andrew. "There you have it. We're escorting a bunch of teenage girls on their coming-of-age journey."

"Don't laugh. You could be right."

"I wonder if we're going to meet the boys. Or the adults, or any other number of genders."

"One of the joys of research. You never know what you'll find."

The captain entered the com. *Are you happy with the test, Toni? We're getting rather busy, out here in re-ti.*

"What do you think, Roselyn? Can your gestalt handle this?"

"The first four had no trouble at all, but those were my star pupils. I think the rest can do it."

"We're ready, Captain. Do you want to talk to them?"

"Briefly."

Children, Captain Natalia wants to talk to you.

Emotion: eager desire to please.

Hello, children. Thank you for offering to help us. As of now, Major Toni is in charge. You just do whatever she says, and you'll be helping us a great deal. These aliens are not enemies. They are just wild things that don't know we're nice people. Be friendly to them, all right? And once you learn how to do it, you're going to teach your parents how, so they can help us, too. Will you do that?

Emotion: eager desire to please.

Over to you, Major. Contact in five minutes.

Toni took charge of the full gestalt, although she could feel Patches in the background, tweaking and polishing the meld. *All right, children. Soon, NightHawk will go through a group of these aliens, and they are afraid of us. We have to calm them down and show them that we are friendly, and we won't hurt them. Can you do that?*

Emotion: eager desire to please.

Major Toni, I don't think we're going to hurt them from three light years away.

That's very true, Levi, so this shouldn't be hard. Here comes the next formation. Patches has put you in a line, and as you come to the front, I will point to an alien ship. You calm her down. Once she has passed us, you go to the end of the line and wait for your turn again.

Image: children lined up as if for treats.

Thank you, Teacher Roselyn. The treats will come later.

Incoming, three o'clock low. Ten bogeys.

What's a bogey, Major Toni?

Image: alien vessel approaching rapidly. That's a bogey, Levi. Why don't you take that one?

Aye, ma'am. The boy reached out, feeling his way rapidly into the creature's mind. *She's not happy, Major Toni.*

So you calm her down. Tell her how beautiful she is.

Yeuck. Okay, Major Toni. I can do that. He redoubled his efforts.

Who's next? She noticed Patches shuffling the order of the children and didn't take time to ask.

Roselyn's soft presence intruded. Oh, *Lilac. Here's a nice gentle one for you.*

The little girl reached out timidly, but immediately radiated joy. *She likes me!*

Perfect. Toni sent the teacher a wink and took over again. *Keep up the good work. Miriam, I see you're next. This one looks difficult to me. Can you handle her?*

Emotion: confidence. The powerful mind reached out. The creature wavered, thrown out of its anger, then calmed. *Image: small girl riding on back of giant alien, swooping and turning.*

Don't overdo it, kid. There are hundreds more to go.

Emotion: apology.

Never apologize for doing a good job.

Roselyn's aura firmed. *Miriam, that one is long out of the danger zone. You're just playing. Will you go and help Gideon? He has a frightened one.*

Emotion: agreement.

171

Toni began to assign the other children, but another wave of aliens appeared, and soon she was losing track of who was where. As the children got better at their task, Natalia accelerated. They spent less and less time with each alien, but it also meant that Toni had to pick up her pace as well. *Roselyn, I don't know how you do it. How can you keep track of a classroom full of them?*

Emotion: mild humour. Years of practice. And I know them all. Do you want me to take over?

Can you? From there?

Of course. Wait a moment. I've got one in tears. Back in a sec.

She faded from the gestalt, but her quiet, firm presence remained.

All right. Carmel just got attached to her subject and was sad she had to go. Carmel's like that. No worries.

Glad to have you here. How long can you keep this up?

I'll have to start pulling them out after half an hour. The older ones might keep going for an hour, but their attention will waver. Once we get the adults online we can go for longer, but they won't be as good at it as the children are. I assume we don't want to risk one getting through to you, still angry.

Toni reported this information to the Captain. "They're going to start fading in about twenty minutes, ma'am."

Thanks, Toni. We'll take a break in fifteen, then. If we decel a bit we can handle them ourselves.

NightHawk came on the com.

Prepare for flip in twelve minutes. Decel in thirteen.

Toni returned to her duties, watching for children who needed shoring up. As they became tired, the children disappeared from the line, and Toni assumed Roselyn was pulling them from active duty. The gestalt remained strong, though, so they were still functioning at a lower level.

Toni?

"Yes, ma'am."

We have an opening ahead. Tell Teacher Roselyn she can take her children out, now.

Aye, Captain Natalia. Emotion: thanks.

Oh, you're here. I mean there. Just where are you, Roselyn?

I was helping organize the children in the line, ma'am. Patches is a wonderful gestalt leader. It felt like I was right there. Toni is a very strong person, isn't she? And she's almost as small as I am!"

Emotion: amusement. Don't flatter my crew in the middle of a battle. It isn't good for their concentration.

Aye, ma'am.

And in case you're wondering, when you're in gestalt with Patches, stuff from the edges of your mind sometimes slips through. I caught your opinion of Andrew. Did you know that he's my son?

I didn't see any resemblance.

You mean genetic? He's adopted.

I see. Well, whatever you picked up, don't tell him, right? Not good for his concentration.

That's for sure. Thanks for your help. We couldn't have done it without you. When would your gestalt be ready to try again?

I think we should have our normal lunch break. I'll tell the children a story to relax them, and then have a training session with the adults. You can have the ten older ones for a similar session in about two hours, along with ten adults, but we'll have to break those in slowly. We'll see about the younger ones, if you need them. Oh. Make that eleven students. Miriam can do this all day.

"All right. See you in two hours, then."

The Jerusalem gestalt faded slowly as Patches released them one by one.

Toni, we need you back in the front lines now. You've had a nice rest.

"If only you knew, Ma'am. I've finally found a job that's harder than commanding a firefight."

What's that?

"Teaching a class of twenty kids."

34. FINAL ESCAPE

NIGHTHAWK

Two hours later, *NightHawk* and *Barwolf 1* hit the accelerator again with a new cadre of minds, most of them less experienced or powerful than the children. It didn't take Patches long to rearrange the format, using the children to maintain an open line while the adults made the actual contacts, bringing their mature sensibilities to bear. Once the new group settled in, Natalia was able to push her little fleet up to optimum speed and give Toni some leisure to see the process from a distance.

"Roselyn, how are things working from your end?"

Just fine, Toni. Our only problem seems to be trust.

"Yeah, cynical adults don't fall into the gestalt as easily as well-indoctrinated children."

I'm not sure I like the idea of indoctrination.

"You're a teacher. I thought that was your job."

If I was cynical, I'd have to agree with you.

"Speaking of trust, what's with this bunch coming online right now? They read like adults, but there's no hesitation."

Oh. Yes, these are friends of mine. They aren't powerful or experienced, but they are friends.

"Especially that one...oh. Am I treading on toes?"

He's...um...

Emotion: humour. "Don't bother to explain. I get it."

Emotion: uncertainty. It's not like with you and Andrew, though.

Emotion: curiosity. "What do you know about Andrew and me?"

Oh. Am I treading on toes?

Emotion: Laughter. "No, no secrets around here. We're talking marriage. When we can get our lives organized."

Congratulations. Are you...

Emotion: exasperation. "We're trying to run a gestalt here, ladies. Can we cut the chatter?"

Emotion: guilt. "And then there's days when I'm not so sure. Sorry, Andrew, just finding ways to ease the interface."

"No, just gossiping. And when I'm the subject of the gossip, I get to have my say."

"Yes, boss. Back to business. How are things going at your end?

"The Big Boss is looking for a progress report. How long can we keep this up?"

"Roselyn?"

Not at this rate for any length of time. We can't keep the children concentrating indefinitely, even working in shifts. Are we talking hours, days...?

Days. Maybe ten. The faster we go, the sooner we're done. Let's check with Patches.

Image: 15 children in gestalt. Passage of time; 14 children. Passage of time; 13 children. Long passage of time: 5 children and two adults.

"You're saying that as time goes on, we'll need less and less children to run the gestalt, and even some of the adults will learn to do it?"

Image: humans working out, building muscles.

Toni glanced to Andrew, who nodded. "There you have it, Rosy. Patches will cut down on the number of children needed as time goes on. Barwolves aren't very precise about quantifying things, so we don't know how that will work out. I suggest your job is to make sure nobody's getting overworked. You know your people best."

I can do that. How will adults know they've been tapped for gestalt duty?

"Patches will take care of it, and one will inform you at the same time. Fair enough?"

Fair enough. I'll deal with my political problems and keep the gestalt running.

Toni motioned Andrew to back away. He caught her hand and kissed it as he moved. "Thank you so much, Roselyn."

No thanks needed. And I know what just happened.

Tony winked at Andrew. "What do you mean?"

And you didn't fool me with whatever physical communication you just used. When people have been in gestalt for a while, their emotions become attuned as well.

"Go on, tell me what just happened between Andrew and me."

You just made some kind of very subtle physical gesture, right?

"I winked at him."

Of course. And his heart did a complete flip. Right, Andrew?...you don't have to answer, because we all know.

"Rosy, my girl, you are becoming a very scary person. Did you know that?"

Like all the other people around here, I'm just beginning to figure it out. You know, I always swore I'd never be like my mother.

"When do we meet this formidable lady?"

You already have. When the Women's Council took their turn.

Toni glanced at Andrew with horrified eyes. "You don't mean Tirza? That's why she seemed familiar somehow."

Andrew laughed. "I think I should warn you, Roselyn, we have already chosen our candidate for Ambassador Pretoro's replacement."

That's all right. She'll take over when Alison moves on up to Planetary Councillor.

"You know about Alison?"

Yes, Nzinga told me all about her. That cat is quite a gossip, you know. Image: auguar preening in front of mirrored line of images of herself.

Andrew glanced at the viewscreen in front of him. "Tea party's over, ladies. We've got a big bunch coming, and if we can get through them, there's about a six-hour gap on the other side. I think they're finally starting to thin out."

Fine. I'll give the kids a jolt of candy to keep them keen, and during the break we'll reorganize the rotation for the long haul.

35. LAST STRAW

It took a couple of days, but finally they worked out a system and got it operating smoothly. NightHawk *was making a steady .0025 Lights in the proper direction, and the* Jerusalem *emigrants were learning their duties cheerfully. But it was a fluid situation, so it was no surprised to get a contact from Toni.*

Roselyn, we have a major swarm coming up. Can we get a couple more of your hotshots in the mix for about half an hour?

"No problem. I'll just rearrange the schedule. Give me about ten minutes."

Thanks. This is working well. Our crew is starting to feel rested.

"That's good." She felt a familiar presence approaching. Rapidly. "Toni, I have a visitor coming and she's upset. Can I call back?"

Emotion: agreement.

Emotion: thanks. She turned to her mother, eyebrows raised, as the older woman strode into the room.

"Sorry to interrupt, dear. I know you're busy with important work."

Roselyn glanced at her. There was no hint of sarcasm. "It's okay. We have a system running, and it's getting smoother." She grinned. "Isn't it fun to work with experts?"

"Yes, I imagine it is. Especially cooperative ones." Tirza's face set into a frown. "Which is what we are not dealing with on this ship."

Roselyn slumped down on her chair. "What's he up to now?"

"He's been campaigning furiously, focusing on the older members of both councils. The ones who have had the power for so long they've forgotten how hard they had to work to achieve it. Now they feel the younger generation taking over without showing proper respect, and they're very easy to sway to the benefits he's offering them."

"I see. What kind of progress is he making?"

"Enough. Between the ones that support him and the ones who think this problem should be settled in council, it wasn't hard to get the quorum required to call a Full Council meeting."

"When?"

177

"Now."

A jolt of fear went through her. "But we're in the middle of a swarm! Tony has just called on us for more help, and I have three Councillors in the gestalt."

"Nevertheless. You need every vote you can summon. And it's worse than that. He has persuaded the Council that it would be unwise to allow the children to work with the aliens unsupervised."

"He's pulling us all out?"

"Sorry."

"Dammit. This could be bad. I've got to get back to Toni right away."

"Ten minutes, dear."

"I'll be there. And I'll be angry."

Her mother laid a hand on her shoulder. "As you should be, dear."

Roselyn went back into the gestalt. "We have a SNAFU, Toni. A big one."

What's wrong?

The political situation on this ship has been simmering for months, and I'm afraid I'm now the epicentre. They've called a big meeting, and everybody has to be there."

You're kidding. Everybody?

"And they're pulling the kids out until the problem is solved."

Dingo dung! How much time do we have?

"Five minutes, I'm afraid."

Okay. We'll have to cut velocity until you get back.

"I'm working on it."

Do the best you can. We're in good condition right now, but the whole crew will be working at full capacity under 1.5 Gs decel to get our speed down to where we can handle the density.

"That can't be fun."

We're Commandos. We can handle it.

"Back to you ASAP. *Jerusalem's Hope* over and out."

* * *

She made it to the meeting with moments to spare. She couldn't help but notice that Pastor Josia stood proudly in a new position three places closer to the head of the table. He sneered at her as she passed.

Councillor Isaac was just sitting, and she stepped up beside him.

"Head Councillor, I told you last week I was looking for an appropriate time to announce my acceptance of a position on the Women's Council."

"You did. And I advised against it at that time."

"What do you advise now?"

He looked up at her. "Are you determined to take this step?"

"Not completely. You know the tone of the Council. Might one vote make a difference in the present situation?"

He winced. "My reading of the situation is that it will not be required." He raised a cautioning hand. "But it might." He gave a downward smile. "It would be a shame to lose by one vote when you didn't have to."

"Exactly. You'll make the announcement first thing?"

"I will."

"Thank you."

As she turned away, his raised finger stopped her. "Good luck."

She sent a feeling of warm thanks to his augment.

He merely raised his eyebrows, then turned to regard his agenda.

As soon as the meeting settled, Isaac stood. "Before we begin this important meeting, I have one notice of business. Roselyn Jacobsdotter, having recently ascended to her adulthood, will be assuming her rightful position on the Women's Council. We welcome Miss Jacobsdotter, and hope that she will do her share in helping the Congregation govern itself in the Way of the Prophet, in tune with the Voice of the Universe."

He started to clap his hands, and she was gratified at the amount of applause that followed. As it died down, he turned to her. "It is traditional to ask the new Councillor to say a few words, and I feel that this is not a time to dismiss old traditions. Miss Jacobsdotter?"

Roselyn stood. "Ladies and gentlemen, it is traditional for the new Councillor to thank the Council for the honour of a seat, which I do with all my heart. It is also normal for that person to suggest some small way in which he or she would like to contribute to the functioning of the Congregation.

"I'm afraid I'm going to do that in a more serious way. I'm going to do what many of you feared I would. I'm going to turn the orderly business of the Council on its head.

"It doesn't take an astrophysicist to know what you're all thinking about the coming argument. You're doing the arithmetic. Lining up who thinks what, and who owes you what favour you can call in, and who you can bully into supporting you when the final vote comes, and what effect the various outcomes might have on your future position. And you are wrong.

"This is not the way of Barnard System. It is not the way of the barwolves, who will soon be our greatest allies. It is also not the way of the Prophet, in case you didn't notice."

"*NightHawk* and her crew are out there fighting for their lives without our help, because you want to indulge in your usual power games in your nice, safe spaceship, which, need I remind you, they just happened to save two weeks ago. What do you think of yourselves?" She scanned the tables, meeting every eye before going on.

"So, I am going to give you a demonstration of how badly your system works, when taken to the extreme. I'm going to show you what happens when a power struggle goes wrong."

As she spoke, she called up the gestalt that was waiting patiently to resume their work. She brought the children in, one by one. She brought her friends in, inexperienced but determine to help. She even brought *Jerusalem* and Captain Nowak's crew in as much as she could. As she worked, the task became easier and easier, and a fuzzy, multicoloured feline face peered over her shoulder. In the background a black barwolf took a moment from her hectic duties in the midst of a swarm of aliens.

Once her gestalt was firm, Roselyn carefully reached in and started removing Council members, one at a time, from the meld. Their faces showed their shock as each one was suddenly isolated.

Then she spoke to them out loud, the only way they could communicate. "Perhaps now you realize what it would be like if I chose to play your power games. Think of the results, if one person was given the kind of control that I have right now."

Slowly, she relaxed her hold, and allowed the gestalt to embrace everyone. Then she spoke, out loud and in their minds. *"You can see how wrong it would be for anyone to have that kind of power."*

180

"This ship has been our life for thirty years. As long as that was our whole world and the power remained balanced, everything worked fine. That period is over. You must start thinking on a larger scale, or our Congregation is doomed. The barwolves have shown us a new direction, ever upwards, that will lead us to success in the Sanctuary they will provide."

She looked around the room. "So, do you need a vote? Do you wish to line your power up on opposite sides and glare at each other? Or can we just get back to our duties as we know the Prophet would wish?"

She opened the gestalt fully, and was rewarded by a rush of positive energy.

She smiled at them and nodded. "Thank you. I knew you would do the right thing."

Councillor Isaac stood. "I think the reason for this meeting has just evaporated before our eyes. Is there any person here who still wishes to discuss our aid for the *NightHawk* and her crew?"

Roselyn turned her stare to Pastor Josia. He started to rise, then looked around and sat. Hesitantly, he raised his hand partially, scanning the room to see if anyone followed him.

None did.

He dropped it.

"I hereby declare that by unanimous vote, the Followers of the Voice will lend their aid to our fellow Spacers in trouble." Isaac turned to Roselyn. "Will you tell our allies that we are ready to help them again?"

She shook her head. "Feel the gestalt, Councillor. They are already re-engaging. See? Miriam, Abram and Samira are turning aside a group of five aliens without help from anyone else. Captain O'Rourke is about to return to acceleration, and we are officially back in business!"

* * *

NIGHTHAWK

Toni sighed and ran a hand through her hair. "Well, I don't want to go through that again."

Emotion: relief. I was too busy here to pay any attention. What happened?

"Our allies have just been pulled firmly to heel, ma'am. Our little friend Roselyn has just showed her teeth, I suspect."

From what I can see, the aliens are melting away in front of us. We can settle down and make some progress. "NightHawk, Prepare for acceleration. We are back in business."

36. PREDATORS

NIGHTHAWK

Three days later, everything was looking up. The swarms were thinning, and Roselyn's gestalt was down to a skeleton crew, less for use on defense of *NightHawk*, and more to allow the pilgrim Sensitives experience in working with the barwolves. They were cruising merrily along in one of the increasingly frequent gaps when suddenly every viewscreen registered a blinding flash of light. Then the overrides cut in and video feeds went completely black.

The crew sprang to their posts, a Red Alert blaring on every channel, and they sat, frozen, waiting for data, keyed up to act.

Soon the screens cleared, showing everything proceeding as normal.

The captain opened com. *"All right, crew. That was not a drill, but well done on your reaction. Analysis, please?"*

First Officer Jones cleared his throat. *"Initial replays indicate an incredible burst of radiation in all spectra originating from a source several IUs away on our ten and 23 degrees low."*

"Thank you. Auxiliary Crew, what happened in Otherwhere?"

Emotion: amazement. Image: incredible burst of energy in all spectra.

Toni glanced at Andrew, next to her in his accel couch. He nodded and spoke on the com. "That's about it, ma'am."

"Dr. Blainey?"

Chief Lundeen and I agree that what we have just experienced was a megakilowatt version of the aliens' defensive attack.

Toni sent Andrew an augment nudge, and he focused where she indicated.

"New data, ma'am. Let's scroll back in the visual record to look what happened just before the blast." *Image: swarms below and to port changing direction.*

Good eye, Diablo. Where are they heading?

Image: small change in direction towards galactic west

"Towards source of blast. And watch this, just after the blast..." *Image: aliens slowly resuming normal courses.*

So, the easy answer is that one of the predators attacked, the others started over to lend a hand, but it wasn't needed, because the battle was already over, win or lose. So, we roll on."

Emotion: agreement.

Fine. All media teams continue your analysis. Bring anything of interest to our attention, but unless otherwise indicated, we're back to normal.

Alwyn's presence came on the com. *Those on intercept duty keep an eye and ear out for any difference in our subjects. If we are getting into a predatory zone, they may be more alert or aggressive.*

Emotion: wry humour. Our civilian expert is telling us our military business, folks. We'd better sharpen up or he'll be campaigning for my job.

Emotions: horror and denial!

Over the next two days the swarms became noticeably less dense, and they registered five battle flashes further away. Toni reported a gradual relaxing in the crew to Natalia.

The captain leaned back in her desk chair and nodded. "I agree. But you wouldn't have brought this to me if you didn't have a solution."

Toni slung herself into the other chair backwards, Andrew-fashion. "I do. We can stop being worried about the swarms. We've proved we can handle them. The more likely enemies, on the other hand..."

"...are the predators. Exactly."

"We still know very little about them. Our limited physical information leads us to suspect they are members of the same or a similar species."

"Right. For all we know, they might be the young males looking to mate outside the proper boundaries."

Toni nodded. "Or they may be a similar species that preys on the swarm. Like a hawk on a flock of ducks, or a lion on a herd of deer."

"Doesn't really help, does it? If they're males of the same species, they will see us as competition. If they're predators, they might see us as prey."

"Or competition."

"But the bottom line is they're definitely dangerous, and we better be ready for them."

"I'll get the Auxiliary gestalt on it right away."

184

"And I'll prompt the *NightHawk* crew."

It was a good thing *NightHawk's* sensors were adjusted for new parameters, because the next blast was almost dead ahead and of a magnitude of ten times greater than the first one. A moment later the ship's gravitation wavered, like she was bucking a vicious headwind. As the screens came back to life, the aliens in front of them, their formations scattered, were silhouetted against a glowing haze expanding at a rapid rate. Slowly, ever so slowly, the creatures regained their positions, and the stately swoop continued. But their courses had changed.

All right, listen up. We have a lessening of density in the vicinity of that blast. It looks like all the aliens in the area are heading in that direction. We can ride in on the tails of those coming from our direction and make better time. We might even get some evidence to tell us what went on. Comments?"

Toni grinned. "Only the obvious one."

Emotion: sarcasm. Maybe it's not so obvious to all of us.

"Sorry, ma'am. Just that we already put ourselves in a hole by following these guys to where they were going."

A valid point. And before you mention it, Andrew, it does occur to me that we'll run into the opposite situation going out the other side.

My Mum is real smart, you know.

Keep it under control, Ensign, or you'll never live to make Lieutenant. We'll be doing as close a flyby as we can manage safely. Any intelligent comments? Emotion: chuckle. Well, that was a real conversation stopper. All right. Let's prepare ourselves. Course change in five minutes. Commander Jones and Dr. Blainey, please confer on the course of least resistance out the other side of this inward spiral we're observing.

Emotion: agreement.

All right. All hands to stations, all eyes peeled, all sensors open. Fill those data banks. Call anything important as it happens.

Andrew consulted briefly with Patches. "Otherwhere radiation fifteen point seven percent higher than the first blast."

Defensive reactions to us in surrounding aliens showing less resistance. It's like we don't count as much.

Thanks, everyone. We're cutting to port of the epicentre, mimicking the path of the aliens. NightHawk, how much time?

Passing epicentre in two minutes, ma'am.

All ears open. Here we go.

It was a tense time, with everyone trying to look everywhere at once. Toni split her attention between the Otherwhere sensors and the barwolves, who were taking care of the alien-calming defence.

Epicentre coming up to starboard...5...3...2...1 We are now outbound.

Thank you, NightHawk. We'll have increased density and velocity in the alien ships, now, so off-duty watch will help out as needed. The rest of you on analysis. Debrief in the Auxiliary Bridge in one hour.

When Natalia entered the secondary bridge, they were still working, but the image moving across the big viewscreen spoke loud and clear. The captain regarded it. "Am I seeing what I think I'm seeing?"

Andrew chuckled. "If you think you're seeing feeding time at the zoo, you'd be close."

Alwyn held up a warning hand. "Let's not jump to conclusions. There are many objects floating in the vicinity, and the aliens are most certainly cleaning up those pieces. Whether they receive sustenance is conjecture."

Andrew lobbed a raspberry at the engineer. "Don't be pedantic, Alwyn. Whether they're cannibalistic or not remains to be seen. They are definitely ingesting the pieces of what is probably one of the predators."

Natalia opened her augment. "Nelson, any word on the size of that blast?"

Difficult to tell when we have no structural data on the object, but the shock wave would indicate ten to twenty kilotons.

"Enough to level a small city. And might I suspect a similar effect in Otherwhere?"

Image: mountain peak blowing off.

"Not quantifiable, but expressive."

Alwyn looked up from his work. "We don't know if it just blew up one predator, or whether the prey were immolated as well."

"Take readings on any piece of debris you see. If our little scavenger friends haven't cleaned them all up. Any chance of overtaking more as we fly?"

"A couple of bits are stuck to our forward plating. We can do an EVA and pick them up, if you like. Shock wave is long gone, and anything moving will keep going forever."

"Thank you for that lesson in Newtonian physics, Mr. Lundeen. We'll leave them there until things settle down a bit."

"*A sus ordines, Señora.*"

The captain dusted her hands. "Good enough. Let's keep our eyes peeled for any predators. We don't know if the explosion was the result of the formation's attack or the predator's store of energy exploding, but we do not want to run into one of those."

Toni had a sudden thought. "I'd better have a chat with *Jerusalem's Hope.* Most of this would be incomprehensible to them."

"Fair enough, Jacobs. You are officially detailed to calm ruffled feathers. Everyone else, back to business."

Emotion: agreement.

As they wove their way out of the thinning swarms, they noticed other changes. In the first place, the formation movements changed.

Alwyn was the first to note it.

"Toni, did you see that?"

She glanced at the viewscreen. "Obviously not. What's going on?"

"I'll do a replay. Watch that four-pack as we approach."

She watched. "Hey! They changed course."

"That's right. It wasn't much, but they just shifted enough to stay clear of us."

They start to see the more trios, and once a pair, which upped the frequency of their wingbeats and sheered away from the Space Arm fleet.

Toni brought it up the next time the Auxiliary Crew was together. "Does anybody have an explanation?"

Dr. Blaney nodded. "If we relate this to Earth animal behaviour, this is what happens at the edge of the herd. These are the outliers: the weak, the ill, the genetically inferior, who often become the sacrifices while the average beasts escape the predator."

Andrew took over the augmental matrix . "All right, how about this?"

Image: blank space, stars in the background, dimly seen flights of aliens in the foreground. Then, down in the corner of the screen, there came a bright flash. A pause, and then three dimmer ones, evenly spaced. Then nothing.

Toni regarded him. "That's all?"

"I wouldn't think so, but it's the third time we've seen that pattern."

She nodded. "Something to watch for. If we see one close enough to take a look without losing too much ground, I'll ask the captain for a course change."

* * *

They didn't have to wait long, because that pattern occurred with increasing regularity. Soon one happened close to their course, and they angled towards it.

Soon the source became apparent. "It's a predator." Andrew upped the magnification. "About average size. And an expanding debris field."

Toni regarded the screen as they flashed by. "*Diablo*, will you analyze the trajectories in that field. It didn't look like a normal explosion."

Aye, ma'am

Soon the ship came back on.

You were right, ma'am. It's debris from three separate explosions, a short distance apart, and timed similar to the three flashes observed earlier.

Toni nodded to Andrew. "Three is not enough."

"The first flash was their combined power, which didn't work, and then he picked them off, one by one.

"That's the best guess."

"Was the big one feeding?"

"Didn't look like it. Just flying. Slower than usual."

"Maybe recovering from his injuries."

Natalia's entered their bridge. When Toni had explained their findings, she sat sideways on an accel couch, musing. "We're seeing a whole lot of these interactions lately." She regarded them. "Ideas?"

Toni shrugged. "We've been going on the theory that this is the herd/predator interface. That's the natural assumption."

The captain nodded, then raised her eyebrows to Alwyn.

"I suppose there is one other possibility."

"Spit it out, no matter how strange."

He held up open palms. "The only anomaly in the natural progression of the aliens' lives."

"Us."

"Right. We don't know whether this is natural or not. It's possible that the predators are sensing a weakness in this area because of our activities in Otherwhere. Anything that upsets the prey makes an opportunity for the predator."

Andrew nodded. "Common research problem. The presence of the measurer skews the data."

"Let's put our two ships and Patches on a long-range scan." Toni was already setting up the parameters on her screen. "See if they can get a frequency pattern for the whole area."

The captain stood. "Let me know. And seeing us as an anomaly makes me think. There's a fifty-fifty chance that the predators will see us as a problem and run away."

"And an equal chance they'll see us as possibly weaker, and attack. I get the message, ma'am." Toni turned to her crew. "Let's decide where the new data fits in, and then get back to work on those defensive tactics."

The captain nodded and, without further comment, left the room.

* * *

Now that the swarms were so thin, the auxiliary crew was excused from defensive duties, so they spent more time honing their battle tactics. As they worked, another attack lit up the vicinity.

It was close to their course, and they slingshotted around the blast, observing a feeding swarm again. They were too late, and the blast had been too large, to get any data on the debris paths.

But in the third attack, they had a stroke of luck.

Flash at three o'clock, seven degrees low.

Toni clicked into the com. "Thank you, *NightHawk*. Any..."

Flash at three, seven again, ma'am. Similar intensity.

"Analysis?"

Both were three-ship volleys, ma'am

"Captain, requesting course change. Something interesting going on."

Natalia came on immediately. *Send NightHawk the coordinates. What do you have?*

"Two flashes at three-ship intensity. No response."

Let's go take a look.

They focused on the area as they approached, but received little data.

Predator. Moving away to galactic north. Normal tempo.

As they got closer, more details were available.

Andrew jabbed a finger at the screen. "There's a group of three."

Toni did the same a moment later. "And there's another one."

The Auxiliary crew regarded one another. Andrew shrugged. "Not to belabour the obvious, but it seems that a three-pack got attacked by a predator, and another three pitched in and helped drive it away."

Alwyn nodded. "Our first real indication that the formations help each other."

Andrew returned to his screen. "Let's add those factors into our battle plans. They might affect us."

They went back to their gestalt, but soon Andrew threw up his hands. "I think we're wasting our time."

Toni pulled back into re-ti and regarded him. "Why would you say that?"

He sighed. "Because the captain has her own way of doing things. It's rooted in traditional Space Arm tactics, which is what she studied, so you can't blame her. But Space Arm's basic premise is that we will be fighting against an enemy that is equally determined to destroy us."

Alwyn nodded. "And any aggressive approach puts us exactly in that situation, so her tactics seem correct."

Toni frowned. "When actually we are perpetrating the attack. That's what happened with the formations we tried to study. The big question: dealing with a predator, what else can we do?"

Andrew shrugged. "Use the only defensive tactic proven over millenia to work."

"A formation of at least four vessels."

"Exactly. We have enough data to infer that formation of four in a flat diamond pattern doesn't get attacked."

"We think." She pulled up an image on the viewscreen. "We have no idea what perpetrates the mutual destruction attacks."

Alwyn grinned. "And being the engineer, I get to do the math. We have exactly eight vessels in this flight. We need to change our formations."

The two men looked at each other. "Who's going to tell her?"

Andrew shook his head. "Not me. She has made that abundantly clear. A mere ensign has no right to question the captain's tactics. Over to you, Doctor Scientific Expert."

"And her partner. If you don't mind, I'd rather not."

Toni glowered at them. "And baby makes three."

"What?"

Alwyn grinned. "An old expression. It means the two of us have ganged up on poor little Toni."

Andrew reached over and put an arm around her. "And you are the senior officer on this assignment."

"Actually, Alison has five months seniority..."

"But she is very diplomatic about it..."

Andrew shook his head. "Sorry, love. It's got to be you. Mum trusts your judgement over anyone's."

Toni sighed. "All right. But we've got to have a solid plan to present. I can't go in there with just some philosophical argument."

"I caught that dig." Blainey grinned. "Boots on the ground it is...that's the military expression, right?"

"Sort of. Let's get planning."

* * *

Picking what she thought would be an appropriate moment, she tapped on the chartroom door.

Natalia looked up. "Why so polite, Toni? Bad news?"

"Not really. Just some new tactics the auxiliary team has come up with."

The captain put her enterpad down. "Good. Let's see them."

Toni called up an augmental VR image above the desk. "We're still working on the assumption that sooner or later one of these big predators is going to attack us."

191

"I've been working in the same direction."

"So, here's our analysis. The standard Space Arm approaches are too aggressive. We observe what's been working for the aliens. It hasn't escaped our bright scientific minds that their typical defence is a formation of four, and usually they don't get attacked. We have exactly eight ships. Our primary setup in case of an attack should be two four-packs, close enough together to lend a hand in case of need."

"I see." The captain's face registered nothing, so Natalia ploughed on.

"So, when we're developing our approaches, we should start with that basic formation, hoping the predator will sheer off. If it doesn't, then we make plans for what we would do next."

"It's quite a departure from the usual tactics."

"We're in quite a different situation."

"Granted." The O'Rourke tipped her head to the side and regarded her officer. "And they sent you to argue with me because the others are afraid to."

"I came to present the Auxiliary Team's scientifically-derived position on the subject. I am the senior Commando officer. It's my duty."

"Fair enough." Natalia sat back and lifted the enterpad she had been looking at. "But as it happens, you're wasting your time."

Toni's heart dropped. "I am?"

"Yes." The captain twisted the pad in her capable hands. "As I said, I've been making some plans for a possible attack. Rather creative ones as well, I think. You'll be interested to hear them."

There seemed to be nothing to say, so Toni said nothing.

"As you so rightfully put it, we are in a very different situation here, and the old style of operation won't cut it. We need a new approach. Patches put me through to Admiral Mira for a chat," Natalia waved the pad, "and this is his response."

Noting a twitch to the captain's lip, Toni again said nothing. *She's having fun with this.*

After a moment's silence, Natalia dropped the pad on her desk. "You are just impossible to tease, so I'll tell you straight out. It's a battlefield promotion. You're temporarily assigned to Commander's rank. If we survive to get back to base, it will become permanent."

"What?"

Now the captain did smile. "Finally, a reaction. What do you think of that?"

"I don't understand."

"Simple. In case you didn't notice, I have been superseded. In all the recent encounters with the aliens, you have been in charge. I simply command my ship as a member of the flight. Standard Outback rules, actually. This is not the place for Space Arm tactics and training. We need direct input from those of you who know the situation best. If you want to look at it another way, the Auxiliary Bridge has been the Command Bridge for the last few weeks. Admiral Mira agrees with me, but he doesn't think a major should oversee such an important operation." She spun the pad across the desk so it ended up facing Toni. "So, you can do anything you damned well please, because from now on the wing's tactics are all on you. Says so right there." The captain grinned. "And how does that feel?"

"A little scary." Toni picked up the pad. "Can I borrow this? They're not going to believe it, otherwise. Especially when I put them to work picking holes in their own ideas."

"That's the attitude, Commander. Get on it."

* * *

"Will you look at this?" Andrew flipped a forward view onto the screen

"Oh, dingo dung. Is that ever a big one. Course?"

"Headed across our bow ten degrees and a bit...wait a minute. Course change. *Diablo?*"

New course intersects ours in twenty-three minutes, sir.

Toni grabbed full com. "Red alert. Red alert. Predator attack in twenty-three minutes." As Natalia's image came up in the gestalt, she fed the captain all the data.

Any chance a course change will work?

"Please try, Captain."

After a short pause, the ship came on again.

Enemy course change, ma'am. New contact time, twenty-one minutes.
The wing is yours, Commander.

"Aye, ma'am. Major Rowell, get *Diablo* in the air. Take Joe as copilot." *Barwolf One, prepare to split.*

193

Eager desire to please.

"All right, everyone, we will execute Camo One. That's operation Camo One."

Image: Red 1, 3, and 5 in formation with Diablo, Blue 2, 4, and 6 with NightHawk. Chip in lead, slivers on wings, larger ship at rear.

Diablo here. We are launched. Starting Camo One.

"All right. Synch with Battle Control Augment. Operation starting...Now."

The ships assumed formation and sailed on. Soon the huge, dark shape looming off the starboard side was easily visible on the screens.

Contact in fifteen minutes.

"Commander Jones, ready the FOF transmission."

FOF ready, Commander.

"Dr. Blainey, do we have any formations in the vicinity?"

"Five within easy range, all crossing left to right, three degrees down."

Commander Jones and Patches, start the FOF, please."

"FOF on line."

Image: communication spreading from Black Bird in all directions.

Jones clicked in. *Increase in Otherwhere transmissions, Commander.*

"From where?"

Various. Too many to tell.

Contact in twelve minutes.

"Captain O'Rourke, prepare *NightHawk* to fire."

Torpedos clear to launch, slug-throwers loaded, plasma cannons online.

"Captain, do you see any indication the enemy is going to break off?"

I do not.

"Thank you. *Image: charge building in enemy ship. Emotion: question?*

Emotion: negative. Image: black barwolf watching enemy carefully.

"Listen up, now. Continue Camo One. *BlackHawk* and *Diablo*, please prepare to fire two torpedos each to intercept the enemy 200 kilometres from contact point. The moment the torpedos explode, every weapon fire at will."

Emotion: eager desire to please.

Torpedos in the tubes.

Torpedos ready to fire, ma'am. Contact in eight minutes.

Enemy changing course, ma'am.

"Good eye, Fraser. New course, *NightHawk?*"

The new course will put the enemy one kilometer off our starboard beam when we close vectors in six minutes.

"Thank you, *NightHawk.* Please aim torpedos to new course and fire as ordered."

"Swarm changing, Toni."

"Thanks, Alwyn. *Diablo, analysis?*"

Five formations changing course. Their new target one kilometer off our starboard beam one minute after we close with the enemy

"Analyze their course as they approach contact."

At one minute before contact, they will be within their attack range of the enemy.

"Listen up, now. Our allies have set the attack time, and they know the enemy. Fire the torpedos to strike one minute before contact."

Contact in three minutes.

NightHawk's torpedoes away... ArIns have acquired target.

Diablo's torpedos away... ArIns have acquired target.

"Fraser, keep your gunsight on that ship. You always catch the first move."

Aye, ma'am.

Contact in two minutes.

Enemy course change, ma'am.

"Well done, Fraser. *Diablo,* analysis?"

Sheering off, ma'am. Wing strokes increased by 50%

"What are the other formations doing, *Diablo?*"

Changing course to follow, ma'am.

"Continue the attack, Captain?"

"I see no other option, Commander. Our allies have committed."

"Listen up, now. We continue the attack. Fire as ordered."

Allies changing to attack formation.

"Any in our line of fire?"

All clear, ma'am. Enemy changing orientation.

Jones came on the com. *He's switching to attack position.*

Image: charge building in enemy ship.

"Too late, I hope. In ten seconds..." A sudden thought brought a chill to Toni's spine. "Now listen up. Change of orders. Keep firing for only five seconds. Got that? Five seconds. Then initiate Maneuver 17. Do you read? Maneuver 17 after five seconds."

It was too late for a response.

Torpedos will strike in 5 seconds...3...2...1...Contact.

The dark hide of the enemy blossomed with a bright line of explosions around the head area, but the great creature continued its movements, trying to orient its arms to fire at *NightHawk*. Then the view of space was extinguished by a torrent of energy from many sources and the visual overrides cut in.

"Now, Maneuver 17. Everybody get out of here! Run, run, run! Maneuver 17, Now!"

The gravity on *NightHawk* swooped as the ship put her stern to the enemy and hit a quick blast at full military override. Behind them an electronic maelstrom poured into the flailing predator from the other aliens.

And then it was all eradicated by a blast that threw the scout ship away like a leaf on a storm. End over end she flew, thrusters groaning in a futile effort to hold her even, main engines straining to provide stability, and gravity fluctuating in gut-churning swoops.

Toni clung to her grav couch, striving desperately to keep her eyes on the viewscreens.

Finally the spinning slowed, then stopped, but the odd heave of her stomach told her that gravity waves were still battering the ship.

But at least she could function. "Report in. *NightHawk, what is our condition? Diablo, sit rep, please. Barwolf 1 report. Emotion: question, question, question?*"

The captain's calm presence came on the augment. "*NightHawk is intact. Concentrate on your wing.*"

"Thank you, Captain. *Diablo*, do you read?"

A rather shaky aura came from Alison. *Diablo is a little light for that sort of fun and games. I have a lot of minor elements in the red, but the main board is orange and green. Propulsion A-OK, life support likewise. Nav has us...700 kilometres farther outswarm than you are. Do you want me to wait?*

"Stand by for now, Major. Analysis and prognosis."

"Aye, Commander. That was some kind of fireworks."

"Agreed."

She glanced over at Patches, bright-eyed and alert in her quad accel couch. *Image: Barwolf 1. Emotion: question?*

Image: Six ships spread across the path out-swarm of NightHawk. Five ships under low acceleration. Red 3 attempting restart.

Image: six barwolves. Emotion:question?

Image: barwolves drinking large amounts of wofnip, staggering around in circles bumping into each other.

Emotion: agreement. Image: humans staggering likewise. Image barwolf with broken leg. Emotion: question?

Emotion: negative. Image: barwolf bounding through forest cheerfully. Image: barwolf bounding through forest in circles, crashing through bushes and bouncing off trees. New image: Red 3 under power.

Emotion: relief. Image: Sliverships joining into one.

Emotion: agreement.

She broke off the communication and looked around the Auxiliary Bridge. "Alwyn, have you managed to track our recent allies?"

"*Diablo* and I are working on it. There were twenty-three aliens in the attack. We can account for nineteen of them."

"So, one of the four-packs got too close to the blast."

He nodded sadly. "When we have time, we'll analyze the video super-slo-mo and figure it all out."

Toni sent a private com message to Natalia. "I guess the battle's over, ma'am. Turning command, what's left of it, over to you."

"Thanks a ton. Considering the size of that blast, I'm happy we still have eight ships with atmo in them. I'd say your Maneuver 17 was the best call of the game."

"I just wish we'd thought of it ahead of time."

"Well, no one considered that our allies would take charge of the operation. Once you lost control, your only choice was to pull out or go with them. We'll talk about it in the debrief, but I'm not going to argue with success. That was the biggest predator we've recorded, by at least fifty metres wingspan and about thirty tonnes in weight. Who knows how many aliens it would have taken to destroy it?"

"Thanks, ma'am. I guess we start the cleanup now."

The captain's response was to take over the com. "Listen up now. Damage reports ASAP. We have another swarm coming through in seven hours, and a few lone four-packs to deal with in between. We need to get our ships back together to ease avoidance maneuvers. We're all going to be too busy doing repairs to placate our alien friends that don't understand us."

"And incidentally, when you're cleaning up, if you come across any tissue samples, bag them but leave them in the outside lockers."

Lundeen came on com. *That's a bit of a problem, ma'am.*

"Why? Aren't there any?"

No, ma'am. There's too many. The slivers have so much gunk on them we're having trouble fitting them back together.

"What do you suggest?"

Short of going EV with a brush, nothing. They do have an electronic sloughing system. That will probably work, but it will fry the samples.

"We're not out of the woods, yet. We need Barwolf 1 back into a single unit. Let's assume there's enough organic matter attached to our ships. We can time our EVAs to go out and collect samples, depending on our situation relative to the approaching swarms."

Wilco, ma'am. Commander Jacobs, do you want to call this?

"Thanks, Chief." *Image: slivers covered with organic material. Image: fire burning it all clean.*

Image: fire burning slivers clean.

An image appeared on the viewscreens. The slivers were grouped in a loose cluster. Slowly they began to glow red, until bright specks flared up, gassing off and then disappearing. In a short time, the slivers turned their usual metallic grey and began to move together.

Health and safety alert, Captain.

Natalia came on the com. *"What is it, Jaunita?"*

The ET organic matter. When Diablo docks and we open the airlocks, whichever one opens first will be exposed to the outside surface of the other ship's door. The usual cleansing spray might not be enough.

"Thanks, Jonny. B'kosa, I guess you heard that. Take some muscle with you and go out and scrub the two airlock outer doors before we attempt to lock together."

Aye, ma'am. Let's reward Fraser for his good eye on the gunsight during the battle by having him swab decks.

You catch that, Specialist Fraser? We need your talents again.

Aye, ma'am. Nice to be appreciated.

The crew swung into action, and soon the wing was back together again and accelerating up to the maximum velocity allowed by the thinning swarms they passed through.

At dinner that night, Natalia pushed her chair back and raised her glass. "I'd like to propose a toast."

They all took glasses in hand, warily observing her grin.

"I'd like to propose a toast to me, for success in an unprecedented action through application of sound leadership principles."

Glasses eased back to the table.

After a moment's silence, Andrew sighed loudly. "We're waiting for the punch line, Mum."

The captain smiled. "Oh, that. In case it skipped your notice, it was my idea to put Toni in command. She was the only person in the whole wing who could have called that action the way she did. So. I'm in charge, I get all the credit. It's all in the official dispatch I just sent to Admiral Mira."

The Chief Engineer raised his glass. "I seem to have a temporary bout of amnesia. I think we were having a toast, but I forgot the recipient. May we raise our glasses to Commander Jacobs, who saved our bacon from becoming crispy this afternoon?"

After the drinks and the cheers, Alison regarded the captain. "A dispatch? Is that what I think it means?"

Natalia slapped a hand on the table. "Damn right it does. Toni just made the most important decision in her career so far, and probably saved half our ships and the lives of half our crew as well. An official mention in dispatches is only the start. They'll be studying our little battle for years, and she'll be the hero." She shrugged. "Whoever happened to be in charge of the mission will barely be noticed. I had to try for my small moment of glory."

"But you did make the original decision to promote her."

The captain snorted. "Sure, I did. Mira said, 'You can't have a major running an operation that important,' and I said, 'So, promote her.' Yep, I take a lot of credit for that, all right."

Alwyn cleared his throat, attracting their attention. "Umm...I don't know if this is a military thing or not, but this discussion of credit is far from the point."

Natalia wrinkled her brow. "By which you mean...?"

"I have never seen a tighter or more cohesive group. If you want an outside opinion, no single person can take credit for anything that happens around here. Hell, most of the time it happens so fast you'd have to do a slo-mo analysis of the whole operation to figure who did what, and you'd still miss half of it."

He raised his glass. "I'd like to raise my glass to the whole damn bunch of us, barwolves, auguars and all. This has been a historic mission, and I'm proud to have been part of it."

"Hear, hear!" Lundeen raised his drink as well. "Here's to all of us. We're heroes, and we'll go down in history as such."

There was a general cheer and an emptying of glasses that continued far past the usual dinner hour. Only the need for a sober operating crew kept the tone subdued.

Toni and Andrew, off-duty for the next twelve hours, retired to their cabin on *Diablo* and closed the privacy screens on their augments, so what occurred there is recorded only in their memories.

37. REAL SANCTUARY

BARNARD EMBASSY

Two weeks later, *Jerusalem's Hope* slid into syched orbit with the Sol Embassy to Barnard. Roselyn and Miriam gazed out the big PermaGlass window from their seats of honour in an out-of-the way corner of the bridge. Right beside them, almost close enough to touch, the former fighter carrier spread out her array of aerials, catwalks, gantries and solar panels. Two huge Space Arm destroyers rode in attendance, smaller ships kept station farther ou, and shuttles and unmanned vehicles of various sizes buzzed back and forth between them all. In the background, the huge, mottled orb of Zeta blanked out the profusion of stars.

Captain Nowak shut down his control panel with a ceremonial gesture and turned to his guests. "Well, we made it. And mostly in one piece."

Emotion: admiration and love

His face reddened. "Why, thank you, Miriam. You did your part as well."

Roselyn glanced around the bridge. "I think you have your own celebration with your crew, Captain. Miriam and I will go and join our friends and relatives in our own rites."

He laid a hand on the shoulder of each as they walked to the door. "Actually, I do have some minor details to attend to." He grinned. "I have to close my flight plan."

They walked down the corridor hand in hand, Miriam swinging their arms in exaggerated arcs as usual and laughing up at her teacher, her augment overflowing with joy.

It was a great relief for Roselyn to stand back and allow others to resume their leadership. Now that the voyage was over, she felt as if a great weight had been lifted from her. She grinned to herself. *As if anybody here needs me anymore. Except my students, of course. But that's not a burden. It's my life work.*

While everyone on the ship was concerned about what the quarantine process would entail, in the end it was nothing serious. It was disconcerting for the younger children when the first off-ship humans they met were wearing hazmat suits, but this team efficiently took their air, water, and medical samples and disappeared.

Quarantined for seven days, the Followers of the Voice entered a strange period of ennui, where everything had changed but nothing was happening. They tended to wander around the ship, going from task to task without finishing anything, staring at familiar scenes, happy that the voyage was over but sad that they would soon be leaving their home.

Roselyn coped by doing her final testing of the children, which focused their minds and hers, at least. Augment contact with the teachers on the embassy helped no end, and they reassured her that her students were doing fine for their ages in most areas and were considerably advanced in others.

She was vaguely aware that the usual paperwork process was taking longer than usual, and the captain seemed preoccupied on the rare moments she saw him, as was Head Councillor Isaac. She put that down to the usual bureaucratic hassles and did not intrude.

As their incarceration came to a close, she was sitting in her office trying to figure out what to teach the next day when she received an augment call from *Jerusalem.*

Miss Jakobsdotter, the advance diplomatic team is now assembling for the initial meetings.

"And you are telling me this because...?

Ambassador Pretoro has specifically asked me to invite you.

"I see. Where do I go, and how do I dress?"

The main shuttle bay. The other members of the team are clad in their finest. By most human standards, your mother is quite striking.

"I'm sure she is."

It didn't take much thought. Roselyn put on her newest teaching dress, brushed her hair back and held it with a simple barrette.

When she reached the main bay, everyone else was assembled. It would be difficult to slide in unnoticed, so she didn't bother. Registering her mother's surprise and displeasure, she chose to stand beside Captain Nowak, who was resplendent in his dress whites.

He glanced down and spoke quietly "I haven't seen you much lately."

She shrugged. "I assumed you would be busy. Everything go as planned?"

"Mostly. I had to be very careful with my legal position."

"The reassignment of ownership?"

"That's right. There was some question as to when the voyage was officially over. When we set out thirty years ago, we didn't have much of an idea what would happen once we got here. It's all done and dusted now, though. Matteo Regio, that young friend of Captain O'Rourke's is a good lawyer."

"And this is now a family business?"

He nodded and gazed around with an air of satisfaction. Then he returned his attention to her. "Rather dressed down for the occasion, aren't you?"

She grinned. "For once, I wanted to be noticed." She tossed her head towards the others. "They're all adorned for their positions. So are you, and you fill the bill admirably, sir."

"Thank you, I'm sure, Miss. But your point is?"

"Who am I?"

"You are the schoolteacher."

"Precisely." She sketched a quick curtsey, flicking the hem of her regulation-length dress with one hand. Then she checked the crowd. Pastor Josiah seemed to be missing.

At that moment, somebody gave a signal, and the delegation stepped forward. Roselyn took her cue from the captain and held back at his side while the important people strode forward. Then the two followed at a more relaxed pace as they filed into the large, official Sol Embassy shuttle.

Soon they were docked in the embassy and moving at a formal pace down a corridor to a reception room, where a small but resplendent group, mostly in uniform, awaited them.

Because of her position in the rear and her lack of height, Roselyn missed most of the preliminary exchange, only aware of a calm, reasonable voice that somehow floated over everyone else's. She glanced up at Nowak with a questioning brow.

Ambassador Pretoro has technology we are unaware of.

She nodded and thought to open her augment further.

Emotion: welcome.

She looked around. *Emotion: thanks...*

Image: brown-and-grey mottled barwolf, female in gender, standing at Human Leader's side, speaking as he speaks.

Emotion: comprehension.

Emotion: plea for patience.

Emotion: agreement.

The barwolf faded out, and Roselyn contacted the Captain Nowak again.

Image: brown-and-grey mottled barwolf standing by ambassador, speaking as he speaks. New technology for sure. She's boosting his message through the Aether.

I see.

Then it seemed the ceremonies were over, because the *Jerusalem* group separated, some going one way, some another. Captain Nowak was courteously invited to follow a Space Arm officer, leaving her standing by herself.

Then Ambassador Pretoro and his barwolf companion started towards her, his aide and Marine guard following two paces behind.

The *Jerusalem* leaders all stopped. *Emotion: careful awareness.*

Pretoro, too, halted.

As Roselyn fully expected, her mother beat Councillor Isaac to the punch.

"What business do you have with my daughter, sir?"

The tension disappeared in a wave of diplomatic charm. "Oh!" He turned toward her. "You must be Tirza Bensoussan. I am so pleased to meet you. But right now, my business is with your daughter. Did she not tell you?"

Tirza tossed her head, and her dark mane of hair quivered. "When your daughter tells you that the moment she sets foot on the embassy deck the ambassador will sweep her away, you don't tend to take her literally."

Pretoro raised his eyebrows at Roselyn, who wondered if there was a small locker nearby that she could crawl into.

Then he smiled. "Am I perhaps listening second-hand to a conversation with a certain Toni Jacobs? Or was it Alison Rowell?"

She gulped. "Maj... um, Commander Toni, sir. And I didn't take her literally, either."

He nodded and again his voice took on a timbre that included the whole room. "Now that your group has reached Barnard, you will find many people here with augments, both electronic and organic. Miss Jacobsdotter is the most gifted human practitioner of augmental gestalts that we have found in the system. We have all sorts of people lining up to speak to her. Only the delicate nature of that communication and the political implications of the interspecies relationship prevented every scientist on the whole station from being here, shouting for a chance at an interview."

He turned to survey the *Jerusalem* group. "You have come at a time of great change, and there are opportunities for you to be part of the change. I see that some of you have mixed feelings about that. It does you credit to be careful, but you are under the law and guidance of the Planetary Community, here. You may run your society in any way that you choose, as long as you do not break any Community laws."

He turned to Councillor Isaac. "I'm sure life in the Sol system was like that thirty years ago, and nothing has changed. In this case, every Planetary citizen must be allowed ones own choice in the pursuit of ones future."

Her mother sniffed. "And I choose to have my daughter accompany me."

Pretoro's smile lost its warmth. "I think you misunderstand, Madam. I am giving Miss Jakobsdotter a choice. Not you."

"But Roselyn is only twenty: a child by our standards. She is still under my guardianship."

The ambassador nodded slowly. "Obviously, this matter needs to be dealt with. We have a change of plans." He paused to use his augment. "...fine. Everyone please follow my aide to our primary meeting room." He indicated the tall, handsome man in uniform, and they began to file out.

"Please, Madam, join us." He placed himself between Roselyn and her mother and followed the rest.

The two women exchanged a glance and paced with him.

They maintained this formation as they entered a large conference room and approached a circular table, ending up with the ambassador seated between them. The barwolf stood on a raised platform with her head between Roselyn and the ambassador's elbow. The aide deftly organized the Head Councillor to sit opposite him, with his supporters lined out in order of precedence on either side. Then he went to stand behind his superior.

The ambassador waited until everyone was settled. Then he glanced down at Roselyn, smiled and regarded Head Councillor Isaac.

"This may be the first time you run into this problem, sir, but I'm sure it will not be the last. Here in the Outback, people have a lot of freedom to set up the rules by which they live. However, Planetary Community laws may not be broken, and human rights are paramount. The rights of children are protected most seriously. Under those laws, the age of full adulthood is eighteen. You no longer hold jurisdiction over Miss Jacobsdotter."

"Are you saying that if one of our children wishes to leave us, there is nothing we can do about it?"

"We would not aid such an action without serious consideration. For example, what if little Miriam decides that she wants Miss Jacobsdotter as her guardian?"

"You know who Miriam is?"

The ambassador raised his eyebrows. "You folks live in gestalt with each other. Surely you realize how difficult it is to keep a secret. Miss Jacobsdotter is only the second most important person on your ship. Now, in the situation I mentioned, the Planetary Community court would have to decide that Miriam understood fully what she was asking for. If the choice was deemed to the child's benefit, then that is where she would go. In the case of such a young child, her progress would be closely supervised, of course."

Then his eyes hardened. "And if the court had the slightest idea that anyone was trying to keep her under their control for political reasons, those people would lose the right to contact her at all."

Isaac swallowed. "But what if all our youth decide to leave us? We are a religious order, and we do not have a large congregation."

The ambassador shook his head. "Cohesive groups who reach Barnard have a history of sticking together. If they don't, then whatever basic premise they were originally formed on was faulty."

He regarded the councillors. "Space Arm and the Planetary Community are in your debt because of the aid you gave *NightHawk* recently. We will go out of our way to see you happily settled. I don't know what you expected when you arrived here, but this is your situation." He indicated a VR image over the centre of the table, which outlined their documentation.

"From our dealings with *Ark of the Covenant*, we know that you have a highly cohesive group with strong beliefs and only moderate technical skills. Thus, your opportunities are limited. There is only one oxy-carb planet in this system, and the *Ark* is already in orbit there, dithering about where and when to land. Many of them are simply afraid to live under the open sky. The course of forced evolution they have practiced over their voyage has not been so successful as yours, but they do have a lot of people able to communicate with the barwolves, and we have been introducing them to that situation in as gentle a manner as we can. They will have similar advantage to yours when they decide to try their chances downplanet. The alternative is to live permanently in your ships and make whatever commerce you could by mining, trading, or haulage."

The Head Councillor glanced around his people. "That does not sound like a match for our desires or our talents, and *Jerusalem's Hope* is now owned by its crew."

"Exactly. So, it is fortunate that your only real choice is to take up residence on Arborea."

Isaac looked puzzled. "Why fortunate?"

Pretoro smiled and indicated Roselyn. "Because of Miss Jacobsdotter and her talented cadre. You spend your lives communing with the Cosmos. Most humans cannot do this, but all barwolves can. Your people will be invaluable for many years to come because of your ability to communicate with our new partners. Your recent gestalt exercise with the *NightHawk* shows how effective you can be. Ladies and gentlemen, you have already begun your new life here."

"I see..."

"So, this is what I suggest. Put your ship in orbit around Arborea. The barwolves are anxious to have you join them, but our Scientific Coordinator downplanet, Dr. Morissa Goodall, suggests that at first, we limit your gestalt's contact to a small group of barwolves. Your Sensitives who have become lost in OtherWhere are a sober lesson to us. An island has been made available near our Barwolf Research Base. We will bring your group downplanet and help you set up your housing there. It will be a laborious process. Most of your people have never lived in the open air, and some will have a great deal of trouble with it."

"Excuse me, sir?"

The ambassador turned to her. "Yes, Roselyn?"

"It won't be that hard at all for those of us with the ability to Listen. I have already spent several hours in the downplanet experience. I was afraid at first, but now I love it."

Ambassador Pretoro had a nice smile. "Let me guess. You've been mind-riding with a barwolf."

"Yes. One's name is Brindle, and one is a great friend of Coordinator Goodall, who has already offered me a position on her research team, creating the educational modules for human/barwolf interaction. And about Miriam, sir?"

"Yes?"

"I was listening to what you said about her making choices. I'm afraid hers are rather unrealistic."

"What are they?"

"She has developed a great kinship with the three kidnap victims. In her opinion, they have suffered considerable trauma through this experience, and she has been working with them daily to comfort and teach them. By the time their vessel reaches here, she will have recovered from her operations, and...well, she thinks she should go and live with them and their families to help them readjust."

"And what do the families, the scientists, and her father think of this plan?"

"Dealing with Miriam, nobody has any idea what to think, sir. They all just want the best for their children."

Pretoro turned his regard to Isaac. "Well, we have the resources of a whole system at our disposal. If we can't make a success of keeping four of our young ones safe and happy, then someone else needs to take over."

The Head Councillor smiled reluctantly. "We have another precept that we don't use much for obvious reasons. *The children are paramount.*"

Pretoro slapped his hands on the table. "Well, there we have it. We'll move you over to Arborea whenever you're ready and start loading you downplanet. That will take a few days to organize, so make yourselves free of our facilities here at the embassy. A shuttle will be scheduled every hour for transport back and forth. Your quarantine is hereby lifted. Welcome to Barnard System."

As everyone filed out, the Ambassador laid a restraining hand on Tirza's arm. "We have some other good news for you. It involves your husband and his fellow-sufferers."

"How do you...? Of course. Rosy told you."

"Yes, we were sorry, of course, to hear about the problem, but it threw some light on similar symptoms we've been having lately in our advanced organic augment recipients. We had already recruited a couple of barwolves. As the *NightHawk* crew discovered, they are subject to the same condition."

"And what progress have you made?"

"Our blended medical team has had great success in dealing with milder cases, using a combination of barwolf rituals and human medication. With your permission, one of the team members will accompany you to Arborea. I'm sure Roselyn and Miriam can help with the interface."

"One of the team...?"

"Yes, a barwolf who has decided on the name of "Doc." Very unoriginal, I know, but she likes the implications. Having added the data from the *NightHawk* experience, our team is confident they can achieve results with your people."

Tirza's face worked, and Roselyn felt a lump burning in her throat. "Thank you, sir. You don't know what it would mean..."

"No, I don't, but I can guess. Now, I have some people you might like to meet." He turned. "Enderby, where's that list?"

Roselyn's mother winked at her. "I doubt if I need a list, sir. I'm sure Admiral Mira is near nearby. Is Councillor Kriver on station? Our family has a connection to Australia, and I've been looking forward to meeting him."

The ambassador nodded. "I see you have done your homework. Do come along."

Roselyn touched Pretoro's sleeve. "If you don't mind, sir?"

"I suppose you want to meet with Doc."

"Yes. How did you know?"

The ambassador lowered his voice and stretched his words meaningfully. "I have seen your file."

"You have a file on me?"

Then he laughed. "No, but Toni and Alison have put me in the picture. They said you were rather...focused."

Her mother smothered a snort.

Roselyn smiled sweetly. "So, you know what will happen next."

"I do. Enderby, you must have a handsome young aide hanging around somewhere."

"Aye, sir." The man waved two fingers and a young, blond officer hurried over.

"Medical Assistant Nilssen, take Miss Jacobsdotter down to the Combined Services labs and introduce her to Doc and Dr. Boening. Afford her all courtesies."

"Aye, sir." He turned and smiled down on her. "Right this way, Miss."

As they started down the hall, she glanced up at him. "You seem cheerful."

"I certainly am." His smile reinforced the feeling, although his augment was not powerful. "I thought I was stuck with some very boring ceremonial duties, and instead here I am, heading off with a pretty girl to meet the famous Doc."

She regarded him askance, wary of this new, handsome man and his forward attitude. "Well, do your duty then. Brief me on why Doc is so famous."

He glanced down to assess her mood. "Oh. Right you are, ma'am. Well, we don't really know that much about her — turn left, here, please — except that she's very good with the poor souls who get lost down rabbit holes. Apparently, it can happen to barwolves as well, and has something to do with their overpopulation frenzy. But I don't know much about that. I'm in battlefield trauma, which is a rather different field."

"I understand. Commander Jacobs told me what happened to the *NightHawk* barwolves when they entered OtherWhere the first time."

He stopped dead and turned to her. "What did happen? We heard rumours, but..."

She gestured down the hallway. "If we could keep moving...?"

"Oh, yes. Yes, yes. This way, please. Just down the slideway." He glanced at her anxiously.

She relented. *He really is a personable young man.* "Well, this is how it happened..." She described what she could remember.

"...and they have rituals to ground them?"

"Yes, Nzinga gave me the impression that they look on it like exercising to build muscles."

"And Nzinga is..."

"...outside the security clearance of a medical assistant, I'm pretty certain. Sorry I mentioned her. Now, we seem to be standing outside a door. Shall we go through?"

He stumbled to open the door, but once inside he regained his aplomb and strode to the reception desk. "A representative of the new arrivals to see Doc, please, Miss."

The nurse looked up at him. "I'm not sure if she's available."

"Ambassador Pretoro's...personal request, Miss."

The girl dimpled. "Oh. Well, if the ambassador said...one moment please." She rose and hurried away."

He looked glum. "They're all like that. They think he's handsome."

She gave him a surprised frown. "Well, he is, don't you think?"

"Not for me to say, Miss."

"And quite rightly so."

And then her attention was taken up with the beast that approached her. She was of stocky build, even for a barwolf, and pale tan in colour, fading to white near her extremities. But it was her mind that took precedence

Emotion: great pleasure. She touched Roselyn's shin with her paw.

Emotion: pleasure and reverence. The girl responded with a plate scratch.

Image: two minds, barwolf and human, equal in size and power.

Emotion: Negative. Image: small girl with large mind.

In an instant, it felt as if Miriam was in the room with them.

Oh, there you are, Teacher. What's happening? This is a very nice barwolf. She's ever so kind.

Yes, she's a sort of medical expert. She's going to help us reach my father.

Emotion: great enthusiasm! Can I help?

Image: young man lying on hospital bed. Emotion: question?

Of course, I will help. Roselyn would never let me try. Your name is Doc, I think?

An older man in a lab coat hurried up. "What is it? Doc just walked out on me." He looked down at Roselyn. "Are you the cause of all this furor?"

She smiled. "I'm afraid not, sir. Your barwolf friend has just discovered Miriam."

"Ah. The little girl on the immigrant ship. What about her?"

Emotion: insistence. Image: tall, lanky Spacer lying still on bed, sinking in deeper and deeper.

211

The doctor spoke out loud and in the augments. *"Yes, I know he's getting worse. We've tried everything."*

Image: Small girl with no mouth speaking to Spacer.

"Well, of course. I'll try anything. But she's so young! Will she be allowed to help? What if she gets caught?"

Roselyn touched his sleeve. "What is the emergency?"

"We have a patient who was testing our most powerful augment, and he went under a month ago. It wasn't that serious; we've had it happen before. We are developing therapies, and they always come out of it eventually. But he suddenly started getting worse about a week ago, and we just…lost him."

"Yes, that happened to my father. He's been like that for three years."

"Oh. You must be off the immigrant ship, too. The question is, if this little girl can really help Spacer Anderson, we should try, and the sooner the better. Who can give us permission?"

Roselyn thought hard. She couldn't approach the council. It would just start another battle, which could take days. *Maybe there is a way. Image: Doc and Roselyn contacting the Jerusalem ArIn. Emotion: question?*

The result was instantaneous.

Hello, Roselyn. Who is your new friend?

"Hi, Jerusalem. This barwolf is Doc. Look, we have an emergency, here. One of their patients has gone down a rabbit hole like Dad did, and they want Miriam to help with him. He's going deeper and deeper every hour. Can you get Miriam's father to authorize her to help?"

Her father? I thought he would have nothing to do with her.

He's still her guardian. Get Captain Nowak to ask him. He's a very persuasive man.

I will do my best. Please stand by, Roselyn.

She looked at the small crowd of people now surrounding her. "I hope this won't take long. It wouldn't hurt to meet the patient. Can you bring us to him?"

"Oh, certainly, certainly. This way please."

The doctor and the barwolf led out, and Roselyn followed. The doctor glanced back. "By the way, I'm Head Surgeon Beoning. Doc has filled me in about you. Welcome to our little hospital."

"Thank you, Head Surgeon. I hope we can be of some use."

"I gather your father's been away for a long time. Our experience is that, as long as the body still functions, there is no physical damage. Theoretically, if we can find them, we can bring them back."

"I would like to believe that...Oh, just a moment."

Hello, again. Captain Nowak will be on in a moment.

Thanks, Jerusalem. Is it good news?

I...think so. Roselyn, the captain took that man by the throat and banged him up against the bulkhead!

He did what?

He said he would throw him out the airlock. Is something wrong with Captain Nowak?

Emotion: glee. No, I would say there's something very right with Captain Nowak.

Here he is to tell you himself.

Hello, Roselyn. I gather you've wasted no time in stirring everybody up.

Emotion: helplessness. It just seemed to happen.

No problem. Miriam's father has agreed to assign you as her guardian.

He what? Assign me...?

Isn't that what you wanted? The ambassador said...

Image: stern teacher look. Captain Nowak, you know very well that was just an example. Now, what, exactly, have you done? How can you threaten a passenger like that? What happened to your non-interference with your clients?

Emotion: wry humour. Not my clients anymore. I told you that problem was dealt with.

Emotion: understanding.

So, I just gave that slime ball one small chance to make up for all the damage he has done to his daughter. He jumped at the opportunity.

Rather than jump out the airlock.

NightHawk, you are a tattletale.

Sorry, sir.

You're not sorry at all. Anyway, Roselyn, you are now officially Miriam's guardian, and she can do anything you both agree on.

Thank you, sir. We have an emergency, here, so we can get the details when I get back to the ship. Now, I must go.

Very well, Roselyn. Jerusalem's Hope over and out.

Doc?

Eager desire to please.

I need to contact my mother. Image: Tall, dark woman.

Again, the contact was instant. *Hello? Roselyn? Where are you?*

I'm in the embassy hospital, Mother. They have a man here who has the same thing Dad has. They need Miriam to help him. Where are you right now?

Just getting back on the shuttle.

When you get to Jerusalem, please go straight to Miriam and stand guard over her. You know why. She's in my classroom. Do you understand? If you have any questions, ask Captain Nowak. He arranged permission for her.

Emotion: confusion. All right, Roselyn. I don't know what's going on, but I will follow your lead.

Thank you, mother. I know things are moving very fast right now, but don't worry. This is going to work out fine.

I truly hope so, dear.

Roselyn turned to Dr. Beoning and Doc. *Emotion: eager desire to please. Image: Miriam sitting in classroom, waiting. Image: Miriam getting on shuttle, coming to embassy. Emotion: question?*

Emotion: negative. Image: Miriam sitting in classroom. Barwolf reaching out, gestalt forming.

Emotion: Agreement.

Dr. Beoning looked around the room. "Chairs, please."

"Aye, sir." A corpsman jumped to arrange seating around the bed.

They all sat, and with a complete lack of ceremony, the barwolf began the gestalt. She brought Roselyn in first, then the Head Surgeon. Then they all reached out to Miriam and the power around them surged.

Doc manipulated the gestalt until it was in the proper form, which seemed to be a shell formed by their minds, held firmly together by the barwolf, with Miriam inside. They were given to understand in no uncertain terms that they were never to loosen this shield.

Emotion: readiness. Emotion: question?

Combined emotions: anticipation.

Image: shell diving into deep, warm water. They floated down...deeper and deeper, darker and darker. Doc was following some thread that Roselyn could not see, but Miriam seemed confident, radiating cheerful attention.

Then, as they travelled, images started to make sense. Shapes floated by, then recognizable objects: a tree, a chair, sparkling gemstones of some sort. Roselyn detected the distinct smell of cedar, exactly like the chest where her mother kept their best clothes. She reached for it, but the shell moved on, dragging her reluctantly away.

Emotion: concentration!

Emotion: agreement.

Think of the man on the bed, Teacher. Picture him in your mind. His name is Bill Johnson. He likes to play globe tennis. What's globe tennis?

Dr. Beoning's firm mind intruded. It's freefall tennis inside a sphere. I'll take you to the courts when we're finished here. Concentrate. We've never lost anyone on a rescue mission, and I don't want to start now.

Emotion: agreement.

Emotion: agreement.

Roselyn pictured the man on the bed, opening her eyes to slits to remind herself what he looked like. He had a fine, angular face and laugh lines around his lips. As she watched, his eyelids moved as if his eyes were searching back and forth.

Emotion: success!

Down in the darkness they approached a lighter spot. It grew and firmed until she could see the face of the man on the bed. Blurry black and white squares covered his features. As they got closer, she could distinguish figures moving on the squares.

He's playing chess. This shouldn't be hard. Dr Beoning's mind reached out and began moving the players. Rapidly, one player left the surface of Johnson's face then another and then one more. As they left, his face became clearer and firmer. Soon there were only five men left: three whites near the nose, blocking two blacks against the edge of one cheek.

Checkmate, Mr. Johnson. You've won the game. Miriam, pick up the rest of the players and put them away. Good, now reach out and take his hand. Careful, now. Stay in the shell. Pull a little, just gently. Good. Let's go back, now.

Coming out was easier, because Roselyn seemed to remember the way. She could resist the lure of the images around her, until she saw her father's face.

She tried to turn and go back.

Teacher!

It's Dad. I see him. Can we...?

Miriam's mind firmed. *It isn't him.*

What...?

He's not there. It's you.

Sorrow rushed through her, with a tinge of fear. *Oh. I almost...*

Time to bring Spacer Anderson home. Then we'll go for your Dad.

Emotion: agreement.

Doc gradually eased them into a normal gestalt. The man on the bed stirred and opened his eyes.

"Oh, hello, Dr. Beoning. Boy, was I having a weird dream. Seemed to go on and on. And then this little girl came along and woke me up. Strange little thing. Hare lip, poor kid. Couldn't talk. But what a mind! You oughta get her in for a scan. Puts me to shame, I bet, new augment and all." He looked around. "Hey, where'd she go?"

He began to sit up, but then fell back. "What's going on? I feel so weak..."

The doctor laid a restraining hand on the man's shoulder. "You've been flat on your back for almost a month. You ought to feel weak."

"What? Oh, no. Did I do the rabbit hole number again? A month, this time?"

"Twenty-nine days."

The patient relaxed back into his pillow. "So, what happens now? You gonna take the augment out?"

Emotion: cautious optimism. Image: small girl holding Spacer by the hand, leading him through a maze of stars.

"Who is that kid?" His eyes fell on Roselyn. "You were there too." He relaxed and a smile formed. "Who are you?"

Hoping to hide her momentary flutter, she put on her polite teacher voice. "I'm Miriam's guardian. I supervise her when she helps patients."

"Oh. Well, wherever she is, I guess I owe her." Then his eyes fell on Doc. "Hey, you're familiar, too. Why is that? I never met a barwolf before. I dreamed you, too, didn't I?"

Emotion: agreement. Image: barwolf trying to pull Spacer out of water. Spacer slips back in.

"Oh, yeah. You kept bugging me to come back, but I wouldn't. Sorry about that. It was just too...I don't know.

Roselyn couldn't stop her curiosity. "Were you really in there playing chess the whole time?"

"Chess? Yeah...sometimes...I think I remember winning, just at the end, there."

"Why chess?"

The surgeon shrugged. "Who knows? Perhaps a metaphor we all agreed on."

"But I don't know how to play chess."

"And you mostly saw his face, right? You didn't see the game."

"That's right. I see. I suppose."

Beoning regarded her. "You seem observant. Did you notice anything else?"

A deep gloom settled over her. "I'm afraid so..."

"Well...?"

"Um...tell me, did Spacer Johnson take that nosedive eight days ago?"

"Yes, that's right. How did you know that? I said a week."

"Because that's when we arrived."

"And what does that mean?"

"Now that I remember, my father was doing isolation exercises with Miriam when he was lost."

"Ah. You think she might be the agent of the effect."

"Well...no, but...well...maybe?"

He smiled. "Well, no, actually. Not all by herself. We have noticed that close contact with a number of powerful Sensitives does increase the likelihood of an accident. But it's much more likely that it was the whole of the Followers that caused the problem. Did you hold a celebration of some sort?"

"Yes, we had a Service of Thanksgiving the moment we arrived."

"And of course, that involves communion with your deity. All of you."

"The Voice of the Universe. Yes."

"There you have it. I'll bet we check the time of the service and the time Johnson started his dive, they'll match up."

Roselyn's mind was working. "But wait a minute. Does that mean if we take Dad off *Jerusalem* and away from the Congregation he'll come back?"

"It's not that simple, but it will certainly help. One thing for sure, you don't want to take him downplanet on Arborea any time soon."

"So, what do we do? Where can we go?"

The surgeon had a quick exchange of images with Doc.

"There we have it. Doc is very interested in your patients. She will hitch a ride with you back to Arborea and work with them enroute. There's a Habitat in orbit around the planet with plenty of free living space, now that its inhabitants have moved downplanet. That ought to be far enough away from the planetary gestalt. Can you and Miriam arrange to stop there for a while?"

"Of course! Anything to help Dad. And the others, too."

"Well! We have a lot to arrange, and not much time to do it." He clapped his hands together. "Let's get this ball rolling."

38. EPILOGUE: WEDDING

BARWOLF BASE, ARBOREA
8 months later

Toni glanced up at her fiancée as the dust from Alison's landing blew off the field. "So. The two most important people in the Barnard System have arrived for our wedding."

It took Andrew a moment. "Oh. You mean Alfino and Miriam."

They stepped forward as the ventral lock opened and the ramp dropped smoothly.

Ambassador Pretoro stepped out of the Harrier and gazed around Barwolf Base. He nodded with satisfaction. "A rather rustic spot for a wedding. Beautiful, though."

Toni strode up to him and linked arms. "I heard that."

"As you were meant to." He regarded the mass of ships that cluttered the landing field. "Busy spot."

"Everybody wants to be here for the wedding of the century...well, of the decade, anyway. Usually it's completely bare, since Alison's wing was transferred to the Arborea City Spaceport." She cocked a thumb at the Wing Commander, who was finishing up her post-flight check. "She and Jackson treating you all right?

"Yes, they helped me choose a wonderful site for my embassy. Pleasant, yet imposing, I'd call it. We will build it with native materials, and given that this is the Tree Planet, I think it will be quite impressive. Jackson also has some very nice plans for the Planetary Manager's residence, when he and Alison get married. If they ever get around to it."

"But I thought, now that she's at the new port..."

"Oh, you didn't hear. She's been given a promotion and a new ride. An In-System Reconnaissance Sloop based at the capital, but on system-wide patrol. So, their wedding gets postponed again."

Alison sauntered down the ramp in time to flash her two Commander's comets, and the two friends exchanged sharp salutes, grinning.

Toni glanced back into the ship. "Where's the omnipresent Enderby? I didn't think you could move a step without your aide."

The ambassador chuckled. "I'm afraid he does give that impression. However, I am here on personal business, and I have left him back in Arborea City with sixteen very important tasks to accomplish in my absence."

"Well, I'm glad you came. Maybe you can talk to Andrew about houses."

"Houses?"

"He hasn't lived downplanet in a real house since he was about four years old." She grimaced. "He has the strangest ideas about what our new home should look like."

Andrew shrugged and wisely said nothing.

"I'll do what I can, but I suggest you recruit Jackson. When it comes to architecture, he's your man."

"He did a pretty good job on the capital city."

"That he did." Andrew grinned. "You can hardly tell most of it was pre-fabbed in Jupiter orbit ten years ago."

Toni turned to Alison. "I hear you have a new ride."

"A pale imitation of *NightHawk,* meant for insystem patrols. More room to accommodate Marines, lighter armament and no Otherwhere Sphere. She's coming out from Jupiter Space Dock on a carrier."

"Not stopping at Freighty for modifications?"

Alison's face reddened. "Well, no, but you may have heard…about my father and Freighty?"

"The Asteroid Project."

"They have finished hollowing out their little moonlet and spun it up to point seven Gs. An ideal venue for a fabrication plant."

Toni shook her head. "Gotta get the cash flow moving. Return on investment."

"That's my father, all right."

Toni looked up the ramp. "I thought you had another passenger or two."

Alison looked back. "Oh, yes. Roselyn's having trouble getting her ward to stop talking to every barwolf on the base. She demanded to meet them all."

Toni grinned. "I can solve that." She opened her augment. *Nzinga, where are you?*

Image: auguar running.

A small, shrill voice came from inside the Harrier. "Nuzzzinga!"

The auguar blasted towards them across the field, bounding towards the small child running down the ramp.

Emotion: caution!

Her warning did no good. The two met in what should have been a crash, but the auguar swerved at the last moment, the girl threw her arms around the cat's neck, and they rolled over twice, the child protected between the animal's front paws. They ended up with Nzinga on her back and Miriam lying on her chest, laughing.

"Nuzinga, I never realized you were so big!" *Image: huge cat standing over small girl.*

Emotion: feline laughter. Image: girl riding on auguar's back.

Immediately they scrambled to their feet. Miriam mounted and clung firmly to Nzinga's neck fur as they galloped smoothly around the whole field.

A pretty, red-haired woman followed down the ramp at a more sedate place and regarded Toni, laughing. "And I never realized you were so big."

"Me?" Toni looked down at herself. "Big?"

"Well, you're a whole lot bigger than your augment persona."

"You're playing games with my head!"

Again, the trill of laughter. "And you've been telling tales about me to the ambassador. You'd better watch your step!"

"I'm not worried. We've been in full gestalt. I know what a softie you really are."

"Fine. Just stop telling people."

"It's a deal. And you're much prettier than your persona. No wonder you have all the trouble with men." Toni suddenly stopped laughing. "Say, how's your father and those others? I hear they got a barwolf specialist working on them."

"They're all fine. Dad finally came downplanet with us today, but there's no way he would risk this emotional morass, so we dropped him off at Sanctuary Island enroute. Alison's a great taxi driver. Whatever you want, wherever you want. Of course, my mother's been here a day already, glad-handing everyone.'

Toni regarded the smaller woman. "Why didn't you tell us about your father? That must have been horrible."

"And make you feel sorry for me? What good would that do?"

"I suppose. But he's getting better, now."

"Yep. Mostly working on getting his muscles back." She shook her head. "Real gravity hit him pretty hard this morning."

"And how about you? Ready to settle down?"

Roselyn waved a hand at the men unloading luggage from the Harrier. "Miriam and I are moving into Base accommodations here, and I'm starting on the educational materials with Morissa after the wedding's over. Brindle is some character, isn't one?"

The two of them stopped as Nzinga and Miriam came to a sliding stop in front of them.

"That looked like fun."

Image: cat with rumpled fur.

Miriam grabbed a fistful of neck hair and pulled. "I've got a very nice brush in my luggage. Captain Nowak gave it to me, and he wouldn't mind if you used it."

Toni gave a "go ahead" flick of her fingers and the auguar stalked away with her usual grace, her little friend bobbing along beside her. "They're giving me a very nice room, all to myself, over there in the main building. I haven't seen it re-ti, yet, but Brindle took me for a walkaround last week. The whole place is ever so much lovelier in person. You know, barwolves see colours very weirdly. Oh. Here comes the luggage." She turned to look back and gesture. "Andrew, can you get this nice man to get my suitcase out for me..."

As Andrew moved to do the girl's bidding, Roselyn laughed. "If she wasn't so good in gestalt, I'd be worried. Since they fixed her lip, she hardly uses her augment to communicate at all. Chatter, chatter, chatter, all day and most of the night, if I let her."

Toni shook her head. "You think that was a reunion. The Three Musketeers hit the embassy last week. They're up on *NightHawk* right now. Natalia will bring them down in plenty of time to get oriented before the ceremony."

"Are they recovered from their ordeal?"

"Who knows? They've just spent almost a year with humans at a very key point in their lives. It's bound to affect them." She shook her head. "And no telling how Miriam has affected them."

Roselyn laughed. "If I was the whole barwolf species, I'd be worried about Miriam."

* * *

The next day was clear and balmy as usual, and the bride and groom left their quarters after breakfast, Toni putting herself under Alison's care to "get pretty," whatever that meant, and Andrew going to what grooms traditionally do to get their nerve up for the ceremony.

At eleven hundred hours the bridal party came out of the building to walk across to the mess hall. The Barwolf Base sign over the door had been modified by the addition of "Ballroom" underneath. Inside, anyone who was anyone in Barnard System was seated awaiting them, but out in the foyer, a few minor details had to be straightened out before the bride's procession could begin.

Toni had spent the last eight months valiantly trying to grow her hair, and she had developed enough to pin a veil and a few short-stemmed flowers on. She had opted for a regulation knee-length uniform dress because anything longer would be completely out of character, though she insisted on a leg slit that would allow her to do a reasonable side thrust kick, should one be required. The seamstresses in the embassy made no comment, having dealt with the military mind for years.

She peered in the door of the former mess and spoke over her shoulder. "Looks a bit different from the last time we were here, hey?"

The lounge had been decorated with the flags of the squadrons represented in the System and the banners of various other Barnard organizations. An honour guard of Commandos stood easy at the back of the room, and a simple podium graced the front.

Roselyn lined up her four charges. *Image: three barwolf pups walking down the aisle in a tidy row, Miriam following, spreading flowers.*

"No, no, Teacher. These are barwolves."

Toni grinned and sent a private call to Roselyn. *She sounds exactly like you.*

Don't remind me.

"Barwolves don't stand in lines. They don't need patterns to follow. They only need to be connected to their people, and nothing can go wrong."

Alison chuckled. "If I know anything about weddings, something is bound to go wrong, and a few barwolf puppies gamboling around will be the least of your worries."

"You're in charge of them, Miriam." Toni looked in again and smiled. "Now, Andrew and Alwyn are already in position waiting for us. I'm going to start the wedding march. Get them down to the front of the aisle the best way you can."

Emotion: eager desire to please. The little girl turned to her charges, and her augment communication echoed through the gestalt. *No! Commander Toni and her mate do* not *want you talking to all those people. Walk down that aisle like good puppies, and don't go anywhere else or talk to anyone. And no, you will not chew on my shoes. These are the first new shoes I ever had, and I love them almost as much as I love you.*

Toni glanced at Alfino, tall and dignified at her side. "Ready for action, sir?"

"Ready when you are, Commander."

"Then let's get this mission started." *Sound: music playing.* The familiar Wedding March rolled out, its tones echoing through everyone's augments.

Miriam looked down at her charges. *Emotion: frown. Now go away and be cute.*

The pups glanced at each other and immediately tangled into a rolling ball with flying legs as they tussled down the aisle. When they reached Andrew, they disengaged and lay, panting, at his feet. Not quite in a row.

Miriam followed at a decorous pace, taking her task of strewing flowers very seriously, to the point where Toni wondered if she'd ever get there. The congregation didn't seem to mind, talking and gawking in equal amounts.

As the women watched, Admiral Mira strode out to the podium and nodded to Miriam, who went to stand opposite Andrew. The little girl gestured to her empty basket and gave him an impish grin, her lips repaired to perfection by one of Space Arm's finest surgeons.

Alison stepped forward, moving down the aisle with a model's grace.

Emotion: anticipation. Patches and Roselyn followed at a dignified pace. At the front, the barwolf arranged herself in a tasteful arc around the puppies, and they all watched the ceremony with intense interest.

The ambassador leaned closer. "Do you think it's a good idea to be commanding the operation at your own wedding?"

"Considering the number of possibilities for SNAFUs, it's the only way to make sure the mission doesn't deteriorate into hand-to-hand engagement."

"It's not a mission, Toni. It's your wedding."

"You maintain the ceremonial feeling, sir, and I'll keep the details on track." She took his arm, and Nzinga stood at her other side. "Shall we?"

They strolled down the aisle to where Andrew and a new life waited.

THE END

If you enjoyed this book, do the author and other readers a service and go to your favourite retailer and post a review. Even a rating and a few words is great.

ABOUT THE AUTHOR

Brought up in a logging camp with no electricity, Gordon Long learned his storytelling in the traditional way: at his father's knee. He now spends his time editing, publishing, travelling, blogging and writing Fantasy, Sci-Fi and Social Commentary, although sometimes the boundaries blur.

Gordon lives in Tsawwassen, British Columbia, with his wife, Linda, and their Nova Scotia Duck Tolling Retriever, Josh. When he is not writing and publishing, he works on projects with the Surrey Seniors' Planning Table and is a staff writer for <indiesunlimited.com>

MORE FROM GORDON A. LONG

Available at most retailers

"Factory 4-80" Freighty Novels 1
"Outback Rebellion" Freighty Novels 2
"Asimov's Laws" Freighty Novels 3
"Occam's Razor" Freighty Novels 4
"Slivership" Freighty Novels 5

"Ocean of Grass" Petrellan Saga 1
"Waves of Stone" Petrellan Saga 2
"Path of Water" Petrellan Saga 3
"Zoysana's Choice" Petrellan Saga 4
"The Innkeeper's Husband" Petrellan Saga 5
"Mercenary's Dream" Petrellan Saga 6

"Out of Mischief" World of Change Book 1
"Into Trouble" World of Change Book 2
"Mountains of Mischief" World of Change Book 3
"The Trouble with Tents" World of Change Book 4
"Queen of Mischief" World of Change Book 5

"A Sword Called...Kitten?" Romantic Comedy with an Edge
"The Cat with Many Claws" Cat with Many Claws Book 2
"Cloud Cat" a Sword Called Kitten Book
"Why Are People So Stupid?" Social Humour with a Point

Look for Gordon's books, selected reviews, poetry and short
stories at <airbornpress.ca>
Gordon's opinions on humanity are at
<https://airbornpress.ca/arepeoplestupid/>
Find his weekly reviews and his ideas on writing at
"Renaissance Writer" <https://airbornpress.ca/newdir/>